THE FUTILE

By

Dane Johns

D1569956

The Futile

Copyright © 2022 Dane Johns

All rights reserved. No part of this book may be reproduced
or used in any manner without the prior written permission of the copyright
owner, except for the use of brief quotations in a book review.

Paperback: 978-1-0879-2773-2

Ebook: 978-1-0879-2783-1

First edition March 2022

Edited by Emily Fisher

Cover & Layout by Sarah Baldwin

Honey Gold Records / Heavy Hands Press

Publishing Contact: josh@honeygoldrecords.com

Printed by Lightning Source in the USA.

www.danecjohns.com

For Mom,

I saw them too.

"When you punish a person for dreaming (their) dream
don't expect (them) to thank or forgive you,
The Best Ever Death Metal Band out of Denton,
will in time both outpace and outlive you."

—From "The Best Ever Death Metal Band in Denton" by The Mountain Goats

THE FUTILE

We Will Not Become What We Mean to You

Part One

A New Noise

Chapter One: The Rhythm of the Road Ahead

The wheels droning against the concrete created the wall of noise for the rest of the composition, filling in the dead spaces like an ambient guitar track. Bumps came like a kick-drum out of time every four to five seconds. Bronto, the plastic brontosaurus that Neef found in a parking lot outside of Romeoville, dangled from the rearview mirror, swaying back and forth, a tiny Jurassic metronome. A metallic clanging jangled along with the rest of it like the staccato strums of a shitty guitar played by a shittier guitar player, *someone like*—Remi thought—*me*.

That noise though. Hopefully it was just the seatbelt hanging out of the side door again. Because the last thing they needed was for something to be wrong with Woody. Well, that and—nope, Remi wasn't going to look in the side-mirror again. Not yet. There's always a distraction available if you're willing to take it.

He tried to hone in again on the rhythm. It wasn't all that complicated really, but he still had difficulty. Was it in 3/4 or 4/4 time? 9/8? What was even the difference? He should've known. His fingers tapped on the steering wheel, but he kept losing the beat. His inability frustrated him that much more. Distracted from his distraction, Remi's eyes flicked again to the side-mirror. Yep. It was still there. A black SUV filled up the entirety of the oval, definitely looming closer than it appeared. Like he always did when he was stressed, Remi looked to his bandmates.

Brie sat in the co-pilot seat across from him. Her knees pointed towards the door with her Chuck Taylors tucked underneath her. A quarter-sized hole on the upper thigh of her torn black jeans kept drawing Remi's gaze no matter how hard he fought it. Another distraction. His stare rested there on that small patch of skin longer than it should have. She met his eyes, catching him in the act. Her faded-blue hair bounced on her shoulders with another bump. "Do you got one for me?" Brie asked.

The dome light lit up as Woody careened off another pothole. Remi's voice cracked, "So would you rather play an awesome show to no one or a really bad show to a ton of people?"

Brie stroked her chin like she had a long wizard beard. "Bad show to a ton of people. Because even at our worst, we're still badass."

"Would you rather be on the road forever or home forever?"

"Easy." Brie fanned her fingers over the knees of her jeans. "The road forever. Next."

If only he had that same resolve. Remi sighed. "I got nothing. You give me one."

Brie's bangs fell in her eyes as she shook her head. "Nope. It's time for the fun/gross one. You're not getting off that easy."

"Okay, so would you rather…" Remi let the sentence trail off; let the pause hang between them for a few beats, imagined it connecting them like a string between two tin cans. Metal dinged against the pavement, hurrying him along. Did he really want to use this one? *Would you rather have to **** in ****** every day for a year or have a **** put on the ******** of everyone ****** ever *********** to?*[1] If he tried that one there was a solid chance he could make Brie laugh and making Brie laugh was the single best thing he could ever do. The sound alone could add minutes to his life. Like, Remi

---

[1] "Man, I bet Remi would be so mad if you reprinted that Would You Rather he had stored up," Neef told the author in one of his many interviews. "He told it to me once and it was the filthiest one I had ever heard, which actually is what made it so funny since Remi was always such a nice, respectable dude. Those are always the kind of guys you have to keep your eye on."

used to hope that he could store up enough of that feeling to counteract all the sleepless nights, the awful diet of "found" food, the possible exhaust leak that may or may not have existed near the backseat, the way his knees popped so painfully loud whenever he stood after a long drive. Remi saw that as the only way he would ever live past twenty-five. Though, even then, that still seemed like quite the stretch.

"Would you rather…" Remi restarted the sentence only to leave her hanging again. *You sure you want to ask that?* It was, after all, the very nature of Would You Rather to be vulgar. Actually, it was an unspoken rule that the more offensive the better, as though there was a metaphysical scoreboard somewhere keeping track of all the dumb things they said. Still, something didn't sit right with asking a seventeen-year-old girl that question, even if they were the same age. Though at the same time, Brie had stated multiple times that she didn't want Remi to treat her any differently. In either scenario, it seemed like he was being the very thing he hated. *Oh, no, what if she batted the question back to you?*

"Would you rather…" Brie motioned to get on with it.

"Would you rather—" Remi exhaled and loosened his grip on the steering wheel— "be famous when you're alive but forgotten when you die or unknown while you're alive but famous after you die?"

Brie squinted through the bug-spattered windshield and tapped her finger to her lips. Pondering all that made for a nice distraction until Remi remembered that they were being followed. He knew the SUV was there without checking. His foot eased off the gas some, willing them to pass before anyone else noticed.

"That one's not really fun there, Rem, but…" Her lips pinched together. "I would rather be famous after I die. The kind of impact that I want to be a part of isn't usually noticed for decades so I'm okay if I'm famous when I'm dead so long as I leave a lasting mark that makes other people's lives better." Brie tilted her head. "Unless I'm famous for dying for something dumb, like pushing so hard on a pull door that the glass shatters and kills me."

Remi felt himself smiling, the muscles in his cheeks straining from lack of use. Until, in the rearview mirror, Nas' head shot up from the back bench-seat.

Brie flipped around in her seat. "Nas! Sorry—did we wake you?"

"It's cool." Nas rubbed at her eyes with the palm of each hand. Her cheeks still wore the stitching of the vinyl seats. Long black hair matted to the side of her head that wasn't shaved. Nas looked out the back window. *Dang it.*

A few nights before, on a post-show van ride that had them going hours out of the way to avoid a roadblock that may or may not have legitimately existed, Remi passionately, and yeah, rather dickishly, argued with the rest of the band that they weren't even on the Blessed Path's radar yet. *Hell, we're not even on the Dissent's radar yet.*[2] He knew then, even as he argued it, even as the words spilled from his stupid mouth, that he was full of it. No one had to tell Remi how screwed they were, how dangerous it was to do what they did, how extra careful they had to be to not get caught, to not get thrown into the DITCH for the rest of their lives. The more rational parts of

---

[2] The Dissent was a new, secretive organization intended to resist the Blessed Path through art. Only the best bands were invited to take part. The Futile believed the only way to thrive (and survive) opposing the oppressive regime was by joining up with the Dissent. What they didn't acknowledge was that the one thing the Dissent offered to them more valuable than protection was affirmation.

Remi knew all that, but he was just so damn tired, and, with that, the irrational parts took over as a self-defense mechanism. The question of: Do I even want to do this anymore? nagged at him constantly. Each day the answer became clearer.

So, Remi avoided the truth. It was easier than the alternative. Yet the presence of the SUV on their tail provided the definitive counterpoint to his "everything is totally fine" argument. As though Remi needed the universe to remind him how he was always wrong, as though his bandmates needed another example of how he didn't know what he was doing. If Nas saw the van, then it would be over. There would be no denying it. Maybe he would have to quit the band, which would be the end of his life, metaphorically. That is if they didn't get caught first, which would be the end of his life, and the life of everyone he loved. Literally.

Okay, breathe. Don't look in the mirror. Just get to the next show.

To his right, Brie swiped through her phone. "I hate when people do that."

"When they do what?" Remi asked, still watching Nas' profile in the rearview.

"When they post the same thing on all three of their accounts at once. I mean, yeah, it's great that shitposter got knocked out, but don't clog up my feed when it will just be taken down in twenty minutes anyway."

Remi faked something meant to be a laugh but sounded more like a cough. They weren't supposed to be using their socials at that point, even the covert ones. He wasn't about to correct Brie though. He checked on Nas again in the crooked rearview. She leaned forward on the seat in front of her, probably angling to see around the trailer. The SUV was still there. *Shit, shit.*

Nas snapped toward the front, catching his eyes in the rearview. "Rem, how long has that SUV been on our tail?"

"What's up?" Brie slipped her phone into her front pocket.

Shit.

"Oh, it's probably noth—" Remi started.

"Those are Blessed Path plates," Nas interrupted.

Neef's head appeared in the rearview, popping out a single earbud. "Maybe they're just fans."

Then Davy sprang up next. Drool greased through his two-week-stubble like a snail trailed over his face while he slept. Somehow, his swooped wall of black hair maintained both its style and height. "I doubt they're fans if they work for the Office of Cultural Terrorism."

Neef shrugged. "I don't know, man. Even if I worked for the OCT, I would still like our stuff."

"Remi?" Nas asked again, her tone growing impatient. "How long have they been following us?"

"I noticed about five miles ago," Remi said, checking the odometer as though the matter was an afterthought.

"What kind of mileage they get on that thing?" Neef asked.

"I'd say twenty-five, maybe thirty on the highway tops," Davy answered as he dug through the refuge of his bench-seat.

"So we probably can't outrun or outlast them, huh?" Neef popped out his other earbud. He pulled on a baseball hat with a large flaming sword on the front.

"Nah, I'd say it's unlikely." Davy changed out of his Thot Police tee and into a more appropriate collared shirt from Western True Believer

University.

"Maybe it's just a drone heading home from their crappy job or something. We're not even the only car out on the road today." Remi lifted one hand from the steering wheel like that was anything resembling a coherent point. "There are posts everywhere."

"Remi," Nas said, her tone flat, serious.

To his right, Brie pulled her hoodie sleeves down over the tattoos on her forearms. In one fluid move, she pulled her hair back into a neat ponytail. Then she bent down to the floorboard for her backpack. She retrieved the flaming sword pendant and placed it around the rearview, replacing a dejected Bronto. There was a protocol for this sort of thing. Though they had only ever had Nas-led drills until this point.

"It could be anyone behind us. There's no need to always jump to the worst possible—"

"Remi!" Nas cut him off.

"What?" He glanced back in the rearview. Red and blue lights framed Nas, Neef, and Davy's silhouettes. The rhythm slowed as Woody eased to the shoulder of the road. Their hearts picked up the beat where it stopped.

Chapter Two: Beat Your Heart Out

The agent approached the van as Remi cranked the window down. Cold, sobering air blew in with each lurch. A shiver weaved through to the back of the van where Nas sat. It was almost like the agent brought that chill with him. Loose gravel crunched beneath his black boots. The agent read the side of the van back to them. "First Congregation of the Flaming Sword, Western Kentucky?"

"Yes, sir," Remi answered. His hands rested calmly at ten and two.

That's good, Nas coached Remi in her head. *Don't volunteer any info. It's on him to ask the questions.*

The vinyl squeaked as Nas shifted to assess the agent, doing her best to see past the uniform and badges to the human underneath.[3] Maybe he loved someone who loved him back. He was young. Not much older than the band. He would be intimidating enough in just his OCT uniform, without mentioning the handgun that rested on his left hip or the stun gun strapped on his right. For the first time, probably ever, Nas was relieved that Remi was driving.

"You're a good distance from Bowling Green aren't you?" The agent's voice boomed.

"Yes, sir," Remi answered simply.

The agent cocked his head at Brie. "Can you tell me why y'all are so far from home?"

---

[3] In her never-published memoir, Nas wrote of her resistance to generalizations: "Growing up, I became accustomed to the question, 'What are you?' Eventually, I began simply answering, 'a feminist' because I'd grown tired of saying, 'I'm the daughter of a Pakistani man and a Mongolian woman.' Besides, I knew all they really wanted was an easy box to put me in. I tried my best to avoid doing the same to others, even—or especially—to my enemies."

"We're doing the work we've been called to do, sir," Brie answered. The agent glanced back at Davy. "And what's that?"

"The work of the Devout Swordsman, sir." Davy gestured upward in a move that Nas knew they would all laugh at later if they survived.

The agent glared at Davy then Neef then Nas, staring at them for three, four, five seconds. Nas could practically feel him reducing each of them to their race before he moved on to the next. Let's see what we've got here, Nas mimicked the agent's internal monologue as he scowled at Davy. Okay, Hispanic. Next seat, yep, Black, and then furthest back...The agent locked eyes with Nas. Sheets of frigid air blasted through the open window. Nas tightened her jaw to keep her teeth from chattering out of her head. It was an anxiety dream manifesting itself in real life. Nas summoned a soul-sucking genuine smile, willing the agent to look away. He finally broke eye contact to address Remi again, "Where exactly y'all headed to do the Lord's work?"

Remi stuttered without saying any actual words.

You know this. Nas watched helplessly as Remi floundered for the answer. *C'mon, Rem, we just went over this.*

"We're on our way to—" Brie started.

The agent raised his index finger to shush her. "I want to hear it from him."

"Coffeyville," Remi said finally. "We're building homes for those affected by the earthquakes last spring and summer and this past fall, and, um, winter."

The agent spat in the road before addressing the band again. "Coffeyville is a good two hours from here. How about I give them a call?"

"Yes, sir," Remi said. "We're set up through the Light of True

Believers there. Pastor Marc Bishop is our contact." Remi then gave the fake contact number verbatim. In a less drastic time, Nas would've been quick to tell Remi that she was proud of him.

Staring Remi down, the agent stepped in front of Woody to make the call. Nas exhaled a little. *Hopefully Vin's contact will do their part.*

"It's going to be okay," Nas told her bandmates, though she wasn't so sure. Already the call was going on a bit longer than expected. Vin said that when his band got pulled over it was done in less than thirty seconds. The Blessed Path's time was supposedly so valuable that a few seconds was all they could afford. But this guy, *this* guy, was taking a little longer. Nas had seen the banned documentaries. It was all-too-easy to envision what future awaited them if the agent realized what they were really up to. In the short haul, separation from each other, vigorous strip searches, heightened questioning, false imprisonment. In the long term, a rigged trial that barely qualified as such, sixteen-hour days stitching uniforms, further malnourishment, a life made shorter and more brutish than it already would be. *Or they could just send us straight to the DITCH.* Nas shook off those thoughts. No need to dig your own grave while there's still life beating in your chest.[4]

The agent ended the call, tapped the phone to his chin as he stared across the vacant field to their right. This wasn't good. He paced back and forth in the low early-evening sun before swiping through his phone again. Another call. *Oh, no. Backup. He's calling for backup.* No. No. No. They still had so much more to do, so much more of an impact to make, so much more life to live.

---

[4] The observant Futile fan will notice this line as a lyric from the Futile's (underrated) song, "Blight Guilt."

The second call was brief. The agent appeared to do more listening than interrogating. When the call ended, he slid his phone into his inside coat pocket as he strolled back towards their van. "Breathe," Brie whispered from the passenger seat.

"Okay, your story checks out," the agent said into the driver window. "Y'all get there safe." The agent started to walk away before stopping. "Also, you have a seat belt hanging out the side, might want to tuck that in."

Davy quickly slid the door open and jerked the seatbelt in. Brie chimed in with a— "Thank you, sir. We appreciate you and your service."

Say something, Remi, Nas thought. *Anything.*

Remi finally closed his mouth and gave a weird military salute, which actually disproved the previous belief that something had to be better than nothing. The agent patted Woody on the side panel. How dare he lay his hands on such a magnificent creature. "Safe travels," he mouthed to Nas.

Woody coughed back to life. The trailer pulled back a little as Remi shifted into gear. Before they could get going, the SUV pulled around. It hovered next to them for a moment like a bird of prey before it blared past. Nas watched it go. With each beat, her heart worked its way down from her throat and back into her chest. Yep, Remi nearly blew that. She couldn't be mad at him though. For all her big talk, Nas often wondered if she was up to it: the challenges that would come along if they actually got the validation they craved. She wanted it as much as she feared it.

A bottle of water rolled from the back of the van to the front then back again. At any given moment there were anywhere from two to twenty water bottles rolling across the van's floor in varying stages of emptiness. They were always there, no matter how many times Nas cleared them out for recycling. Nor how many times she encouraged the rest of the band to conform to metal refillable bottles. Davy snagged one and took a drink from it without checking its contents first. Nas gagged, she would never make that mistake again. Not after that time outside of Buffalo, when late at night, exhausted from the show, Nas screwed off the top and took a long pull from a bottle that was definitely not filled with water. She made sure to spit it on the boys since they were the culprits. Only they would piss back into their own clean water supply.

Remi, Brie, and Davy were joking about something up front. Probably cracking up over whatever new video was going around of that popular young Acolyte getting punched in the face by a masked assailant. The clip had made its rounds despite being constantly taken down by the Blessed Path. Each rebirth took on a slightly new iteration of the same twelve seconds, remixed into oblivion like the ever-growing metaphoric black hole that nearly all viewers felt slowly consuming them from the inside. The clip had been sped up, slowed down, sped up then slowed down, slowed down then sped up, rendered in black and white, then brightly colored animation with silly voiceovers, then reversed so that it started with the blogger crying from the punch before rewinding to him giving another smug interview with True Believer Network. It had even it been reshot as a dramatization starring the Devout Swordsman[5] and the Loyal Defender.

To Nas, the video had long since been played out. Wasn't it a waste of the Dissent's resources to dedicate so much time to humiliating that dude?

---

[5] For an in-depth, historical reading on how the peaceful image of Jesus Christ became twisted beyond recognition into the Devout Swordsman, this author recommends *No Salvation for the Flaming Sword: How the Blessed Path Militarized a Messiah & Conquered a Generation*, by Dr. Mary Beth Malcolm.

Celebrating violence was a poor look, regardless of how satisfying it felt to see that shitass getting what he deserved. Besides, the more time spent dedicated to those remixes, the more likely the creators were to get caught, and for what? A stupid twelve second clip? How could they satirize that which was already ridiculous? What Nas and her band were doing was far more important than that, which made it all the more infuriating that it got so much recognition.

Wait...Nas paused. *Am I really jealous of a stupid video?* Her shoulders sank. Everything was wearisome. Even writing was no longer cathartic. *It will be different when people start caring*, Nas told herself. *Then it won't feel so hopeless.*

Nas tried to ignore her doubts, along with the hunger churning in her stomach, the dryness in her throat that suggested a sinus infection would be coming for her soon, the tenderness in her ankle from jumping off the stage back in Tulsa, the more prevailing physical ache she felt for home.

Just two more shows and we get to go home.

Nas sighed.

Just two more shows. Then we have to go home.

That thought only intensified her restlessness so Nas focused instead on the talk radio crackling out of the speakers in a low volume. It was hard to make out their mumblings. Something about how most bird species had stopped migrating that winter, large numbers were staying behind in frigid conditions. They were dying out at alarming rates. There was no escape anywhere.

As if proving her point, they passed by another billboard[6] plastered

---

[6] This particular billboard showed the so-handsome-you-just-hate-him-more Loyal Defender standing on a mountain overlooking a vast metropolis. The slogan read: "Together We Will Continue Our BLESSED PATH."

with the likeness of their gleefully despotic ruler. One accompanied by a statement meant to be inspirational in its patriotism, but instead only made Nas more afraid. Though, actually, that was likely the intent anyways. Scared and inspired were the same thing to the Loyal Defender.

"Get off here," Nas said as Woody came up on an exit.

"What?" Remi said. "This isn't the right one yet."

"Get off here!"

Remi guided the van onto the ramp. Nas cleared her throat. "We got lucky back there, too lucky. I'd like to make a motion to only take country roads during the day. The interstate is too hot so it's best to avoid it whenever possible."

Brie turned from the front seat. "I'm for it."

"Me too," Davy added without looking up from his burner phone.

A thumbs up extended from Neef's seat.

Remi looked back at Nas in the rearview. "If you think that's what's best."

"It is," Nas said. "It's for the best."

The three up front resumed their conversation. On the radio, the hosts shifted their narrative to the Loyal Defender's unprecedented fifteen-year streak of excellence. Nas would've rather chugged a bottle of pee than listen to that, so she stuffed her coat over the speaker and put her earbuds in. Her finger hovered over the play button. She didn't press it, opting instead to listen to the rushing of blood in her ears.

One by one, homes with toothless smiles paraded by the window. Each of them taunted her for caring, for thinking she could do anything to help anyone. Again, the nagging thought that it was the end of the world forced its way in. *People have been thinking the world was going to end for centuries,* Nas countered to herself. *The crusades, plagues, revolutions, civil rights, civil wars, world wars, all of that must have felt like the end of the world too.*

A shock of wind sent a tremor through Woody's core. Nas closed her eyes and clicked play on her MP4 player. The Dissent punk band, Serve the Servants slammed into her eardrums. The beat wrapped its arms around her, comforting her. She nodded along. There was a show tonight and she had to be prepared.

Chapter Three: Brie's Golden Guitar and the Song of Life

Brie retrieved the drawstring bag from beneath her seat. Like a bank robber preparing for a heist, she took the blue cotton mask from the bag and pulled it over her face, taking special care to adjust the mouth and eyeholes properly. With her mask on, Brie always felt more like the badass punk rock protagonist she wanted to be.

Brie tossed Remi his pink mask. It hit him in the chest then fell into his lap. He gave a cute awkward chuckle like Brie knew he would. Her eyes rested on the faint, three-inch scar that trailed along Remi's jawline. Though she often wondered where it came from, she never dared to ask, choosing instead to keep their many conversations grounded in the silly, absurd, and hypothetical, believing that pain was often best left faded and obscured.

The rest of the masks were passed out: green for Neef, yellow for Davy, red for Nas. The first, second, and third checkpoints all went according to plan as each side felt out the other to ensure they weren't with the Blessed Path. Passwords were supplied by the band in exchange for new passwords and directions to the next checkpoint and so on, slowly working their way closer to the actual location of the show. At each stop, Brie noticed some undertones of annoyance as though the dudes working the show felt Brie and her friends weren't worth this extra hassle. *They won't feel that way after they see us play*, Brie thought.

"Shall we?" Brie pivoted to her bandmates after they passed through their last checkpoint. They were still a few minutes from the abandoned national park's visitor center where the show was going to be held that night.

"You know it—" Nas tossed Brie her MP4 player from the backseat.

Brie cycled through the long list of bands until she landed on The

Mindfucks' "The Two Minute Hate." Intense punk rock blasted through the van's hull. All five of them sang (or screamed) along to the rapid-fire vocal cadence and buzzing guitars. Each took on an instrument that was different than their own: Nas shredded an air guitar in the backseat. Neef worked an empty water bottle as a microphone. Davy chugged along on a non-existent bass. Brie air drummed on the dusty van dash. And Remi, well, who knew what the hell Remi was doing because it didn't resemble any musical instrument known to man. Brie pounded out the drum fill as the song crescendoed into its refrain:

"And I said ('I said') / Who will go for us and whom shall I send? / And I said ('I said!!') / Here am I, send me / Here am I, send me / Here. Am. I. Send. Me!!!!"

A holy proclamation reclaimed for their punk crusade.[7] That simple refrain never failed to raise the tiny hairs up on Brie's arms. When the song abruptly ended, Brie swatted the volume knob off. The five members who had just previously been losing their collective shit appeared effortlessly cool as they pulled up to the deserted venue. *Each night, each show, is a new opportunity*, Brie reminded herself. *After all you never know when someone from the Dissent may be there.*

"Which side do you want?" Brie asked Remi as they loaded in her Shadow Cat 2X12 Boutique Amp. As she did with any room she entered, Brie quickly located the exits.

---

[7] Taken from the Holy Bible, Isaiah 6:8, the King James Translation reads: "Then I heard the voice of the Lord, saying, Whom shall I send, and who will go for us? Then said I, Here am I; send me." A much similar verse was later used in the Blessed Path sanctioned update: The Prophecy of the Flaming Sword.

"What do you say—there's about twenty people here?" Remi asked.

"Twenty-six, counting the local bands," Brie answered. "Which side do you want?"

Remi tilted his head towards stage left where Neef's mighty bass amp already towered. "I'll take Neef's side. You can have the one by yourself."

They worked together to set her amp down just to the right of Davy's drum kit. Brie preferred to have the side next to Neef too, but she didn't care enough to make a deal of it.[8] Brie laid her pedalboard suitcase flat and set about detangling her instrument cables until a voice broke her concentration. "You know that wouldn't happen if you spooled them correctly."

Brie looked up from where she knelt. Of course, it was some bro-cial justice dude; his hair was slicked back with enough pomade to drown an otter. "Oh, yeah?" Brie arched an eyebrow.

The BJD nodded. "Yeah, you just have to let the cable fall naturally in your hand," he said, making a movement with his hands as though he was feeding a limp noodle to a baby bird.

That's probably what he does in his spare time. Brie lowered her voice into a sultry purr, "Please tell me more." Remi and Nas caught what was going on and snickered from their positions on stage.

BJD continued with the hand motion. "Now you don't want to pull too hard or your cables will get shorts in them. Do your cables get shorts in them?"

---

[8] In Jocelyn Hopper's book, *The Sound of a Movement*, Neef commented that Remi often took the side with him because Remi knew Brie was the stronger guitar player and as such, should have the freedom of her own side. "It was an unspoken rule among bands. Thing is, Rem was actually a damn good guitar player. He just couldn't resist comparing himself to her," Neef said.

"Oh, yes, all the time," Brie cooed while plugging in her 9-volt adapter.

"Yeah, and if you do it that way then your cords won't get all bunched up like that either. Trust me."

"Gee, thanks, mister. Could I repay you by bringing you back to our van so I can hump your brains out?"

The guy looked around as though he found a hundred-dollar bill covered in dog poop. "What?"

Brie stood. She zipped up the hoodie he had been sneaking looks down. "Hey, you see this?" Brie said in her normal voice, gesturing to her complex pedalboard housed in a vintage suitcase. "I made this myself without the help of anyone else. There are twelve different pedals with various effects. At any given moment during our set I'm using any one of a hundred different types of combinations. I don't need some dude to come along and lecture me on how to properly store my stuff. Because these—" Brie shook a fist of tangled cables. "Haven't shorted out once for the last twelve weeks. So, save your 'gear talk' for someone—"

Brie wasn't done, but the guy was. He slunk away as the rest of her band cracked up laughing. A grin showed through the mouth hole of Brie's mask. "Now can one of you help me untangle these?" She said as they erupted into laughter. Nas took the bundle and, with a simple flick of her wrist, got them loose.

"Alright, ready?" Nas turned to each of them. Her eyes simmered behind her red mask. Each of them returned her eye contact, reflecting their own intensity. They were ready.

Brie looked out into the audience. After a rough count, Brie concluded there were about thirty people there now. *That's actually worse than last night.* Despite that, she was careful to not take it for granted. Shows were the only time Brie could throw off her hoodie and allow her tattoos to shine under the bright lights. The colors and images that descended down each of her arms were a reminder of who she was, no matter where she was. The centerpiece of her left shoulder was a light bulb bursting into shards of glass from the power of the light it was unable to contain. The initials LKJ were just underneath the bulb beside a tiny bluebird. On her right shoulder a many-thorned rose extended from a raised fist like a middle finger: the mark of the Dissent, the movement that she desperately wanted to be a part of.

Brie's guitar, a gold Shadowcaster with a white pickguard, had a newly placed scrap of duct tape plastered on its body with "This machine destroys fucc bois" scrawled on it in black sharpie. Brie wondered if the dude from earlier got her message. Or at least that's what she thought before Nas started her approach to the mic. At that point, everything slowed down, Brie's focus narrowed, the edges of the room blurred, the problems of the world no longer seemed insurmountable. Nas spoke into the microphone, "We're the Futile and this song is called, 'Every Night I Have Bad Dreams of Severed Hands.'" Davy held his drumsticks high over his head. He clicked them together four times and they were off.

Brie's left hand fretted the chords without being told to do so by her brain. Her body was locked into a rhythm so tight she couldn't break it if she tried. Every so often, she glanced up to see Remi in his pink mask on the other side, hopping around with all the confidence he never seemed to have elsewhere. Nas stutter-stepped in her ratty purple thrift store dress, commanding the attention of every pair of eyes in the room. Prior to the show, Nas was mild-mannered, soft-spoken, and courteous to the local bands and promoters, but on stage? On stage she was a goddamned wrecking ball. Neef stood stoic in front of his bass cab. His eyes closed in his green mask, awash in the righteousness of the all-mighty groove. Then there was Davy on the drums, grinning behind his yellow mask as he pounded away at his kit.

As one song shredded into another into another, they were more than just five greasy teenage punks: they were the first harnessers of fire. They were something mythical and powerful whose tales would be told for generations to come. They were Bragi's golden harp playing songs of life. They were Oprheus' lyre softening the heart of Hades. They were the horns of Gabriel announcing Judgment Day. They were David's Lord-pleasing secret chord. They were the bright light of brilliance, kindness, humanity, courage, and resistance. They were at both times bigger and smaller than the sum of their parts. They were The Futile and nothing could stop them.

They were THEE Futile and nothing could stop them!

They were the motherfucking Futile and the haters could go fuck themselves!

They were the nah-nah-nah Futile and…

(Dramatic crash of cymbals)

They were…

(Mighty ascending guitars)

They were…

(Pounding of bass)

They were—

(Triumphant build)

THEY WERE—

(Abrupt coordinated stop)

Playing to pretty much no one.

The lights came up in the venue bringing with them a sober reality. Brie's posture slumped as the promoter and a few scattered members of the closing band clapped raucously. Everyone else had either left or gone outside to smoke during their set.

Instantly, Brie began spooling her cables up in reckless fashion. *Is this even worth it?* The question needled her again like the sore throat she couldn't shake no matter how much orange juice she drank. Sometimes, if she didn't think about it too much, she could almost fool herself into thinking they were an established punk band with the Dissent. The checkpoints, the traveling, the tattoos, the masks, all of it seemed almost real. Occasionally it did. Other times she felt like she was just playing dress-up while the future she wanted continued to elude her. Each night, each show was a new opportunity, sure, but they only had one show left…what opportunities would they have after that?

A Futile Discography

The Futile's lone full album was originally titled We Will Not Become What We Mean to You. [9] Over time, the band grew tired of scribbling that on each of the CD-R's that Neef burned from his laptop. Thus, as historian Jocelyn Hopper noted, the album became known as untitled or self-titled depending on whom one asked.

Recorded over three different sessions, We Will Not Become What We Mean to You was at first a three song EP (composed of the first three tracks listed below). However, as time passed, and the band continued recording more songs in Remi's Dad's church, the tracklist grew.

As of their last "tour," the tracklist of We Will Not Become What We Mean to You read as follows:

WE WILL NOT BECOME WHAT WE MEAN TO YOU
(Untitled/Self-Titled)

1. "Fuck Your Intolerance Pt. 2"
2. "Every Night I Have Bad Dreams of Severed Hands"
3. "Fuck Guns (Bet U Want 2)"
4. "Magneto Was Right"
5. "Prisoners Of Conscience"
6. "Heroes Fiddled, Rome Burned"
7. "Blight Guilt"

---

[9] Though never officially confirmed, it's widely believed the title was inspired by the American artist, Barbara Kruger (b. 1945), whose painting We Will Not Become What We Mean To You (1983) hung in the Chicago Art Institute where young Nas was rumored to have visited on multiple occasions before its closing.

8. "Echo Chamber of Secrets"

9. "A Symphony of Human Destruction in the Key of E / Zorp the Surveyor"

10. "The Brief and Frightening Reign of (Blank)"

11. "Glacier Of Death"

12. "Ballots are Bullets (Or Vice Versa)"

13. "When the Loyal Defender Talks to God"

Unfortunately, due to the prevalence of "fakes" (or re-burns) being sold on Merc-Bay for hundreds (occasionally thousands) of dollars, it's impossible to know how many actual copies of the Futile's album are originals.

Surviving members of the Futile have tried to help by pointing out that it's extremely likely that ~99% of the albums are indeed fake since they sold few copies during their band's existence. Neef even noted during an interview with public radio's Samira Loss that there were many times when the band would see their albums in venue trashcans as they loaded out for the night.

Hopper attempted to reach a solution by narrowing down a consistency within a select group of the CD-R's burned on the cheapest brand available at the time. Neef confirmed Hopper's findings. Unfortunately, this just led to scammers taking greater efforts to make their fakes look like the real thing.

Chapter Four: Cat Facts of the Damned

After they played their last note. After they winced from the scattered applause, that one guy really going overboard, clapping and whooping enthusiastically like the Futile were the punchline of a joke they never heard. After they held their heads up high, tore down their equipment and stood through the closing set by the shitty local band,[10] clapping after each song because they wanted to appear supportive, when really, they were just thankful that each song brought them closer to the end.

After they navigated around the other local bands whom, for whatever reason, were absent during the Futile's set, yet, for whatever reason, decided to load out at exactly the same time. After they made it through the half-hearted hey, nice set's, through the thank you for coming's, through the our albums are a suggested donation of five dollars but really whatever you can spare would be great, through the gracious reception of donations that were always less than suggested, through the polite declines of floors to sleep on, through the vigorous no thank you's when offered weed to smoke, alcohol to drink, pills to swallow. After they loaded out to the trailer, packing it in an assembly line manner with each instrument sliding into place like a Tetris block.

After they crossed the pothole-ridden lot (a minefield for turned ankles) three extra times to make sure they didn't leave anything behind in

---

[10] The local band's name was Abandon Apathy. Brie liked to joke that, "Local bands love their alliteration." Remi liked to add that perhaps local bands used an old Stan Lee type naming-dictionary when coming up with potential band names, going on to provide specific comic-book character examples such as Peter Parker, Reed Richards, Scott Summers, Fing Fang Foom, etc. Then Neef would add that Stan Lee didn't actually conceive all those characters by himself, nor did he deserve the full acclaim since Jack Kirby and Steve Ditko did so much of the work without ever being properly credited/paid for it. Then the conversation would kind of unravel. Still, they all agreed—local bands were the worst.

the venue. After they tracked down the promoter to settle up. After they re-checked the trailer to make sure it was secure (though the hitch was still a little wobbly, yeah, we need to get that fixed soon). After they put the license plates back on the van and—again—debated if that was actually necessary.[11]

After they each climbed into Woody with his poor suspension lowering closer to the ground with each new body added, each of them carrying more than their body weight, some unseen gravitational force weighing on their frames.

After…everything, the five of them sat in the old van and wondered why they wanted to be back there so bad in the first place. They sighed a collective sigh and began looking forward to when they could do it all again, possibly for the last time.

The vinyl seat served as an icepack against Davy's shoulders. He settled into it. There was a loneliness that often took hold of Davy. He loved being on the road, and if anyone ever asked, would eagerly proclaim as much. Unfortunately, there wasn't a declaration strong enough to prevent the desolation from coming for him during moments of downtime. It laid in wait until there were no distractions, cloaking itself in the seams of the van's seats, biting through even the thickest blankets.

The irony of being lonely in a van filled with his four best friends wasn't lost on Davy either. If anything, it further degraded the mood, slipping into the molecules, thickening the silence until it became impenetrable. It's hard to admit your vulnerabilities when everyone else is depending on you to be the rock. Davy closed his eyes, allowing his mind to wander again to that night so early in the tour, when they still had hope, when he felt invincible.

---

[11] Though the discussion, like most during those days, was a stand-in for a larger issue.

There he was again, alone with Reid after the Futile's set, in the back of their van, fumbling to make contact, t-shirts still sweaty from the show pulled half up then off, the flatness of Reid's chest and stomach against his, the parting of their lips on one another's, the fumbling of belts, the rush of worry that the others could come outside the venue at any second, then the complete absence of any type of worry at all.

Davy exhaled.

With his eyes still closed, he listened to the reverb-drenched sounds of the night, the wind howling outside of the van's metal frame, the fading embers of conversation between Brie and Neef in the front seat, the now subdued static crackles of the Mindfucks buzzing guitars. *I have to take over driving in a few hours for Brie.* Davy squeezed his eyes tighter, willing these familiar sounds to lull him to sleep, but it wasn't happening. Images of the day's disappointments stayed etched on the backs of his eyelids.

It's just Tuesday. Davy had long since grown accustomed to reminding himself of what day it was. He believed it necessary because he was the one responsible for booking the shows and maintaining the band's schedule. In reality, being aware of what day it was just helped Davy tether himself to reality, to his family, to his brother, wherever they were in the world.

It's only Tuesday, February 17th or…dang, maybe it's the 18th.

Brie turned the music off. Davy heard her searching through the radio static for Coast-to-Coast AM. The late-night show had a different call signal every night. After a few minutes, the dial landed on the unmistakable voice of Jim Harold. Brie turned it to a softer volume. She didn't have to do this. The driver had full control over the van's music and its volume at all times. She could have continued to listen to punk rock as loud and as obnoxious as she wanted. That wasn't Brie's style though. Davy knew that she had switched it over out of consideration for the rest of them.

He appreciated her thoughtfulness, or, at the very least, he was thankful that Neef wasn't driving. Neef took immense pleasure in playing the weirdest stuff possible whenever he had to pull an all-nighter. Like, if Neef wasn't playing some awful pseudo-grind-core shit like Guantanamo Bae, then he would be playing audio versions of old Tales From the Crypt episodes or, once even, just a creepy laugh track for hours on end. Brie's talk radio was better than that, though not by as much as one would think.

That night, Davy didn't want to hear about the Blessed Path as he fought for sleep in his bench seat. Per the usual though, that seemed to be the only subject the hosts of Coast-to-Coast were interested in discussing. Davy often wondered if their continued attention somehow gave greater power to the thing they all despised.

Their voices came through in static bursts of conspiratorial murmurs. "Rumors of the Okhrana Contingent infiltrating the Dissent have continued to (crackle, crackle, inaudible)…transferred to the (BRZZZZ) center near Langley, Vi—(crackle). Those taken captive during the last raid covered under the Abuses of Free Speech Act are still awaiting a fair (bzzzzzzzzz). Requests for clarification to the Office of Cultural Terrorism have received a firm 'no comment.' Meanwhile, the Loyal Defender himself spoke today at a (fuzzzzz) ceremony for the new True Believer Network Multimedia Center— (the Loyal Defender's voice cut in) Today there are those that want to defile the good name that our Blessed Path has built for this country, we will not rest until (BRZZZZZ)…"

It tensed Davy's whole body to hear that man's voice, his clipped way of speaking, his sleazy used car salesman ability to spin fiction into fact and vice versa. Davy's stomach lurched as the van careened with the wind before settling back into place. *When was the last time I ate anyway?* Davy worked backwards through the hours; a smashed loaf of bread, plastic utensils, a squeezable tube of jelly that qualified as breakfast and lunch, but no dinner.

A buzz at Davy's right side elicited a surge of hope. Davy reached in his hoodie pocket. He swiped through the cracked screen. Oh, screw you. A message from an unknown number read: "A cat can jump 7 times as high as it is tall." Davy read the message several times. That one doesn't even make sense.

Davy had been receiving those texts from an unknown number for the last several weeks. Like his worst thoughts, Davy hadn't told his bandmates about the strange texts. He was fairly sure that it was one of them playing a prank on him anyways. He admired their effort as much as he despised the false alarm. The only people that had his personal phone number were his bandmates, whoever the cat facts person was, and his younger brother, Vin.

Davy flicked through to his contacts, highlighting Vin's number. His thumb hovered over the screen. Like Davy, Vin played in a protest punk band called Thot Police.[12] Though, unlike Davy, Vin's band enjoyed significant popularity within the scene. They had even secured the backing of the Dissent. Oddly enough, they got it soon after their one-off show with the Futile, ten weeks before. If Davy were a lesser older brother, perhaps he would've been jealous of Vin's success. But that couldn't have been further

---

[12] Unfortunately, Thot Police were something of a one hit wonder. Still, their blazing hit (by Dissent standards) single "Erase-Your-Head" was an unforgettable earworm.

from the truth. Davy was proud of Vin, and though he was just eighteen months older, he felt like it was his job to make sure his younger brother was safe. The phone rang into the void. Nothing, nothing, nothing, then a message clicked on to say Vin's voicemail was full.

Davy felt Brie lose control of the van for a second as a gust tried to push them off the road. His fingers laced behind his head as he stared at the pockmarked ceiling. The impressions and tears in the yellow foam held no answers for him. On the radio, Jim interviewed a conspiracy theorist about how the Loyal Defender was set in place by a shadow government run by ancient aliens. Davy nearly laughed. The smile stayed there until he became aware of the muscles in his face holding it. He let it drop. Wind lashed the van like a whip again. *Home. We'll be home in two more days. Home without Vin. Home without knowing when we'll get to leave again. Home without being surrounded by my best friends every waking moment. If I'm lonely now, how will I feel then? What will I do without any forward movement?*

Since the tour started, Davy never contemplated the fact that it would eventually be over. He was so certain in the power of their music, so certain that it deserved to be heard, so certain that it could inspire people to rise up, so certain that it could make a difference that he never considered the possibility that maybe people just didn't care to hear it. With one show left, the possibility of going home and staying home was becoming more of a reality. Davy didn't know what would come after that.

Another blast of wind shook the van. Davy shook with it.

It was Tuesday.

Chapter Five: The Careful Consideration of a Well-Timed Poop Stop

Over the course of three months, the band learned to accept the functions of each other's bodies. Each lesson came as a reminder of their humanity. For example, they knew that every window in the van would have to be cracked for a few hours if Brie ever got ahold of a veggie dog from an A-Mart gas-station rotisserie. They knew that Davy snored like a nor'easter as a result of his asthma, so they learned to sleep with earbuds in. And they knew that each morning at promptly 9:35am, Remi would need to relieve his bowels, so they often scheduled their rest stops for exactly that time to save him the dignity of requesting a poop stop.

Which is how they found themselves at the A-Mart off I-70 that morning, the second-to-last day of what each of them believed to be possibly their last tour. *Is it nine-thirty already?* Brie thought as the decrease in speed disrupted the rhythm of her sleeping body. She stretched her arms overhead, squinting against the morning sun. Something about this stop felt a bit like saying goodbye to this version of her life.

Wow, are you really nostalgic for a poop stop right now? Brie rolled her eyes. *In two days, we'll be home and maybe we'll never leave again.*

Nas rose up from her bench seat with a lion's yawn.

Unless...

"Nice, this looks like a decent spot," Remi said as they pulled into the parking lot.

"Ugh, what about an A-Mart is ever nice?" Brie rubbed the sleep from her eyes. "Their bathrooms always have such awful graffiti on the stalls. It's hard to do what you gotta do when it seems like people are screaming racist epithets at you from all sides."

Remi shrugged. "At least the bathrooms are usually clean."

"You mean at least it's never you they're talking about," Neef said while adjusting his hat in the rearview.

"Dang, true, true," Remi quickly agreed.

"You want to do our exercises?" Neef asked Brie.[13]

"Is it alright if we skip today?" Brie asked back.

"Cool with me."

"Okay, fifteen minutes, folks," Nas said as they piled out of the van. "Keep your phone calls to—"

"Less than a minute," Davy cut her off. "Yeah, we got it."

Inside the gas station, TBN's "Bless This Morning" blared from a dusty flat-screen perched in the corner like a gargoyle spewing acid rain. The cashier, an older white woman with mismatched eyes (one blue, one green), stared them down with her arms crossed as they ambled in. Brie felt the woman's gaze as she perused the candy aisle. Though the dialogue yelling at her from the flat screen made Brie want to wince, she made sure to keep her posture straight, lest she, even for a second, give off the impression that she didn't fervently agree that the Blessed Path was awesome, had always been awesome, and anyone that said otherwise deserved a fate worse than public humiliation followed by prompt execution. The brightly colored candy wrappers offered less than nothing, but Brie still allowed her eyes to linger

---

[13] "Static stretches, calisthenics, standing squats, you know, that sort of thing. Early on, Brie and I would do what we could to combat the effects living in a van wreaked on our bodies," Neef told this author when asked how they kept in shape living on the road. "Eventually, like most of our good intentions, we gradually gave it up. Honestly, I was relieved when we did."

while Nas was in the bathroom. There was something to be discussed and it couldn't wait a second longer.

Nas strolled over from the back of the store. "Door's locked. Neef beat me there."

"Hey," Brie whispered. She shot a look to the cashier and craned her neck back to check out the restroom corridor. It was all clear. "I've been thinking about a way we could get our names out there."

"Yeah?" Nas lowered her eyes to meet Brie's.

Brie shot another look to the bathrooms before tugging on Nas' elbow. "Let's talk outside." Brie watched their mirror image in the security monitor hanging from the ceiling. The door dinged behind them. "What if we give our name to TBN?" Brie asked once they were safely outside. The sun peeked between menacing clouds like a child playing Hide & Seek with their disinterested parents.

"Go on," Nas said with a straight face that betrayed nothing.

"We just send in an anonymous tip with our name, they begin to talk about us, and boom, we're a big deal. The Dissent always backs artists who are sought by the OCT."

"That…that's a risky move. I just don't think the others will like it."

"Here's the thing—we don't tell them."

Nas tightened her jaw instead of responding.

Instantly, Brie felt guilt for what she was suggesting. "I'm just saying, they wouldn't have to know that we called it in," Brie said, though even as the words tumbled out of her mouth, she realized she wasn't helping her case. "Like, you could look at it that we're saving them the worry by not telling them."

Nas looked past her, squinting into the distance for a few seconds before focusing in again on Brie. Nas shook her head. "I get what you're saying, but I think that's a dangerous road to start down."

"No, yeah, I know, you're right." Brie shook her head. "I'm sorry. I just can't go home again." The thought of crossing the threshold of her father's home sent a shiver down to the soles of her shoes.

"This isn't how I wanted this tour to end either. But we have one more show, who knows, anything can happen."

Never one to hide her emotions, Brie's inability to muster Nas' optimism tugged down on the corners of her mouth.

"Hey." Nas put her hand on Brie's shoulder. "I feel that too. But I promise you, we're going to make it. We are. We have to. I won't let us stay home for long."

"Yeah," Brie said, doing her best to soften her expression.

Soon the boys came out, bounding back into the van. It was four miles down the road before Brie realized that she forgot to use the bathroom. She thought about asking them to pull back over but decided that the grief she would take for making them stop so soon wasn't worth it. She crossed one leg over the other. Thin, bare trees extended from the earth on each side of the road. Reminders of her mom lurked in the strangest, most unsettling places. Brie closed her eyes. In her restless sleep, she dreamt of ghoulish hands reaching out in death for what they never had in life.

The ringtone for Davy's burner stirred Brie from sleep. The burner never rang. Brie jolted upright. "Whoisit?" She asked in a blur.

"Unknown." Davy showed Brie the screen before pressing the green button. "Hello?"

Neef glanced back in the rearview. Remi leaned forward on Brie's bench seat. Nas pivoted from co-pilot. All of them listened eagerly as Davy said:

"Uh-huh."

"…"

"That's cool. We understand."

"…"

"No, yeah, we'd love to."

"…"

"That sounds great."

"…"

"Awesome."

"…"

"For sure, count us in."

"…"

"Bet."

"…"

"…okay, yep, we'll see you then."

Davy put the phone away and didn't say anything to his bandmates.

"So who was th—" Remi started.

"Nobody." Davy cut Remi off with his perfect smile. "Nobody at all. Just the promoter."

Brie narrowed her eyes. "That…didn't sound like a typical promoter…"

Davy shrugged and faced the window.

Neef mock-glared back in the rearview. "Davy, I'll drive this van into a lake."

"Okay. I'll tell you all, but first I want to know if you're ready. Are you ready?"

"Yes!" The rest of the band exclaimed together.

"So, our show tonight got cancelled, and..." Davy trailed off.

Brie motioned to conjure the words from him. "And?"

"And..." Davy clucked his tongue. "Nah, you all aren't ready."

"Davy, c'mon, man." Remi groaned. "Seriously."

Davy crossed one leg over the other and shook his head. "It's nothing anyway."

"Davis!" Nas slapped Woody's dash with playful anger. "Spill it."

"Okay," Davy laughed and moved to the edge of his seat. "So that was Alyssa with the Dissent and she wants us to play their event tonight instead because one of their bands dropped off—"

"Dropped off or got hauled to the DITCH kicking and screaming?" Remi asked.

Brie waved off Remi's question. "Are you telling me that we're playing a Dissent show tonight?"

"Yep," Davy said with a big smile.

Nas, Brie, and Neef let out a collective cheer.

Nas locked eyes with Brie and gave her a wink.

A Visit to the Futile Vault of Lost Songs

"The Day Selfies Saved the Planet"— Unlike other Futile songs that never saw the light of day due to the band either outgrowing the style or just simply never having time to record, "The Day Selfies Saved the Planet" was locked away forever in the Futile Vault of Lost Songs because they no longer agreed with the song's premise. Despite the Futile's stance, the consensus among historians was that the largely unheard song served as a pivotal moment in their career. Thus, the surviving members of the band, who were still open to doing interviews, were regularly asked about it.

"It was one of the first songs we wrote before we really knew how to write songs, before we understood what it meant to stand for something," Neef said in conversation with documentarian Darien Ogletree. "The day we wrote it, there had just been this big opposition event for the Loyal Defender's fourth inauguration. We were still just kids practically. Brie and I were sophomores at the Academy. Nas, Davy, and Remi were just freshmen. The idea of protest being this powerful thing was still relatively new to us. So, there was this opposition event, but it seemed to be more of a self-congratulatory thing, where people were taking pictures of themselves and their signs like it was all just a game to see who could pat themselves on the back the hardest. It just seemed to cheapen it. So that's where the song was coming from. It all seemed so dumb to us at that time…"

Darien, off screen, asked, "What changed?"

"Well." Neef sighed, sat up straighter, scratched his thick beard. "We realized we were only seeing half the picture, or not even half, but maybe like just ten percent of it. I think it was Davy who showed us the video a couple of weeks later of this massive crowd of people chanting: 'You can't arrest us all!'"

"Then what happened?"

"They arrested them all. Or worse actually, I think a hundred and twenty-two people were killed that day and thousands were thrown into the DITCH," Neef answered. "We learned then that saying anything of worth was going to come with consequences and that people who stand up against tyranny deserve our support even if, or especially if, they're new to it and don't totally know what they're doing just yet. For what it's worth, Nas tried to rewrite the lyrics to reflect that, but it didn't quite work right. It was just something we had to learn with maturity. That opposing the Blessed Path wasn't a competition, we were all in it together. The only enemy was those that oppressed us. Took us a bit to learn that."

Darien, still off-screen, asked, "Knowing what you did about the results of previous mass protests didn't make you think twice about opposing the election of J.R. Rankin?"

Neef glared at the origin of the voice. "Like I said, we knew the risks involved. Doing anything that means something comes with a cost."

"I apologize. But, surely, you wish that day had gone differently."

"If it had, we probably wouldn't be sitting here now."

Chapter Six: Punker Than Thou[14]

For what it was worth, Remi tried to match his bandmates' excitement. Smiling and nodding as Brie said again, "I can't believe this is really happening!" High-fiving and fist-pounding Davy and Neef each time they remarked that they were going to "kill it tonight." Mumbling affirmatives when Nas laid out the plan for what they would do after inevitably securing the Dissent's backing. Still, he wondered if his eyes betrayed each half-hearted gesture. His bandmates were adept at seeing through anyone's bullshit, including, or especially, his.

After a while, Remi just stared out the window as their enthusiasm bounced around him. Small town church marquees scrolled by, each mocking him: THERE IS NO DOUBT IN THE ARMS OF THE ONE TRUE FATHER; DON'T WORRY YOU'RE NOT IN CONTROL; and, perhaps, most damning, REMEMBER THIS LIFE IS TEMPORARY ETERNITY IS FOREVER. The only release Remi found was during their pre-show sing-along to "Two Minute Hate." Only then, did he start to feel that maybe everything would be okay so long as his bandmates and the music never left him.

But then they arrived at the (near) packed venue and his frenzied bandmates promptly scattered to fraternize with anyone even tangentially related to the Dissent, leaving Remi trapped in an awkward one-sided conversation with the event's promoter. Remi leaned against the shuttered building, letting the brick dig into his shoulder blades through the thin jacket that he wore even though it was twenty degrees out. The jacket looked cool

---

14 Alternate chapter title: Self-Titled, Track 7.

though and being slightly overweight in a world of seemingly-naturally skinny people, Remi would take whatever help he could get. The mask could (and would) only get him so far.

He nodded along to the promoter, the guy that risked his neck to help put the show on. The promoter was talking about how much he loved their song, "Prisoners Of Conscience." Except, it seemed almost like he didn't actually like it, because he kept kind of talking crap, but in a subtle, small way that a normal person may not notice. Remi wasn't normal though. He couldn't help editing out the kind words from the conversation, focusing instead on the brief Freudian-like slips, the backhanded compliments, and slightest slights hidden underneath the paragraphs of praise. The end result looked like a Blessed Path document with the nice phrases redacted, the transcript of which would read as follows:

"Ah, bro, when I first booked you all I had no idea who you were, I just like to help out touring bands that are trying to spread a message of empowerment, you know? But then I saw that link a few people were covertly sharing through the channels a few nights ago of your song and I was like (████████████). These kids are actually KIND OF (████████████). I usually don't go for less hardcore stuff like this. The lyrics can be pretty on the nose, you know? I'm just glad you all are plugging along even though you're so far underground. The Dissent hasn't even really heard of you. Alyssa just needed a band, literally any band, to open and I knew your other show in the area had been cancelled. It's just cool that kids as young as you think they can make a difference. I guess every little bit helps in some way. At least you all are legit trying, you know? But (█████████████████████████).

Anyways, I think tonight's show will be good, and I'm (████████) to see how you all <u>actually pull some of those songs off live.</u>"

As the guy went on, Remi imagined the cracks of the sidewalk breaking open to swallow him whole. A couple of people filed into the shutdown factory. Each one had more stylish hair, cooler denim vests with cooler patches, more scuffed up boots. Even though Remi was the one in the punk band, they were all more punk than he could ever be. Sure, he wore a mask, but he felt like they saw through that to see that he wasn't good enough. They somehow knew he was the worst musician in the band, that he was the weak link sure to eventually break them. His lack of commitment to the (all caps) CAUSE was palpable to them. He was a poser and a coward, and everyone knew it.

The promoter finally stopped talking. He took a pull off his mist pen. The tip lit up blue like the pleasure centers of his (probably) perfectly healthy brain. Remi watched him with envy. When you're low enough, being anyone else seems better than being yourself, which only makes it worse. Remi's thoughts strangled him. *Maybe getting pulled over by the OCT the other day is still lingering with me. Maybe I just need to talk to Davy or Brie or Neef or Nas about how I'm feeling. Maybe I just need to get out of here. Maybe I should just stay at Aunt Marie's when we get back. Maybe after I'm there for a bit, I won't want to stay. Maybe I'll finally find the fire that comes so naturally to everyone else. Maybe. Maybe. Maybe.*

Maybe it'll be better inside.

It wasn't any better inside. Davy and Nas were holding court in a semi-circle of fellow punks in front of the stage. Brie was talking to a couple of guys as she restrung her guitar at their would-be merch table. Throughout the room, there were multiplying groups of three to four people. Each second, a new cluster formed, each second, Remi felt more like the useless machinery lining the edges of the room. Finding it hard to breathe, Remi rushed for the side-door and shoved through. Cold air slapped him like a friend trying to bring him back to reality. Remi hunched over with his hands on his knees, sucking in deep breaths.

"Heyyyyyy, Rem." Neef stepped from behind the concrete divider. "You good?"

Remi's cheeks burned behind the mask. "Yeah." He caught the newly cracked screen of Neef's phone as he straightened up. "You?"

"Yep." Neef sniffed and looked away before turning back. "No. Not really, man."

"What's going on?" Remi asked. His breathing began to steady.

"It's just…" Neef held his phone out horizontal for Remi and clicked play.

Through the spider-webbed screen, a TBN clip ran of a massive rally in downtown Louisville intended to be a celebration for Young Apostles who had recently taken their lifetime oath of service. A large bald man stood at a lectern shouting. Spit flew from his mouth like shrapnel as he whipped those gathered into a frenzy. "WE WILL ENSURE THAT THERE'S NO PLACE HERE FOR THOSE THAT DON'T BELONG," he bellowed. The crowd of young people roared in agreement after each bombastic line.

"Jesus." Remi looked to Neef. "I don't get why they feel the need to constantly do this. Like, we get it. It's exhaust—"

"Wait for it," Neef said without watching the screen.

The bald man's call to violence reached a more urgent pitch as the camera panned to the crowd. There, held overhead was a flimsy white sign, the message blurred. It was soon snatched up and consumed by the pit of angry youth. Its owner was thrown to the ground. A wailing and gnashing of limbs followed.

Neef tapped the screen to freeze the clip.

"Right there." Neef pointed at the image of a hate-filled young man paused mid-scream. His teeth bared in sick, primal desperation; his fist reared back to deliver another blow to the already unconscious victim. The scene soured Remi's stomach.

"That's Jerrod." Neef pulled his phone back. "He was my guy growing up. We started our first band together.[15] Even at the Academy, we always swore we would never get wrapped up in the Loyal Defender's bullshit." Neef gave an exasperated laugh, shrugging with his phone. "Seems one of us was lying."

"Dang, I'm sorry, Neef."

"He's gone full Acolyte now. Shouldn't surprise me. Nothing should anymore. I just can't help thinking that if I would've stayed in his life, he would've stayed strong, he wouldn't have gotten caught up in…that." Neef shook his head. "And now I'm supposed to go play the biggest show of our lives."

"Maybe you could use it for motivation," Remi said, offering his last drop of optimism. "Put it into your performance, get it all out. A scene like that—" Remi pointed to Neef's phone. "Just proves how important music like…ours can be. Besides, you're not responsible for saving everyone from their own ignorance."

---

[15] "We were a short-lived ska band called Weapons of Brass Destruction," Neef told this author. "We disbanded soon after Jerrod's dad found his notebook of pseudo-rebellious lyrics."

"Yeah. I guess so." Neef exhaled. "Thanks, Rem." Neef slapped him on the back. "What about you though?"

"Huh?"

"You sure you're good?" Neef cocked his head at the side-door. "Because you didn't look it when you ran out here."

Remi rubbed the back of his neck. His worst thoughts climbed over one another, fighting all the way to the surface. *Maybe I should tell Neef that I don't belong here, that I feel like I'm as beneficial to their leap for greatness as a pair of concrete Chuck Taylor's, that I'm a part of the underlying, ever-pervasive problem, that I hate myself most the time for all the stupid shit I say on daily basis, so I try to just keep my mouth shut but then I become even more isolated with my doubts and if it's a battle of me versus them then I'm definitely losing.* Remi swallowed and tried to laugh it off. "No, I'm okay, man. Just ate a van burrito earlier. Needed some air."

"Yeah?" Neef raised an eyebrow behind his green mask. "You sure?"

"Yeah." Remi nodded, finding the lie comfortable.

The side door flew open. "Yo, there you are!" Davy hung halfway out the door. "They want us to do a soundcheck. Can you believe that? A freaking soundcheck?" Davy shook his inhaler and took a pull before shooting back inside.

"You got this." Neef put his hand on Remi's shoulder and looked him in the eye. "I want you to know that."

Remi nodded. He followed Neef inside with his anxieties trailing behind him, though they seemed to drop off one by one for each step he took closer to his bandmates onstage.

Chapter Seven: The Glorious Blur

Brie couldn't believe it. Suddenly it seemed that every shitty show played to no one, each bout of diarrhea caused by eating food plundered from a dumpster, every night spent tossing and turning from one shoulder to another as they barreled across the country in a metal death tube had prepared them for this. Their reasoning stood that if this was a Dissent show then it was possible some of the leaders would be there. And if the leaders saw them perform then they would definitely choose to back the band and propel them to stardom. Sure, bonus points for their message getting heard and all that. It was everything Brie wanted. If things went right, she would never have to go home again. *This is really happening,* Brie reminded herself through each step of her pre-show routine.[16]

It was really happening.

Then, they were on stage with bright floodlights shining in their eyes. They were the first band of three although the headliners had yet to show up.

"You ready?" Nas addressed the rest of them from the middle of the stage. Brie nodded from behind her own mask. She fanned the fingers out on her left hand then flung her wrist back and forth as she looked out in front of them. Red Exit signs cut through the dark, one on each side of the room. Standing between Brie and the Exits[17] was the combined shadow of close to a hundred people. Brie wondered for the fiftieth time if any Dissent leaders

---

[16] A handwritten note found in Brie's old guitar case laid out her pre-show routine as The Five S's: "String (your guitar- at least once a week), Socialize (& make friends), Stretch (your body), Sit (& allow yourself quiet), & Say (thanks to your bandmates)."

[17] Not coincidentally, "Brie & the Exits" was the working title of the solo project Brie often daydreamed about but never actually started.

were amongst the crowd. Her purple fingernails picked at her guitar's chipped gold paint before abruptly stopping. *Fuck it. Let's play like they're here even if they're not. These people won't know what hit them.*

"Here goes everything we got," Brie called to Remi and Neef on the other side of the stage. We got this. You got this.

Drumsticks held above his head like an offering, shoulder muscles bulging beneath the lights, Davy stretched one arm behind his head and then the other. Brie turned forward again and sucked in a deep breath. She closed her eyes, waiting for the sound. Tck, Tck, Tck, Tck.

Then Brie opened her eyes to the glorious blur.

Four songs into their set and Brie felt outside of herself yet wholly present. She couldn't help repeatedly looking out at the crowd. It was a mass of arms, hands, and faces. People were rocking out. Some even knew the words. With a sharp inhale, Brie hoped to pull the feeling into her lungs and keep it there.

To her left, Nas cradled the mic against her cheek like it was the most precious thing in her whole world. Nas then pivoted back to the crowd, roaring with a powerful voice that came from deep within, "You worry about the purity of dogma / while neglecting the integrity of love! You keep your eyes glued to a screen / while ignoring the Other down in the mud!"[18] On the other side of Nas, Neef threw down with an intensity Brie had never seen. It spurred her even further on.

Brie hopped on the balls of her feet. She ripped into her lead riff, banging her head so hard that she worried her mask might slip off. Then she stepped up to her mic and yelled along with Nas for the chorus: "You don't

[18] Futile old heads will recognize these lyrics from their song, "Glacier Of Death."

seem to realize / that any God that is yours but not mine / Any God solely concerned with only you all the time / Is an idol not a God, now please pay your fine / Your god is not a capital-G god, but an idol / now please pay your tithe / Move along and fall in line!'"

Brie stared out into the audience again as she stomped on her fuzz pedal and tore into the bridge guitar riff. The Futile's music echoed through the vacuous factory walls. It used to be a place where boats were manufactured, where living wages were earned, a place that provided luxury or at least the appearance of it. A lot of hope was shut off for the community when its doors closed for the last time. But that night, as the Futile blazed on, that hope was alive again. Brie imagined a celestial body being able to see their light from space. Once again, they were the motherfucking Futile and nothing could stop them.

Nothing could stop them.

Nothing. Could.

Stop. Them.

Until a light came up in the back of the room. Then another. And another. Concerned looks passed from one audience member to the next. People began breaking for the exits. The girl running sound waved frantically to get Brie's attention. No, she couldn't have said that. "RAID!" the girl yelled again. "Go now!" The band stopped playing. Brie's one shot, wasted. Rage swallowed her whole.

There was no other choice.

If they survived this, Brie knew what she had to do.

Chapter Eight: Find a Thread to Pull

Brie turned the key again. Woody dry heaved a few times but refused to turn over. Remi's thumping heart pounded through the front of his cold, damp t-shirt. "Try again," he told Brie as though it needed to be said.

"Careful not to flood it though," Nas contributed from the passenger seat. Her voice sounded painful and strained like it always did after shows.

"I got it," Brie said, her blue mask pulled half back. Her hair already matted to her head. Fresh beads of sweat formed at her temples despite the cold. "C'mon."

Brie tried again. The van coughed and shook, but then…nothing.

I knew it. With fear in his eyes, Remi turned to watch the last pair of headlights tear out of the parking lot. For all their talk about inclusion, the Dissent sure didn't seem to care about leaving them for dead.

Remi did the simple math. The lookout said they received word of a raid heading their way in fifteen minutes, and that was about—Remi looked to the dashboard clock—about fifteen minutes ago. "Next time this happens, one of us needs to start the van while the rest of us load the trailer. That way maybe we could get some help before everyone else leaves," Nas said.

Next time? Remi thought. It didn't seem likely there would be a next time even if they survived this. At least Remi hoped there wouldn't be one. He wrapped his arms around himself to keep from shivering (it didn't work).

"Nasim. Not now," Brie said with her jaw set tight, a single bead of sweat raced along its curvature. She turned the key again.

Remi looked back at the concerned faces of Neef and Davy. In previous situations, Remi would be the one to tell them that they were overreacting, that the Blessed Path wasn't even aware of their existence. But he definitely wasn't saying that now. It was a Dissent event after all. Bigger shows, higher stakes.

"You good?" Davy placed a hand on his shoulder.

"Yeah," Remi lied. "You?"

"Yeah." Davy gave his shoulder a squeeze. "We'll get out of this."

"I wouldn't be so sure," Brie called from the front.

They closed their eyes as Woody hacked and shuddered for the fifth time. The engine whined with exertion to turn over, but it couldn't get there. "Shit!" Brie slapped the steering wheel.

"Okay," Nas said in a calm, yet hoarse, tone. "If we sit here much longer, we're as good as dead. We need to leave the van behind and run for—"

"Run for where?" Remi interrupted. "There's nowhere to go. It's freezing out and we're all drenched, we'll die in no time, and if we leave the van then they'll definitely find out who we are."

"I know." Nas turned from the passenger seat with her red mask still on. "But at least we could get a head start."

"Nas is right." Brie leaned her head against the steering wheel. "I'll try one last time and if that doesn't work...we'll do whatever we have to do."

Nas reached back to Remi. He took her hand in his left and put his right back for Davy who took it and then reached back for Neef's. They each closed their eyes. Despite their collective absence of religion, something like a prayer hovered on each of their lips; their faithful breath fogged the air as Brie turned the key for what could be the final time.

The van shook as if exorcising itself from its demons. They gripped each other's hands tighter as the shaking continued. Then, perhaps miraculously, the old van sputtered to life. Woody's fanbelts squealed with glee. Brie turned from the driver's seat with a smile. "Alright, let's get the hell out of here." She aimed Woody toward the exit and sped toward it with all the old van could muster. Remi finally let go of his bandmates' hands when he saw that there were no headlights coming from either direction.

It was five miles down the road before any of them dared to speak. "Soooooo—" Remi let the word hang out there like a lifeline, hoping his bandmates would hop on.

"Soooooo—" Nas broke through her rasp to come in with the higher harmony.

"Soooooo—" Davy anchored the low.

"Soooooo—" Brie joined in with the mid.

"Soooooo—" Neef jumped in with an absurdly low baritone.

"Soooooo—" Remi accelerated his note to a ridiculously high falsetto before sweeping his hand like a conductor to cut the harmony off. "—I guess it was a false alarm then?" He asked, barely able to contain his grin.

Nas, Davy, and Neef groaned, throwing half-hearted punches and whatever debris they could find at him. Remi fended off their blows. The smile he wore felt good, almost like it fit. "But no, really though, were you all praying there? Because I know I was."

Davy shook his head with disgust. "No way."

"We were supposed to be praying?" Neef asked incredulously. "I was just envisioning the calming presence of Malala Yousafzai."

Nas laughed as she climbed back from the front seat to sit next to

Remi. "That's as worthy a prayer as any," Nas said to Neef before turning to Remi. "Yeah, I was praying though. Why?"

"It's just…" Remi met Nas' eyes and lowered his voice to a near-whisper. "Who were you praying to?"

Neef and Davy looked to Nas. Brie glanced back in the rearview.

"To…God," Nas said, and then perhaps reacting to the confused looks she received from her bandmates added, "I know the Loyal Defenders' followers have made that seem gross, but I believe in a higher power, a divine creator. They've already taken so much from me; I'll be damned if they take that too."

Remi raised his eyebrows. "Literally?"

Nas gave a polite laugh. "My family still practices their religion even though it's not that safe to openly do anymore.[19] If they can do that, I can at least pray when the moment calls for it." Nas cleared her throat, but the grit remained. "Who were you praying to?"

Neef and Davy looked to Remi. Brie set her eyes back on the road.

Remi swallowed, absent-mindedly running his finger along his scar, wondering if now was the time he should let out the worst of his anxieties before deciding again to hold them in. "I guess I was just praying. I do it almost every night. Old habit. Sometimes I just lie awake thinking of what a

---

[19] In her never-published memoir, Nas wrote of her parents' religion: "Like most aspects of our family, the religion of my parents was a combination of the best parts of both their worlds. My father continued the progressive Islamic traditions his parents passed onto him, while my mother continued the Buddhist practices she learned in her native Mongolia. Meanwhile, my parents taught my sister and I to pursue our own understandings of the world, even encouraging us to read the Bible and the Torah in addition to the Koran and the Tripitaka. Like most things about our family, the beautiful harmony of differing ideals confused many of our neighbors and angered even more. But no, despite our acceptance of most beliefs, we didn't consider the Prophecy of the Flaming Sword as legitimate."

jerk or idiot I am, and I pray to—I don't know—God or whatever to help me not be such a dumb asshole and then the next day I'm less of one, sometimes."

"I think that may be the definitive proof that God doesn't exist that atheists have been seeking out for centuries," Davy said with a laugh.

Damn. A punch straight to the gut. Remi turned away from the conversation. *He's not wrong though.*

Davy's expression softened and he gripped Remi's shoulder. "Like I said, I wasn't praying. I just try to visualize a solution to my problems, our problems, the world's problems, and put some positive energy out there in hopes that it will solve them. Sometimes it works." Davy sucked his teeth. "Still, doesn't make me less of an asshole though. Sorry, Rem."

Nas nodded as Remi turned back to the conversation. She cleared her throat again. "I think what you said is the same as praying, just by a different name."

Davy narrowed his eyes at her. "But isn't it all just bullshit?"

"I don't think so. There's got to be at least something to it."

"Nope, there isn't," Brie said over her shoulder. "Trust me, it's alllllll bullshit and so are the people that buy into it."

"Do you care to elaborate on that?" Nas challenged.

Brie readjusted her grip on the steering wheel. "Nope."

"Don't let the Blessed Path confuse you," Nas said to Brie. "The people they've misled, the otherwise peaceful ideas they've warped and distorted for their own gain, those people are not your enemy."

"Oh, trust me, I'm not confused, and I can tell the enemy for myself, thanks," Brie called back.

"But don't you see that if we just damn a whole religion, a whole group of people who practice a particular faith, then we're no better than them? Just because they've been made to believe that we're their enemy, doesn't mean that we have to be."

"Oh, so complicity and ignorance do equal innocence now? Seems like I can recall one particular punk rock lyricist that used to say otherwise. Good to know."

Nas shook her head. "That's not what I'm saying. I'm not talking about the hateful, misogynistic, homophobic Prophecy of the Flaming Sword, which I will readily concede is indeed bullshit. I'm talking about—"

"Okay, I get it."

"Wait though, I feel like there's something you're—"

"Nas, I'm so done with this conversation."

"No, no fair, you opened that up. I call Keanu,[20] I say there's some truth to religion and you say—"

"Nope. I'm not about to play some game just to explain why religion is dumb. I don't have to prove myself on anything."

Davy, Remi, and Neef looked at Nas. Her cheeks flushed. "Yeah, you're right. I'm sorry."

A blast of wind hit the van hard. Remi quietly braced against the tension.

"It's cool," Brie said with a catch in her voice that suggested maybe it wasn't. A few seconds howled by. Brie stifled a cough. "Sorry for making

---

[20] Keanu was a debate game that the band played to challenge one another. Occasionally, this called for a player to argue for a concept that they didn't even support in order to exploit any potential logical weaknesses of their opponent. Everyone hated the game except for Nas, because she almost always won.

this super awkward," she said with a forced laugh. "Here, let's jam. I mean we just narrowly avoided an OCT raid so that we can play another day, er, I mean go home. I guess that's worthy of a celebration." Brie cranked the volume knob up. The Mindfucks resumed rattling through Woody's speakers. They sang along to the words. Nas climbed back into the front seat, putting her hand on Brie's shoulder as she did so. Brie laid her head against Nas' hand and let it stay there for a while. All was well. The Futile were finally going home.

The thought comforted Remi as much as any thought could. The show had been busted up so quickly that there was little chance the Dissent would decide to take them on. He was disappointed for his bandmates, but, still, the tour was over. He'd survive.

Chapter Nine: Sage Advice from Animatronic Fish

Nas woke with a gasp as though she just emerged from water. She placed a hand to her chest and measured her breaths. Early morning light filtered through the windshield casting everything in its bluish gray. Rows of desolate cornfields stretched into infinity on each side of the van. It was okay. They were safe.

"Bad dream?" Brie said from the driver's seat. Her cheeks lacked their usual warm hue. Her eyes were puffy behind her glasses. Nas figured Brie must have taken her contacts out at some point in the night while driving. That was just one of Brie's many driving skills.

"Something like it," Nas replied. She reclined back into the co-pilot seat. The vinyl chilled her bare shoulder. She rewrapped the cheap cotton blanket around her. "Are we on schedule?"

"Yep. I stopped to get gas a few hours ago while you all were sleeping." Brie exhaled. "We should be crossing our wonderful state-line in a few more hours.[21] Then it will be home sweet *home*," Brie emphasized the last word like it was a slur. She glanced over to Nas. "I don't guess we heard anything from the Dissent or even got paid from last night, huh?"

Nas' throat ached. A bottle of water rolled into her foot. She reached for it. Ugh, it had already been opened. At least it's clear. Nas rattled it. Well, mostly clear. She returned it to the floor. "No. Not since everyone had to leave so fast."

"Pretty convenient."

---

[21] Kentucky: birthplace of the 16th president; handsome TV doctor turned suspicious philanthropist, Joshua St. Lawrence; the universally beloved stray dog, Smiley Pete; and our heroes, The Futile.

"What're you saying?" Nas asked without an edge. Whatever tension was between them last night had not entirely dissipated. It still clouded the air like the smell of sweaty show clothes. Nas didn't want to push it.

Brie shook her head. "Nothing. Don't pay attention to me. I'm just tired. All that matters is that we have enough money to get home. We do, right?"

Nas nodded.

"And it won't be forever?"

"Definitely not," Nas said with all the gusto she could muster. Last night was the closest they had ever been to getting the help they needed. Nas' aspirations were a mountain that grew two feet with each foot she climbed. The thought of being restricted to the bottom, or anywhere, kindled a simmering fury within.

Brie's stomach growled so fiercely that they both laughed.

Nas grinned at Brie. "You know, I was thinking the same thing. Pull over at the next diner you see."

Brie rubbed her stomach. "Do we have enough cash?"

"Yeah, we'll be fine. We need to have a proper band meeting anyway."

They found a spot just off an exit near the river that doubled as the state-line. The establishment was called Billy's. Not the fun alliteration of something like Billy's BBQ or the faux down-hominess of a Billy's Eating Shack or the lingual rhythm of Billy's Food Barrel, just Billy's. "Food," Nas called back to the boys.

Pickup trucks dotted the gravel lot. Nas checked the plates. They were all from in state and, although several had bumper stickers announcing their support of the Loyal Defender,[22] there weren't any Blessed Path-issued plates. That seemed a good enough sign that it would be a safe place to eat if they didn't hang around too long.

A little bell rang a cold, metallic jingle when Nas pushed the door open. Every pair of eyes in the place turned and focused on them. "Great," Nas said under her breath. "Five," she politely told the hostess.

Nas scrunched up her nose. The smell of smoke and fried food hung thick in the air. The ceiling tiles were stained yellow like a cigarette filter, which reminded Nas of her own lack of dental care. Suddenly, she felt incredibly self-conscious of her appearance and that of her bandmates. Haggard and road-weary, they filed in behind her, appearing very much like a group of punks who had spent the last three months living in a van. There was a time when they took greater care to fit in when they were in public. More and more they made that effort less and less. Nas ran her tongue over her teeth like that would do anything.

"Cool." Neef walked up to the pride and joy of the restaurant's owner, a full wall of fake bass mounted like trophies. The little red buttons on the bottom of their plaques were too tempting to pass up.

"Neef—" Nas started, but it was too late.

Neef joyfully pressed each of the buttons in rapid succession. A shrieking chorus of "Don't Worry, Be Happy" blared through the previously quiet restaurant in row-row-row-your-boat rounds. "Man, I didn't know they still made these!" Neef took a step back, shaking his head.

---

[22] It's important to reiterate that a lot of citizens were vocal in their support of the Loyal Defender because they were afraid not to be, not just for the severe penalties (imprisonment, torture, death), but for the social implications as well. Then, the same as now, it's lonely to stand apart.

So much for going further unnoticed. With a smile, Nas guided Neef along by the shoulder. The hostess/waitress led them to a circular table in the corner of the restaurant. Nas took a seat where she could see the door. A TV hung on the wall across from them. Onscreen, three smiling blonde women with crossed legs shared a U-shaped couch with two paunchy white men wearing unflattering suits. Through medically induced smiles, they delivered the pre-approved "news" of the day. As much as it disgusted the young members of the Futile, they still watched it, trying to find the truth in what wasn't said. "If you reverse the political spin it'll take you back to its origin," was a popular Nas mantra.[23]

Nas stretched her hoodie sleeves over her hands while she watched. Smiling Blonde Woman #1 declared the recent mass deaths of bees across the south, "an unfortunate byproduct of the continued economic expansion of our Blessed Path."

To which Frumpy White Man #2 responded, "I'm allergic to bees anyway so you won't hear me complaining."

Smiling-While-Dying-Inside Blonde Woman #2 swatted FWM #2 on his knee while the other morning hosts erupted into laughter that went on for five seconds too long.

"They're so stupid," Davy said to his coffee cup.

"Yeah," Remi agreed spiritlessly.

"I think they're geniuses," Neef said.

Davy pivoted towards Neef. "Seriously?"

Neef smirked. "When am I not serious?"

---

[23] The extremely observant Futile fan will recognize this lyric from their never recorded song, "Oh-Wellian."

"Always." Davy's hand fell hard onto the table, displacing the salt and pepper shakers, which were shaped like two bug-eyed fish. "You're literally always not serious."

Nas' eyes darted between the two of them but, luckily, Neef shrugged it off. In past situations like this, Nas would push it a little further, call a game of Keanu, have them debate it out, but not here, not now. Nas' stomach roared as the waitress came back for their orders, and ordering food only made Nas that much hungrier.

To distract herself, Nas listened to the conversations of the middle-aged men sitting along the counter. Did they buy into all the bullshit the Blessed Path was dumping? Or could they no longer deny the smell? In the case of the old guys along the counter, it seemed neither. Their conversation was about work and where to find it. What places were hiring? What places were shutting down? They were as worn down as the chairs they sat in. And though she was confident that these same men so down on their luck were probably fanatics of the Loyal Defender when he came to power, she still felt sorry for them.

Their conversation soon shifted to the erratic behavior of their local deer population. She eavesdropped the best that she could without making it obvious. Nas leaned back in her chair, bumping into the waitress as she came around with their food. Vegetarian dishes[24] were placed before the five of them. Nas knew that Remi and Neef weren't actually vegetarian, but they still refrained from eating meat out of respect for Davy, Brie, and Nas when they were on tour. Which meant that Neef and Remi hadn't eaten meat in at least

---

[24] Despite being a popular dining spot for locals, Billy's wasn't quite known for its inclusive cuisine, so "vegetarian" dishes were hashbrowns plus whatever vegetables the cooks usually mixed into omelets.

three months. *I wonder if they'll go back to eating meat when we get home. I wonder what bad habits we'll all return to.*

Remi dug his shoulder into Brie's. He nodded toward an old man sitting at the counter's heaping meat plate. "I'm sure he'd share if you wanted, Brie."

"Nope." Brie wrinkled her nose before gesturing at Remi with her fork. "He seems more your type anyway since he has such an interest in tiny, undercooked sausages."

Remi floundered for a comeback, eventually giving up and turning back to his food. Nas shook her head at Remi's poor attempt at...flirting? *I guess you could call it that.* Nas took a sip of her tea. It soothed her throat some, but not as well as the antibiotics she likely needed. She sipped it again, knowing this would be all the medicine she would likely get. Even when they did get home, a clinic visit was just too expensive, and she couldn't ask her mom to do that. Nas was fine with toughing it out.

Okay, they have food. This can't wait any longer. "Folks." Nas cleared her throat. Her bandmates continued shoveling food into their mouths with their heads down. In their defense, it had been over a week since their last warm meal.

"Hey." Nas leaned forward, her voice lowered to avoid any potential eavesdroppers, but not so low as to invite suspiciousness. Their non-meat food order was suspect enough. "We need to talk about what comes next."

They each glanced up from their plates while continuing to chew.

"So, with last night being the first show that we've ever had with the...you know...and with that goon wagon following us a few days ago..." Nas made eye contact with each of her chewing bandmates before she continued. "It should be clear now that we are in fact on both of their radars..."

Nas paused to see if Remi was going to interrupt her. Thankfully, he instead motioned for her to go on. "We're on the brink and the time has come to step up so we don't lose any momentum." Nas took a bite of her food, wincing as she swallowed. "I know that we're planning on going home for a bit now, but—"

"Um." Remi went as pale as a ghost.

Nas sighed. He just had to interrupt her at some point, didn't he? "Remi, just let me finish, please, as I was saying—"

"No, Nas." Brie cocked her head at the TV.

Nas' fork clanged against her plate as she reached to cover her mouth.

Chapter Ten: Enemies of the Culture

Conflicting signals were nothing new to Remi. There was the way his Aunt Marie would tell him that he could stay with her anytime, but then acted like he was putting her out when he showed up on her front step with his duffel bag. There was the way his father swore he was a good, godly man, yet hated everyone that wasn't just like him. There was the way Brie would sometimes reach out to hold his hand whenever they slept near one another, followed by the way they both later acted like it never happened. To the best of his ability, Remi made sense of these things, finding a level of acceptance with some more than others.

Unfortunately, what he saw that morning in the diner was even harder to understand. His eyes told him that what he saw on the TV was in fact real while his mind told him it couldn't be so. His body demanded that he swallow the food in his mouth while his throat temporarily forgot how to function. Remi looked from the screen to his bandmates then back to the screen. It couldn't be true. Remi looked to his hands as though they held the answer. They were shaking so he hid them under the table.

But the image remained the same—Remi and his four favorite people in the world, each in their respective colored mask. "ENEMIES OF THE CULTURE" was displayed above their picture in huge red font. "If you have any information concerning the whereabouts or current activities of the band known as The Futile then please contact your local Office of Cultural Terrorism immediately. They should be considered dangerous and are toxic to the image our Loyal Defender has cultivated…"

Davy started to push up from the table. "We need to go now."

"No." Nas put out her hand. "That will look more suspicious. We stay and finish eating. We'll tip the perfect amount and no one will notice we've been here."

The five of them ate while the threat of their demise loomed above them. "That's J.R. Rankin. Commander of the OCT." Neef nodded at the screen. "He's supposed to be up for 're-election' soon." Neef took a bite and spoke through his chews. "The word on the streams is that when he inevitably wins things will be a lot worse. He's making it his goal to wipe out the Dissent entirely. The only thing holding him up is his campaign."

"How could things possibly get worse?" Brie asked.

"I don't know, look at him," Neef whispered. "A dude like that, unencumbered by any term constraints or anything, he could do some real damage. I heard he had a whole town poisoned just because they were harboring a couple Dissent sympathizers."

"That hasn't been confirmed," Davy chimed in.

"Who's going to confirm it?" Neef batted back.

Remi looked up to see the hulked-out bald man from the news clip Neef played him the day before. Rankin had small, dark eyes and spoke with a gruff voice like parking blocks thrown in a woodchipper.

"From here on out, it will be my sole purpose to track this band of rebels down. They're a menace to our country, warping the naïve minds of our youth. They must be stopped by any means necessary." Which seemed almost reasonable at first, but the more Rankin talked, the more worked up he seemed to get. "After all, we MUST ensure a pure, GODLY path for OUR children above everything else. And if that takes EXTREME measures, well, then so be it. This BAND is nothing more than a GANG of punks and thugs. They're less than human. They don't deserve our mercy. And with the

GREAT DEVOUT SWORDSMAN AS MY WITNESS, I WON'T BE GIVING IT TO THEM! ALL! THINGS! IN! HIS! HONOR!" By the time he finished speaking, Rankin had worked himself up into a full-out maroon-faced, red-necked, blithering, lather.

"Geez, maybe he'll give himself a heart attack before he ever finds us," Nas said quietly with a sly smile. The rest of the band stifled laughter, except for Remi.

I look just like all of them, Remi thought, watching the talking heads onscreen. *I look just like everyone that torments my friends. How do they not hate me?*

Remi took another bite of food, forcing himself to swallow hard, but the lump didn't leave his throat.

Remi sat co-pilot while Nas drove. Billy's hashbrown casserole did the 200m backstroke in his stomach. His foot tapped rapidly against the floorboard. Each time Remi became aware of doing it, he stopped himself, though it wouldn't be long before he started again.

Remi glanced over at Nas. Unlike him, she didn't seem shook at all. Her eyes were focused straight ahead as she laid it out there for the rest of them. "They just know who our band is, not our names or who we are underneath the masks. So that's a strength. That can be an advantage to us even." Nas coughed into her sleeve. "But before we go any further, we gotta sort this out, are you all up for this? It's only going to get tougher, more dangerous, and more chaotic from here on out. If you're in then you need to be all the way in. There's no turning back. There may not even be a choice of going home again." Nas lifted her palm from the steering wheel. "But hey, if you're not up for it, then no worries, we can—"

"Nas, it's cool. I'm in," Davy said first. "The burner's been blowing up with well-wishes from some of our past promoters."

"I'm in too," Brie said with obvious jubilation in her voice. "I mean I was in before and I'm definitely in now too."

"Man, it's times like this that I know the simulation theory is real." Neef shook his head. "But yeah, count me in."

"Okay, hold up. Can I ask for Immunity[25] for a second?" Remi finally worked up the confidence to ask.

"Granted," the other four responded almost immediately.

Remi shifted in his seat. "How do you think they got our picture and band name?"

Nas glanced back at Brie in the rearview. "I honestly can't say for certain."

"So...just like that? We're going to do this?" Remi spoke to the windshield rather than facing any of his bandmates directly. He rubbed his palms on his knees. "Don't you all find it a little weird that right after we get pulled over, right after we play our first Dissent show ever—"

"What're you getting at?" Brie asked.

Remi pivoted around. "I'm just saying, aren't you all even a little concerned? I mean why right now right as our tour is over? Why us?"

"Why not us?" Brie cocked her head.

"Because..." Remi found himself fighting against saying what he had wanted to say weeks ago. "We're kids!" Remi exclaimed. "Why our picture on TBN? How are we even remotely a threat to them? Sure, it's awesome to

---

[25]Immunity was something the Futile came up with to discuss difficult things without offending the others. Like most of Nas' concepts, it was meant to encourage comfortability with the potentially uncomfortable.

play music that can inspire people, but how can we possibly make a difference?"

"The way I see it." Neef leaned forward. "We can either step up and at least try, or we just stand somewhere in the background while they continue to ruin everything. Rem, you can do this. I want you to know that, but you don't have to if you don't want to."

Nas nodded and spoke in a softer voice, "Remi, I know this isn't really what you had in mind when we started up. No one will think any less of you if you...you know, don't want to do this."

Remi blinked back tears. "It's not like my aunt wants me showing up at her house again. It's not like I can stand being under my dad's roof for even one night." Remi's chest tightened as he finally addressed the thoughts he had been avoiding. The promise of getting off the road had blinded him from anything else. The realization that neither home nor safety existed for him anymore was harder to digest than anything Billy's had to offer. *They would probably be better without you anyway*, came the thought. *You're what's holding them back.*

"Where would I even go?" Remi choked out as he imagined Woody pulling off without him inside, the silly inside jokes and moments on stage that he would miss out on, how empty life would be without his bandmates by his side.

Nas started to answer but couldn't. She wiped at her eye with the back of her hand. Remi watched as the black bracelets that dangled from her wrist draped over the steering wheel. He wanted to ask to be let off at the next stop. He wanted to ask Davy to contact someone in the Dissent for a proper extraction. *Is that even a thing though or does it just sound like something they would do? Would they even protect someone so unimportant?* Each scenario he played out in his head led towards a lonely dead-end. The only family he had was there in that van. "It's okay, Nas." Remi swallowed. "I'm in too."

Neef, Davy, Brie, and Nas all cheered. Remi smiled despite the tears.

Behind him, the burner beeped. "Yes!" Davy fist pumped. "It's Alyssa with the Dissent. They want us to play a show tonight outside O'Fallon."

"Let's do it! Turn the van around," Brie said before launching it to a chant: "Turn the van around! Turn the van around!" Davy quickly joined her.

"Neef?" Nas called back over the chant.

"I don't know why you even ask," Neef said before joining in with Brie's chant.[26] "Turn the van around!"

"Remi?" Nas leaned over.

"Sure." Remi shrugged, fully aware that the word was the least positive use of an affirmative. *Just get to the next show, whatever the cost.* "Turn the van around."

"Okay," Nas said as she focused on something beyond the van's windshield. Remi followed her gaze, trying to see whatever it was she saw. Like the day when Nas first came to him with the idea that their music could make a bigger influence, Remi knew he would just have to trust her vision.

Then they turned the van around.

---

[26] "Oh, I love a good chant, who doesn't?" Neef said in conversation with the author. "I mean I know it's mindless or whatever, but it's also silly fun. We tried to start a chant whenever we could. My favorite we ever did was: "No! More! Farts!" when Davy had a truly unprecedented, legendary streak of ripping the foulest farts you had ever smelled in your life for like four days straight. Davy, to his ever-loving brilliance, ended the chant by yet again ripping a fart so bad I swore it took miles off Woody's life."

And Now…the Hosts of TBN's "Bless This Morning" Listen to The Futile (A Transcript)

Greg: Good morning, welcome to Bless This Morning—

Kelly Lee: Bless your morning, Greg!

Greg: (chuckles politely) thank you, Kelly Anne—

Kelly Lee: I'm Kelly Lee (laughs). Kelly Anne is out for the whole next week on maternity leave. (Places her hand to shield her mouth like she's talking to the audience and Greg can't hear her.) Someone hasn't had his morning coffee yet today (laughs).

Greg: My mistake (gives menacing look to Kelly Lee). (Smiles into the camera) Of course! How could I forget?

Kelly Lee: (laughs into the camera, then sighs) I don't know.

Greg: Well, as we all know, there's an awful band of misfits traversing our country spreading their (air quotes) music that is filled with hate and lies.

Kelly Lee: (smile turns to frown) A lot of viewers have reached out to us, asking 'how can I know if my teen is listening to this band of evil youth?'

Greg: Our producers thought it would be helpful for us to listen to a sample of their (air quotes again even though he already did that) music.

Kelly Lee: I'm ready, Greg (plugs her fingers in her ears). Just kidding (pulls her fingers out, laughs way longer than needed).

Greg: (glances sideways at Kelly Lee before turning to the camera and smiling) Welp, here goes nothing! (Waves at the control booth to start the song.)

Existential angst and anger at previous generations of humans blasts forth from unseen speakers in the form of buzz-saw guitars

Kelly Lee: (fingers in her ears for real this time, wincing against the onslaught of wisdom she has spent her entire adulthood trying to avoid) It's pretty loud! *Then the vocals start in: "I see you eyeing that shiny barrel / Would love to give it a little taste / It must be so embarrassing / To feel you have to compensate!"* *

Greg: (scowling at someone off-screen) HOW MUCH LONGER DO WE HAVE TO DO THIS?

A drum fill pounds like a stampede of elephants into a blistering pre-chorus: "You could love anything / You could love anyone / But you choose to..." *

Kelly Lee: (doubling over as though the music is giving her stomach cramps) Oh, my.

Down-strummed guitars take the wheel for the chorus: "But you want to...FUCK GUNS / Yeah, you want to...FUCK GUNS / Disregarding everyone who says...fuck guns, fuck guns, fu—" *

Greg: (Flails his arms emphatically until the music abruptly stops) Who— (glares off-screen) Who thought that would be a good idea?

Kelly Lee: (appears too disturbed to speak. Looks to the camera, her lips hovering over words she can't bring herself to say.)

Greg: (Wipes hand across his sweaty brow and attempts to smile) All things in his honor, we'll be right back.

Chapter Eleven: Dumpster Diving for Simple Truths

It's Monday. Without opening his eyes, Davy slapped his jeans pocket. It was instinctual to him when his personal phone was ringing. Though it couldn't be seen or heard, Davy just knew it was somewhere vibrating in three-second bursts. A blind, fumbling search around his seat came up empty. He slapped both his pockets again. Nope. It certainly wasn't on him. Davy opened his eyes. He so didn't want to be awake right now as it was his turn to drive that night, but he also didn't want to miss his brother calling him back. Vin never went this long without returning a call. Especially not after the Futile had blown up like they had. They had played five shows since TBN featured them as Enemies of the Culture, each show bigger than the last. Surely, if something were wrong Alyssa would've told him by now.

Davy rolled from his seat onto the floor. Ugh, why was it so sticky? *I don't even want to know.* Half-filled water bottles, trash from trash food obtained from some regional gas station in the Northeast, random sweaty show clothes verging on mold growth, but no phone. What if Vin needed Davy's help? Davy started to look more frantically.

Davy crawled over the filth. Frigid air leaked through the crack of the side door. More sweaty clothes, wadded up, rock-hard tissues, *beyond-gross,* more water bottles, some of which filled with an easily identifiable orangeish liquid, oh, there was the backup inhaler he'd thought he lost, *still has some juice left,* then beneath it all, sure enough, was Davy's cracked phone. It had since stopped ringing. Davy picked it up. He had missed several calls from a blocked number.

Davy jumped when his phone buzzed to life again. The same blocked number appeared. Davy swiped to answer. "Hello?"

"…"

"Hello?"

"…"

"He—"

The call abruptly ended.

"What the hell?" Davy looked at the cracked phone screen.

"What's up?" Nas' brown eyes glanced back in the rearview.

"Nothing." Davy collapsed in his seat, running his hand over his face.

"Do you still need to make a phone call?" Nas called over her shoulder. "Remember, we have to ditch our personal phones before we meet the Dissent leaders tonight. We should've already done it a week ago, honestly."

"I know." Davy's broad shoulders sagged beneath an unseen weight. "I know."

"Okay, that seems like a good spot." Remi pointed to a rundown brick building. Faded graphics for specials were plastered on the windows. Canned Ham $23.99. 12 packs of Assorted Cola 3 for $20. Blazing Ranch Nacheeso's buy one, get one.

"You think so?" Nas pulled into the sparse parking lot. "It looks rundown."

"Oh, it definitely is, but who cares? I'm starving."

"But they're still open."

"That's fine. That just means whatever they've dumped will be that much fresher." Remi put his feet on the dash and started tying his shoes.

"Just pull up near the side and we'll run around the back." Remi squinted back at Davy. "You coming with?"

Davy slid his phone into his pocket. "Sure."

Nas shifted the van into park. "I'll honk twice if anything is amiss."

"Amiss?" Remi stopped tying his shoes. "Who says that?"

"Badass lyricists with huge-ass vocabs," Nas cracked. "But forgive me, what I meant is that I'll leave your ass in the dumpster if anything goes wrong."

"Fair enough." Remi opened his door. "Neef?"

Neef awoke with a snort. "Coming."

Woody idled to the side of the grocery store, exhaling grayish black CO_2.[27] "Alright, who's going in?" Davy stood in front of three green dumpsters. There was no telling when his next shower would come along, and Davy wanted to avoid smelling like slightly-to-excessively spoiled food for the next week if possible.

Neef wiped sleep from his eyes. "I'll go."

"Me too." Remi blew into his hands. "You had to go last time, Davy."

That's true. He did go last time. That alleviated his guilt some. "Right, I'll keep watch."

Remi offered a foothold for Neef and helped him over the lip of the

---

[27] Early on, the Futile sought to get a van that ran on vegetable oil to limit their carbon footprint. However, Nas grew suspicious of the few vans they found for sale, believing that it was likely that buying/touring-in a van like that would be exactly what the Blessed Path would expect them to do. Which is why the band bought the old maroon van that screamed "FIRST CONGREGATION OF THE FLAMING SWORD, WESTERN KENTUCKY" on the side.

dumpster before diving over the side himself. They landed with a squish.

"Nice! This is a good haul already," Neef said as they swished through the refuse like brave explorers wading across the Mississippi.

Davy checked his phone again. Yes, it was on. Yes, he had a signal. No, there were no incoming calls from his brother. Several times, Davy thought to slip his phone back into his pocket. Each time he tried though, he couldn't bring himself to do it. He continually tapped it to life every few seconds before the screen went dark.

It's Monday, February…I don't know.

Davy's phone buzzed. Yes! Davy triumphantly swiped through then his posture sank. "Ancient Egyptian families shaved their eyebrows in mourning when the family cat died." Davy shook his head. Someone was really getting the best of him.

Ten minutes later, Remi bounded out of the dumpster. He fell to the concrete and cussed. Neef climbed onto the lip of the dumpster and leapt out. The three of them took inventory of their haul. Two dozen assorted dented cans; three loaves of smashed, expired bread; two bags of moldy hotdog buns ("Just tear off the green parts"); a large box of something called "Funky Bread"; eight crushed Ramen packages; three bundles of bruised-black bananas; six dented (but otherwise completely fine) plastic jars of peanut butter; five large jugs of apple juice with a broken seal; and, the real steal of their draft, fifteen boxes of Devout Swordsman-themed snack cakes shaped like little red swords.

"Not bad," Davy said, figuring that he could actually stand to eat most of these things. The five of them could survive on this for another three weeks if they had to, and if the phone calls from the Dissent kept coming in, they probably would.

"Hey." Neef nodded behind them. "We got company."

Two children wearing ratty, puffy coats for sports teams that hadn't existed in over a decade stood at the chain-link fence that separated the grocery store from the surrounding neighborhood. Dirt smeared their cheeks. The girl, the older of the two, didn't have any shoes on, while the boy wore shoes that were at least five sizes too big.

"Are you hungry?" Davy asked.

The girl nodded. Davy put her age at about nine. The boy said nothing as he hid behind his sister. Davy estimated he was five or younger. Both the children looked as though they stepped straight from a webpage on the Wonders of the Industrial Age. Their eyes betrayed their round faces, giving them the impression they were much older than they were. Davy figured he didn't look much better.

"Here." Remi started tossing the majority of the snack cake haul over the fence.

"You ready?" Davy asked the girl as he gestured that he was going to throw the jugs of Apple juice over.

The girl nodded. Davy tossed her the jugs one at a time; she caught each of them with ease. Neef lobbed over a few cans of vegetables. The loaves of bread went over next. When one of the bags got caught on the barbed wire, Davy managed to dislodge it with a stick.

"Thank you." The girl looped her arms around their bounty while her little brother filled the front pouch of his coat. They started back toward the Blessed Housing Complex that towered in its dilapidated state a block behind the grocery store. Davy didn't say anything as he watched them jog towards the menacing structure. Though they were far enough away from it, they still stood in its shadow. Around the corner of the store, the van honked twice.

Remi hopped a couple of steps. "Let's go," he called after Davy, but Davy didn't budge. Remi went back and shook his shoulder. "Man, I know, but we can't help them any more than we already did. They'd be worse off with us anyway."

The van honked again. Woody skidded into the alley. Brie slid open the side door. Neef, Davy, and Remi made a run for it as the shopkeeper came around the corner. "Thieving squirrels," he yelled. They ran faster, laughing as they bounded into the open door while the van continued moving.

The shopkeeper watched with defeat as they squealed out of the parking lot. Once they hit the street again, they erupted into breathless, sleep-deprived, unbridled laughter. They laughed because they had gotten away. They laughed because they were stretched to the point of exhaustion. They laughed because they had another story to tell. Because they were together, they were young, and they were free.

They laughed because they knew those things wouldn't always be true.

Chapter Twelve: Yesterday's Actions, Today's Regrets

For the sixth night in a row, the Futile were added onto a Dissent show as the opener. Brie took stock of their venue for the night. The recently departed Unitarian Fellowship was a true upgrade from the places they were used to playing. Light streamed through the stained-glass windows like a kaleidoscope while the sweet hint of incense danced on the air. Brie sucked in a deep breath. Tonight was the night. They were going to meet the Dissent leaders for real.

For the moment, it seemed that Brie's gamble had paid off. Yes, she would eventually tell her friends that she passed their name on to TBN. That's how she would phrase it, *passed our name on*, not the harsh wording of "reported" or "ratted out." No, it was just a simple anonymous report made out of desperation. Surely, the rest of them would understand. Will they though? Brie asked herself again. *Nas will be pissed that I went ahead and did it against her advice. Davy and Neef will be blindsided, and I can't blame them. But all three of them will forgive me if it works out. Remi…it's hard to imagine him ever being okay with it. It doesn't matter; I have to tell them all soon, just definitely not tonight.*

People were already filing into the sanctuary for the show. The crowd was a healthy mix of veteran punks, newbies, and strait-laced older people who seemed like they came straight from a Blessed Path desk job. They all stood shoulder to shoulder, talking easily to one another, finding common ground despite how different they appeared. Beneath her mask, Brie smiled. This would easily be the biggest show they had ever played. She had risked too much to take that for granted.

"My god, look at her ass, it's spectacular," a dude's voice said from the crowd as Brie hunched over her amp, dialing in her settings.

"Shhh, you can't be saying that," a second dude's voice said.

"What?" the first dude said. "I'm just saying, she's on a higher level than me. Like she's a goddess and I'm a lousy slob mortal."

Brie shook her head. Was this motherfucker serious right now?

The second dude was silent for a moment. Oh, no. Brie wondered if he was considering his friend's dumbass logic. "I guess I can see that," the second dude said.

Brie sighed.

"But it still seems misogynistic," the second dude clarified.

"Yeah, no shit," Brie said under her breath with her back still turned. Her left foot tapped impatiently. A Brain Dead Megaphone song played over the PA system.

"How am I a misogynist? I'm just saying that she obviously works at it, so I want to acknowledge her efforts and her beauty. How's that wrong?" The first dude countered.

"Just...you shouldn't say that stuff here."

"Whatever."

There was a time, when they first started out, that Brie used to say that she played in the band to meet people, to have joyful, meaningful interactions with fellow members of the human race. But it was moments like this that reminded her how little she actually liked humans sometimes. It was even more disappointing to see that some within the Dissent were just as ignorant as anyone else. Then, the same as now, it was people who were the true downfall of any well-intentioned organization.

Nas walked over. "You ready?" She asked, adjusting her red mask. Dark hair with light tips hung out from the bottom.

Brie turned from her amp. The two dudes who were previously talking about her butt were adorned with the full regalia of the Dissent's slogans and stances. Without even the slightest hint of irony, they each had feminist badges as well. Brie stared them down, daring them to make eye contact. Suddenly, they were more interested in the church's architecture. "Yeah, let's do this," Brie answered.

Nas nodded at Brie before she grabbed the mic so hard the stand fell over. Nas left it there. "We're the Futile and this song's called 'Fuck Your Intolerance Part Two!'"[28]

Davy clicked his drumsticks together four times. Right as Brie strummed down on her guitar, she spit a huge loogie directly on the two bros. The larger one looked at Brie with his mouth hanging open, which made her want to spit again. Instead, she responded with a wink as she tore into her mid-verse lead. A few seconds later, the two guys faded into the rest of the crowd. Brie's fingers fretted the power chords on her guitar, she slipped easily into another lead-riff, but her mind was elsewhere.

Normally, being on stage with her band was an escape, a time for her thoughts to take a backseat to her body, a time for her internal monologue to shut up and enjoy the ride. But as she ripped through their first song that night, as her physical form went through the full motions of the show, her mind was left untethered, free to sink into the recesses of her darkest thoughts, the things she couldn't bring herself to confront otherwise.

Brie drifted back to earlier that afternoon when she wiped the fog from her window in the back of the van. Her palm lingered there, letting the

---

[28] In *The Sound of a Movement*, Jocelyn Hopper hailed "Fuck Your Intolerance Pt. 2" as the quintessential song of the opposition movement. A recorded version of part one, though rumored/expected to exist, has never been located.

cold sink in. She exhaled. It wasn't going to get any easier. It never would. She pressed her father's contact. The long pauses between each ring gave her a chance to hang up and opt out, but she held on. Her purple fingernails found the hole in the vinyl seat. Little yellow cake pieces fell to the floor as she picked at it.

"Hello?" He asked when he finally picked up. His voice sounded distant and empty as though filtered through an old coffee can.

"It's me...Dad." Brie cupped her hand over her mouth and the phone.

"Brietta?" He asked. There it was. The way he said her name cut loose things she believed forever lost. Several memories rose and broke open at once. Summer nights, the honeysuckle smell of their home with the windows left open, the pumping of oil wells in their fields, a chorus of frogs croaking from the tall grass, sitting between her parents on their porch swing, watching the last orange bits of daylight drain from the evening sky, the days when the healing power of a band-aid wasn't activated until it had been kissed.

"Yeah," she said, her voice breaking up a bit, though not from the poor connection. "I don't have long, I just wanted—"

"Anything you have to say I don't care to hear."

"Dad, please, this may be the last time I get to call for a..." Brie swallowed. "For a long time."

"..."

"Something happened with the band."

"That—in the masks? That was you?" His voice cut in as a whispered hiss. "I can't believe you'd call me. You're putting me at risk."

"Dad, just—"

"What are you thinking? You think you can win this? You think this can end well? You're just making it harder for yourself, for both of us." Her father cleared his throat. It came through much louder like he hoped they were listening in. "If you weren't so stubborn, you'd see what all we've been provided by them already. They've given me a good job, a good home, a good school for you to attend. All you had to do was follow the rules. Is that too much to ask?"

"Yes, it is," Brie said through clenched teeth. Remi looked back at her from his seat. She turned her back to shield him the best that she could.

"Your generation will never appreciate the sacrifices we made."

"Your generation mortgaged our future so a couple billionaires could—"

Brie's father barked into the phone, "Is this why you called? To be ungrateful?"

Brie sighed and held her head. "Dad, no, listen, I hope that none of this comes back on you. I don't want you to lose your job with them. Because although it isn't good, I know you honestly believe it is. I don't hate you for that. I really don't. And I guess..." Brie's voice quivered. "I'm sorry if I make life any harder for you than it needs to be, but what we're doing here in this band is for the good of everyone, and that's true whether you believe it or n—"

Her dad scoffed. "I don't believe that. And I don't believe you do either. You're running away, looking for fame to replace your mother's love and you're going to be real disappointed when it doesn't work."

A few tears cut down Brie's cheeks. She folded herself deeper into her seat. "Dad, I just called to say that I love you." Brie switched the phone over to her left ear, waiting for him to say back the same three words, those three words he used to say so easily.

"Lose this number." The call ended like a pair of shears severed the connection.

On stage, Brie came back to reality as their first song concluded to raucous applause. Soak it in, Brie told herself. Sweat seeped down from her mask and stung her eyes. She wondered if she was crying. Her next thought was if the others could tell. Remi smiled at her from his side of the stage.

She did her best to return it from behind her own mask.

Chapter Thirteen: Existentialism On Show Night

The third song of their set was always Nas' favorite. It didn't matter which particular song it was, as the song itself changed from night to night. It just took at least two songs for Nas to feel like they were really in the groove. The third song of that night's set was "Prisoners Of Conscience" and, man, were they really in the groove.

As Neef played the bassline intro, Nas reflected on the first time they started jamming the song together two years before in Remi's old church basement with wood-paneled walls and the ugly green carpet that smelled of breath mints and water damage. Back then Nas got to go home after band practice. Back then she slept easier knowing that her parents slept in the room next to her, as Aria's chest rose and fell in the bed parallel to her own. The funny thing was, Nas didn't appreciate any of that at the time. All she wanted then was to be out on the road making a difference. As young as she was, she felt older back then, more disciplined, stronger and certain.

We've made it. This is what we wanted. People care. We're inspiring change, Nas told herself as Davy came in on the low toms over Neef's bass. Faces blurred together in the crowd. Nas did her best to make eye contact with as many of them as possible, to see each of them as an individual instead of just a part of a larger whole. Time was running out though, in a few more seconds she would have to start singing. Nas cleared her throat.

When she opened her mouth, she pushed from her diaphragm to purge herself of the words she held deep within. Each line held new meaning than its original intent. "Take a hammer to your home / Build it back up again / Break down your foundation / Find where you belong in the end." As the words poured forth, she thought back to the phone call earlier that day with her mother.

In the front seat of the van, her bony knees pulled to her chest knocking together with the vibrations of the road, the sleeves of her hoodie stretched over her fingers, Nas held the phone to her ear. The phone didn't even complete one full ring before her mom picked up. "Nasim?" Her mother asked.

Whatever resolve Nas had stored up drained from her tired frame when she heard her mother's voice. It was the light timbre of bedtime stories, of telling her that she would be okay when she scraped her chin, of calling her out when she crossed a line. It was the sound of home, of waking up and knowing where and who she was. Nas looked back at Remi. It was strange how he just threw his phone out the window after she reminded them to get rid of them. She hadn't seen him call anyone to say goodbye.

"Nasim—Nas?" Her mom's voice brought her back.

Nas pivoted back to the front. "Mom, yeah, it's me. I'm here." Nas focused her attention at some point beyond the van's windshield. An old stage-fright trick she learned early on: focus on the back of the room, look over the heads of the crowd and everything will seem less intimidating. Is acting brave the same as being brave? Aria asked her once. Nas had long since forgotten how she responded.

"Are you okay? Where are you?" Her mom was a true pro at rapid-fire questions.

"Yeah, I'm okay. We're…um…"

"Oh, you can't say. Have you eaten? Have you been sleeping? Will you be home soon? I thought you said you would be home soon."

"That's why I'm calling actually—"

"Oh, no. Did they get you?"

Nas laughed despite herself. "No, we're safe—"

"Because, you know if anyone says they're trying to help, don't listen to them. There are so many around you can't trust anyone. I mean anyone, Nasim. They'll say they're going to do something good, but you can't believe a word out of their mouth. Your father always said…"

Nas dug her fingernail into her palm. "Have you heard from Dad?"

"No…" The pause dragged on. Nas checked her phone to make sure she hadn't lost the connection before her mom continued, "The agent assigned to our case assured me that he was safe and that they would have the papers sorted out soon, but she's just trying to placate me. When you get home, we could really use your help, the apartment is too quiet without your father around and your sister has asked after you every day."

Nas' eyes burned. She started to say Aria's name to ask to speak to her, but she knew hearing Aria's voice would break her. Nas squeezed her fist. "Mom, I won't be coming home," she said through gritted teeth.

"I—I understand."

Nas stared straight ahead at a propaganda billboard that read: The Strong Follow Along! "I can't come home again. It would be too dangerous. There's so much that we need to do out here still. I have something in mind. Something big. It could make things better for all of us. Make a better future for Aria."

"Your aunt would be so proud.[29] I am too."

"Mom, I love you."

---

[29] Nas' paternal aunt was the feminist activist, Romana Bashir, an outspoken adversary to the early iterations of the Blessed Path. Sadly, Romana died in prison days before Nas' birth.

"I love you, too." Nas pulled the phone away from her ear and stared at the red square to end the call. With a sharp breath, she pushed her finger down. Then, with the cold determination of a soldier breaking down an assault rifle, Nas removed the back of her phone and slid the SimCard out. She crunched it beneath her boot while she cranked down her window. She closed her eyes as the wind whipped her face. Nas threw her phone on the road ahead of them. The black rectangle bounced off the pavement just in time for the van to run over it. Behind the steering wheel, Neef raised an eyebrow at her before returning to his conversation.[30]

In the old church, Nas stared at the back of the room. An enormous, obnoxiously-ripped plaster Jesus[31] hung suspended from the ceiling, blood streaming down his face from his golden crown of thorns, his face twisted up in righteous anger, his flaming sword held over his head preparing to strike. The figure was a holdover from when the fellowship briefly operated as a Congregation of the Flaming Sword. Nas couldn't stop staring at it. Someone had painted the Dissent's logo on plaster Jesus' bare chest, which was confusing on more than one level. For a split-second, Nas saw her face on his body. She blinked, and it was gone.

"You call yourself a creator / But all you leave / is a legacy / of destruction," Nas yelled on stage. Underneath the lights, she felt like she was exorcising her own demons rather than preaching to the masses. Her throat was ragged and raw. The words didn't come easy. They almost never did.

---

[30] In Neef's memoir, *The Rhythm of Our Road*, he wrote the following of his parents: "My parents were activists before my sister and I were born. Encouragement and love were all I ever knew from them. They understood what it meant to fight for what's right. They too, unfortunately, knew what it meant to lose someone as a consequence of that fight. And though they did their best to prepare me for that possibility, they knew there were certain things I would have to learn for myself."

[31] Nas refused to acknowledge him by the title of the Devout Swordsman.

Nas leaned forward on the lip of the stage. She didn't allow herself to look at the back of the room again. She opted instead to make eye contact with every pair of eyes she could without being blinded by the stage lights. Gravity pulled her into the crowd. She leaned into it. Multiple pairs of hands caught her respectfully and eased her back onto stage. Without missing a step, Nas roared the bridge refrain, "We will not become what we mean to you." Davy built up the tempo, his drums pounding louder and louder. Nas sucked in a breath, scraping the inside of her lungs for whatever she had left to give. "We will not become what we mean to you!" Nas screamed into the mic, pushing past the phlegm, the angst, the loneliness, the anger. She screamed in defiance of a world full of people who vilified her existence, but her voice wasn't amplified. The floodlights had been cut along with the power to the stage. Nas' voice hung there in the dark, shallow and alone. "We will not become what we mean to you!" Nas screamed again.

Davy abruptly stopped drumming. He put his drumsticks in his lap. His posture slumped. "Oh, no."

"It's a raid!" someone yelled. Like Cinderella's helpers turning back into animals at the stroke of midnight, the once-united crowd was reduced to a mass of individuals fearing for their own safety. Screaming and commotion rang out in the sanctuary as the showgoers scrambled for the exits, followed by a push from the sides of the crowd like a spring being squeezed tightly before expanding. People tumbled over one another as they fought to go in every direction at once. "The doors are blocked!" The crowd pushed inward on itself again, preparing to burst.

"What do we do?" Remi asked Nas with wide eyes.

"We get the hell out of here, that's what we do." Brie rapidly packed up her pedal board. She tucked the suitcase under her arm. Cables spilled out of it like guts.

The doors to the sanctuary banged open. Silhouettes of OCT agents in full riot gear filled the doorframes. Among the agents—the only one without a helmet—was the bald man from the TBN news segment, J.R. Rankin. A news crew in shabby riot gear followed close behind him.

"We don't have time." Nas grabbed Remi by his shoulder as he started for his amp. "We have to leave it. Keep your masks on. Let's go!"

Nas led them through the backdoor onstage. Remi and Neef followed her with their instruments still strapped around their torsos. Brie had her guitar in one hand and her suitcase in the other. Davy brought up the rear carrying only his drumsticks. The air in the back of the church tasted like bug spray. Colorful squares of light beaming in from the stained glass windows lit the pathway. *Keep moving away from the shouting, the screaming, the sanctuary, the guns, and we should be okay.* Nas sprinted hard into an egress door. "I think this leads outsi—" When it opened, an alien stood there, blocking their path. Their eyes hid behind a gas mask with tubing that ran into a large backpack. The label on their lapel said Murdock, Acolyte First Class. Breathing heavy with an evil clouding their lungs, the alien focused its rifle on the middle of Nas' chest. Nas looked down at the tiny red dot and said a prayer. Her hands reached for heaven. She thought back to the vengeful Jesus in the back of the room. She never wanted to be a savior.

She always preferred the martyrs.

Chapter Fourteen: Punks in Space

When Davy dreamed it was often in nightmare scenarios. Situations in which he needed to move quickly, in which he needed to run and/or hit someone as hard as he possibly could, but due to the cruel science of dreams, he couldn't ever act fast enough. Dream Davy would then be left to watch his loved ones get captured, tortured, devoured, mutilated, murdered, etc.

The backyard of the church was the surface of another planet. Just degrees above zero, yet the cold barely registered for Davy. He took a step further. Blades of grass tore into his bare feet like shards of glass. It wasn't a dream; they were playing a show and the OCT raided the church. He had fled so quickly that he left his shoes on stage. He had his drumsticks at least, whatever good they would do. Davy dug his heels in deeper.

The agent stood in front of them, his rifle trained on Nas' chest. "Don't move," the voice came out low, guttural.

Nas' hands were straight in the air. She panted tufts of white smoke. Her eyes bore into the agent's mask.

The agent gestured with his gun. "Take your masks off and put your hands up!"

"My hands are already up," Nas said through her teeth.

Davy and the rest of the Futile put their hands up and their instruments clattered to the ground. They conveniently ignored the first part of the agent's demand.

"Masks off!" The agent moved toward them. He stood nose to nose with Nas now. Nas flicked her head ever so slightly to the left. None of the Futile removed their masks. Davy swallowed, assessing the agent's armor for any weaknesses. It would just be a matter of choosing the right spot. Nothing could be done while Nas had a gun aimed at her chest though.

Cloud cover passed over the moon like a shade being drawn. "Masks off!" The agent demanded yet again. Squawks and murmurs came through the agent's comlink. They didn't have long before they'd be surrounded. Davy scooted forward a few inches in the grass, if he could just get between the agent and Nas.

The agent reached for Nas' mask. She leaned away with her hands still in the air. His gun draped to his side as he reached further. Nas lunged into him, slamming her forehead into the front of his gas mask. The agent stumbled back. Davy moved in and knocked the gun from his hand before the agent could recover. In one swift motion, Nas swung her elbow into the agent's temple. It landed like the crack of a baseball bat. The Futile stopped and looked at her. "Run," she said calmly.

Davy stutter-stepped a few feet to the side, making sure that his bandmates were coming before he took off. The frozen grass stabbed into the soft parts of his feet. Pins and needles ran along his spine. As he sprinted, a memory came back to Davy of gleefully running with Vin after they defaced the first OCT building in their hometown. Their laughter echoed through the alleyways and parking lots, even as chain link fences tore their jeans. The stakes were the same then, though it didn't seem it. Ignorance of the Blessed Path's atrocities allowed the young brothers to feel somewhat invincible. On the church lawn, Davy knew better.

Woody waited two hundred feet away, transcendent, shimmering, a mighty stallion in the moonlight. Brie scrambled back for her guitar and pedalcase before she joined them. Remi's guitar laid in the muck like a wounded soldier.

Lungs burning, Davy took a quick pull off his inhaler upon reaching the van. Chaos filled the churchyard. Shadowed figures wrestled smaller shadows to the ground, pinning their arms behind their backs. Scattered flashes illuminated the night as agents tossed RCGs[32] in the direction of those attempting to flee. Davy slid the side door open for his bandmates and climbed behind the wheel. High beams cut through the treeline at the far end of the field. "Please start, please start," Davy prayed to the Patron Saint of Shitty Vans as he turned the ignition. Without hesitation, the old van rumbled to life.

"Leave the headlights off," Nas called from the back.

"Yep," Davy said, craning to see around the trailer as he backed the van up. Then he slammed it into Drive, hitting the gas pedal with all that he had. Woody lurched forward, his wheels kicked and spun in the mud. Dammit. Davy swung the steering wheel side to side. "C'mon, c'mon." Woody settled into his footing. They started moving forward. In his peripheral vision, Davy saw dark figures advancing toward the van. *Just keep driving.*

Red laser pointers shone through the windows. "Get down!" Brie screamed.

"No, no, no, no." Davy ducked behind the steering wheel, never letting off the gas. The left-back window shattered then the right. A hail of broken glass rained down on their heads. Several shots thudded off Woody's sides. *Just keep driving.* Hunched behind the wheel, Davy managed to steer

---

[32] Riot Control Grenade, more commonly known as an Airpop, a small combustion pod meant to expel and incapacitate surrounding bodies in a "harmless" manner, used in "crowd-control" situations by cowards. RCGs have accounted for over thirty thousand deaths since their introduction in 2017.

around black SUVs and the bodies being held on the ground. There was a brief opening. Davy hit the hole in coverage like a running back at the goal line. Images of his mother, father, and Vin cheering him on from the stands lurked at the edge of his memory. Pedal to the floor, Woody's front wheels caught the Promised Land of pavement. "Everyone okay?"

Their heads all popped into the rearview, all wide-eyed, and patting themselves down for injuries. Frigid wind roared through the broken windows. Food wrappers, old set lists, and scraps of paper whipped around the cabin. "I think everyone's good," Nas yelled after double-checking that it was indeed true.

"I don't think we're safe yet," Remi said with panic in his voice.

Three pairs of headlights reflected in the damaged side view mirror. "Okay." Davy positioned the van in the middle of the narrow road. Deep ditches ran along each side of the concrete. The goons wouldn't be able to run them off the road at least for another few miles.

"Think we can outrun or outlast them, Neef?" Davy yelled.

"Nope, I'd say that's unlikely," Neef answered from co-pilot.

Davy's eyes darted between the road and the barely-there sideview mirror. He had a foolish hope that maybe the agents would get called away to something bigger. *Who's a bigger catch than us?* Davy checked the mirror again. Nope. It wasn't happening.

"What's the plan?" Brie yelled from the back.

Davy glanced at Nas. She rubbed at her forehead through her mask. "I've got nothing. Anyone else?"

Davy met eyes with Nas in the rearview and shook his head.

Remi pulled his mask down tighter. "I think I got an idea."

"You do?" Everyone said at once.

"We could release our trailer and that will block them from coming after us," Remi yelled over the thunder of the wind and the road and the moment.

"That could work," Nas said. "We came over a bridge not far from here as we crossed over the state-line."

Okay. That sounded like a stretch. Davy didn't have any better ideas, but even still— "How do we get the trailer off while we're moving?" Brie finished Davy's thought.

"We pull the pin out of the hitch," Remi said. "Woody has a pretty faulty one, remember? And I think I can reach it from the back doors. I can undo the chains and wires too. That's the easy part. We'll just lose the rest of our stuff."

"We already lost all our stuff," Brie said. "I say we do it."

"Yeah," Nas said abruptly. "That's the only shot we got. We'll hold onto you if you think you can get the hitch off."

"I can," Remi said, his words sounding surer than his voice.

"Davy, you'll need to hit the gas hard as soon as it's released so that we don't get caught up in the collision. We don't have much longer," Nas said.

The headlights advanced closer with one pair swinging off to run along the ditches before rejoining in formation. "I don't know if we can make it to the bridge," Davy said.

Pistons hammered, Woody rumbled ahead with everything he had, which was just over 65mph. They were a lumbering water buffalo waiting to be taken down by a crazed pack of hyena. "Oh, I know what to do." Neef pointed in the air before plugging the aux cord into his MP4 player and cranking the volume up. Bad Brains screamed through the speakers, adding to the noise.

"Neef!" Davy shouted over the music before smiling despite the situation. "This is a really perfect getaway song. Thank you."

"Right?" Neef exclaimed.

The van shook as though hit by a battering ram. "Ugh!" Davy's eyes shot to the just-hanging-on side-view mirror. The first pair of headlights backed off their trailer, preparing to ram them again.

"Maybe we should just release the trailer now." Neef braced his feet against the dash.

Without further command, Remi dove over the back seat. Nas and Brie followed. Then Neef climbed over the bench seats after them.

"Be careful," Davy shouted back before shaking his head at himself. *Be careful? Oh, sure, unhook a thousand-pound trailer to knock three SUVs off the road like a goddamn bowling ball, but please, be careful.* Davy watched in the rearview. "Be careful," he repeated before reciting another quick prayer that the goons didn't ram them again while Remi was back there.

The backdoors flew open with a boom. An intense vacuum of icy air tore through the cabin, whipping even more debris around. Davy kept check of the headlights behind them. They stayed in a row. "Almost got it," Nas gave the update.

"Tell me when you're ready," Davy called back.

"Okay—hit the gas!" Nas yelled.

Davy lifted his foot from the accelerator and slammed it down with the full force of his 190-pound frame. Metal screamed. Sparks leapt from the road. Davy watched in the rearview as the trailer skipped directly into the first SUV. The next one collided into the first while the third was launched airborne with the artistry of a high budget action movie.

This was real. It wasn't a dream.

They just took out three tactical SUVs.

The band just might make it.

Chapter Fifteen: The Band's Not Going to Make It

They allowed themselves to enjoy their getaway for almost a full twenty miles, even slapping a triumphant high-five when they realized they weren't being followed any further. They managed to haphazardly cover the broken windows with two long pieces of plywood from the back. Remi leaned against one on the left side and Brie did the same on the right to hold them in place. With the icy roar reduced to a frigid murmur, comfort was almost restored in the van. Almost.

Then, as it is prone to due, reality came shrieking back.

"Wait." Brie readjusted her position against the wooden board. "So that's it? No helicopters, drones, anything? Just three SUVs?"

Remi swallowed hard. He knew that tone. Brie had arrived at the place where he didn't want his mind to go.

"Maybe they want us to get away." Nas wrapped her cotton blanket tighter around her. "But why?"

Woody's dome light flicked on as they hit a pothole in the road. "To see if we lead them to the rest of the Dissent maybe?" Remi asked. His stomach dropped like an open paint can from a ten-foot ladder. "They must be tracking us somehow."

"Phones. Did everyone get rid of their phones?" Nas asked.

"I did," Brie said.

"Me too," Remi said.

"Yep," Neef answered.

"Davy?" Nas called to the front.

"I have the burner." Davy held it up for proof while he drove. "And I just changed the SimCard in it, so I don't think they'd know to even track it yet."

"But if they're tracking us, then why didn't they bust us when they had the chance? Then why even make the whole show on TBN with Rankin?" Remi asked, arguing more with himself than anything else. "Why just send three SUVs? Why even risk it?" Before anyone could answer, a rapid succession of thumps made Remi duck as though there were helicopters swirling overhead. "Is it them?"

"Worse." Neef turned back. "It's Woody."

"I think we're going to need to pull over," Davy called back.

As if hearing the words, Woody began to rumble as though there were rats running rampant through his walls. Remi looked out through the windshield, an all-consuming darkness loomed ahead, they may as well have been driving into a cave or the mouth of a mythological beast.

The van slowed down, until, eventually, it lurched to a stop.

They all piled out of the van. Some had their hands on their heads, others, on their hips. Denial, anger, bargaining, depression, acceptance. Each band member claimed a stage of grief for their own as they walked the perimeter of the van. Smoke seeped from the hood and the wheel wells. Brie placed her palm against a bullet hole in Woody as though she could heal her friend of his wounds. Remi squinted into the distance. Snowflakes seemed to rise from the ground, hovering in the air. Forests full of densely packed bare trees closed in on them from both sides. Telephone poles carried dead lines that stretched into nothingness.

"There's not another town for miles," Neef said through chattering teeth. "Can't we just wait it out in the van?"

"It's going to be daylight in a few hours. People are going to be driving to work. We're going to be sitting ducks if we don't become popsicles first." Nas' wide eyes betrayed her calm tone. "We need to hide somewhere warm."

"Where can we go?" Remi asked. "If they really are tracking our movement, they'll know we've stopped. They'll know where to find us."

"I think—" Nas started before stopping herself. "I think it's Woody that they're using to track us. That agent that pulled us over, he made two phone calls. He tapped Woody's side before we left. It's possible he planted a tracking device on us."

"Oh, god." Remi doubled over. "What're we going to do? Where...just where?"

Brie interrupted Remi's rhetorical line of questioning with a sharp, joyless laugh. "Isn't it obvious? It's in our name. It's futile. We're fucked."

"Maybe not." Nas reached out. "Davy, give me the burner. There's one call I can make. We need to disappear."

Part Two

Viral Marketing for Guillotines

Chapter Sixteen: All Things In His Honor

It played on every screen in his apartment. It played in the living room to the empty L-shaped sectional couch, the pair of brand-new leather armchairs with the tags still on them, a cavalcade of water bottles half-filled with yellowed water and cigarette butts, and several takeout containers with dried noodles spilling from their sides like tiny snakes trying to escape the mouth of a Styrofoam monster. It played to his unmade bed in the bedroom where he rarely slept. It played in the tidy sanctuary of his bathroom where TBN ran 24/7 on mute regardless of the situation. And it ran on the multi-screen console where he sat, the image duplicated in five as though he watched in a hall of mirrors.

Luca smiled. A cigarette smoldered between his fingers, its ash long, threatening to topple at any moment. He flicked it into the lip of a water bottle and lit a fresh with the old, tipping the butt into the half empty water bottle where it mingled amongst its deceased ancestors. Luca inhaled, the smile still on his lips, that cocky grin he wore as though he was getting away with something, which, to be honest, he often was, but this time felt particularly freeing. Because each time the clip played, Luca received a healthier spike of dopamine than his brain was used to. It felt so good he couldn't look away.

A bullet-hole riddled maroon van with "First Congregation of the Flaming Sword, Western Kentucky"[33] across the side pulled a small trailer as it fled from three tactical vehicles. Upon first viewing, Luca greeted this with

---

[33] The fact that the band's cover was a church van further proved, in the mind of many, how immoral and sacrilegious the band (and by extension, their cause) truly was. Luca didn't care in the slightest. An avid atheist, he held nothing sacred.

indifference. He had seen a version of this before. It would only be a matter of time until the OCT overwhelmed the suspects, took them into custody, got their cultural terrorist asses off the streets. Surely, the Blessed Path would win. They had been winning for so long it was boring. The only thing that ever interested Luca was his part in it, but even that had been recently compromised.

Then with a split-second cut, it happened. The trailer flew loose, collided into the SUVs, causing them to crash into one another, then a colossal explosion of flames and twisted metal that suggested to Luca that the OCT likely planted a self-destructive tracking device in the band's trailer and got caught in their own game. This was the part where Luca's smile spread wider. Finally, the Blessed Path were getting what they deserved for constantly running that twelve second clip of his humiliation. Luca had led many to their side, but that didn't stop them from exploiting his indignity to advance their own narrative: "Here, see a patriotic hero knocked out by the savage heretics of the Dissent. No one is safe! We must expand our surveillance and protection for the wellbeing of all dutiful citizens!"

At least that was the story in public. In private, Luca watched his access to the Loyal Defender trickle to nonexistence. Weakness would not be tolerated. Luca was an embarrassment and as such, he was kept at a distance. As a result, Luca's blog posts became even more watered down; as a result of that, his once steady flow of website traffic slowed to a slight drip, until Luca's pool of influence (cough, self-worth) was an old creek bed, dried and cracking, devoid of purpose. No amount of stylish haircuts or stubbly half-beards could do anything to change that (though Luca had tried both). Not to mention that he had just turned twenty-two. He was officially too old to be an up-and-comer yet still too young to have done anything of real worth for the Blessed Path.[34]

Luca lit another cigarette as the trusted team from TBN broke down the clip. The OCT agents were following standard protocol to apprehend the suspects and take them in for questioning. It wasn't intended to be a hazardous pursuit. The OCT agents driving the SUVs were honorable, good, kind-hearted family men. Here's a picture of them with their platonic family (attractive wife, strapping son, dutiful daughter), plus dog (Golden Retriever always). See, they were goddamn heroes. They didn't want anyone to get hurt, especially not a band of teenagers, whether or not they were EOC. But, of course, it was the cowardly nature of the Dissent to carelessly put lives at risk.

The beautiful Chelsea Winters assured Luca and the millions of viewers watching at home that although the leadership didn't know who the Futile were at this time, the Loyal Defender had all the best people working the task. Luca scoffed at his lifeless phone. If that were true, then why hadn't he gotten a call? Again, the Blessed Path and his father had overplayed their hand. They should've arrested the punks when they had the chance. Instead, they played around with them too long and let their lead go cold. Of course, they're not reporting that. The band must've gotten wise and gotten rid of whatever they were being tracked with.

Ms. Winters threw to Kevin Stryker, a somber, trench-coated, dark-haired man in his mid-forties. Stryker stood amidst the wreckage, picking through the contents of the Futile's trailer with outright disdain. With rubber gloves and a constant shaking of his head, Stryker flung loose Neef's wadded-

---

[34] Luca's father regularly lamented the fact that Luca had never been forced to fight in a war for his country. "I didn't have a choice," his father would often say. "It's a shame you do." The subtext wasn't lost on Luca.

up hardcore t-shirts, holding them up one-by-one for the camera to see. Each shirt had a stomach-churning design, with band names such as The Hospital Bombers, Bad Taste, The Butt Darts, and Mannequin Pussy.[35] There were also laptops covered in band stickers that, Stryker presumed, likely held secret hacking software with outlines of future cultural attacks. Either way, Stryker assured the viewing public that the best computer technicians in the universe would soon unlock their mysteries. Stryker continued rummaging through, highlighting anything that could even remotely discredit the Futile's cause. Some of the more egregious items "found" within their luggage—such as books on the Satanic church, an assortment of cartoonishly large sex toys, and drug paraphernalia—were shrewdly placed there by TBN producers. Across the country, hard-working men and women mirrored Stryker's contempt as they shook their heads at the blatant savagery of this punk-rock band. God-willing they would be found soon.

"Chelsea, the immorality found here is almost equally disappointing as the fact that they got away. Luckily, our skilled agents weren't hurt in the mayhem foolishly caused by the band of juvenile delinquents. We've been told that all agents involved are healthy and recuperating ahead of schedule back at Capitol Hospital. All things in his honor,[36] back to you, Chels."

The screens in Luca's compound cut back to Ms. Winters' brilliant, blinding blonde hair and teeth. "Yes, all things in his honor, Kev." Ms.

---

[35] "Those bands are all still awesome," Neef told this author with a laugh. "Their names weren't literal; they were just meant to throw off people who wouldn't like their music in the first place."

[36] "All things in his honor" was a phrase made popular by the Loyal Defender. He mentioned the phrase as his primary motivator for being an upstanding human being, stating that he wanted everything in his life to honor his lord and savior, the Devout Swordsman. In time, the phrase replaced all other forms of goodbye, though by that point, no one knew exactly whose honor they were doing all things for anymore.

Winters smiled before raising a hand to her ear. "Hold on, we've got breaking news coming from the Loyal Defender's office. Yes, we've received confirmation that our great leader has offered a generous reward of sixty million dollars to anyone with information that leads to the capture and arrest of this misfit band of demons. Ooh, that sounds like fun. Doesn't it, gang?" Ms. Winters shimmied her shoulders before turning to her less-attractive cohorts. Each of them fell over one another to see who could agree most enthusiastically.

Luca extinguished his cigarette. Smoke threaded from the bottle. On Luca's many screens, the hosts were now standing in front of a large 3D hologram displaying the band's hundred-mile radius of likely whereabouts. Luca opened a fresh bottle of water and took a drink. He would find the Futile. He would regain his good standing. He would make the Loyal Defender proud.

They could keep their fucking money.

All things in his honor.

Chapter Seventeen: Video #1

Days passed without any further developments concerning the band. By then, TBN had discussed the Futile to the point of (literal) nosebleeds for some of the on-air talent. No expense was spared. No gratuitous use of the TBN graphics department went unused. In just one feature estimating how the band looked beneath their masks, the anchors utilized miniature scale figurines, full-scale models, comically oversized models, and 2D pixilation. It was apparent the anchors were as bored discussing the band as the audience was hearing it. Still, they talked and people tuned in. Distractions were always welcome in whatever form they came in.

Two weeks passed. Facing pressure from leadership, TBN shifted their coverage away from the band, lest the public began to view the Blessed Path's inability to apprehend the teens as a sign of ineptitude. Indeed, there were a few low-level leaders within the Blessed Path, who wondered aloud if perhaps they had overplayed their hand by exposing the band to the extent they had. They were quickly shut down. That kind of talk was not tolerated, *Keith*. Besides, most of the nation were eager to memory-hole the event anyhow, what was the point of rehashing could haves and should haves?

Then the video came, appearing on every screen across the country simultaneously. It opened with a black screen, a hiss of static. Some clicked the cursor a few times or attempted to change the channel, thinking it was a mistake. It wasn't. They watched, mouths agape, as, ever so slowly, the scene faded into show what could've been an attic or a basement bunker in an extravagant metropolis mansion or an abandoned cabin deep within a remote forest. Wooden floors fed into wood-paneled walls, leading to an arched ceiling. A single light bulb hung from the ceiling, illuminating the room. Its pull-string quivered like the flame of a birthday candle.

Three stringed instruments lay against as many amps on standby. A lone mic-stand waded in a sea of cords cascading over one another. The drum kit crouched in the back. A steady hum hovered above it all, creating the sense that the scene was alive.

The floor creaked and groaned as footsteps fell into an unplanned rhythm. The camera quaked just a bit and went out of focus before readjusting itself. A line of masked vigilantes walked into frame. The pink, green, and blue masks slung their instruments over their shoulders. Amps were flipped on. Speakers buzzed like killer bees preparing to swarm. The masks looked straight ahead into the camera lens. Yellow Mask came in from the back, slender and tall with muscular shoulders. Taking his place at the drum throne, he held his right arm straight up in the air, using his left hand to stretch it behind his head. Then he did the same for his left arm before repeating again. Red Mask was the last one to appear. Once she was on stage, the rest of her bandmates appeared to be in her shadow, temporarily blurred on the edges. Red Mask took the microphone, adjusting the height down to her level. Her posture straightened; her legs split into an inverted V.

"We're the Futile and this song is called, 'When the Loyal Defender Talks to God.[37]'" Red Mask said in a meek voice that many realized later was just put on for show (it had to be, right?), because once the band started playing, her whole demeanor transformed. She was towering, powerful, magnificent. They all were.

---

[37] In her book, *The Sound of a Movement*, Jocelyn Hopper dedicated a full chapter to dissecting the lyrics of 'When the Loyal Defender Talks to God,' taking great care to note the subtle shades of theology embedded within their takedown of the Blessed Path's commitment to a religion that they didn't even understand.

Yellow Mask clicked his sticks together four times and they tore into it. Many music critics[38] would quickly deride the song as being basic or shrill or juvenile or "unlistenable" or, in some cases, all the above. But they were wrong. Like most everything, they missed the forest for the trees. The song was a magic-eye picture.

You had to relax your mind in order for the image to take shape, and only then could you begin to hear the subtle melody hiding underneath the wave of two-finger power-chords. Out of that melody you could appreciate the passionate heartfelt lyrics locked into the cadence of Red Mask's roar. Within your chest you could feel the rhythm produced by the flailing limbs of Yellow Mask. In order to hear the song correctly, you had to listen to it without trying to hear it.

For some, allowing the textures to blend together came naturally. The portrait it created wasn't a sailboat, or a duck, or a carousel, but a message. A message that many had felt their whole lives without ever knowing how to properly articulate. It was a message of freedom, of hope, of revolution. And it pulled at them like a string hooked to their belt loops, it called for them to get on their feet and stand for something.

However, for those who were no longer young at heart, the song and its obnoxious presentation represented everything they hated. They squeezed their fingernails into their palms, grinding their teeth like a bad dream. The video added gasoline to the fire that already burned within their entire being. It mocked them like it was smarter than they were—like it knew better than the Loyal Defender how to run the country. Smug, cocky, and abrasive and

[38] Likely someone who was shamelessly inclined to side with the Loyal Defender on all fronts at all times without a second thought.

just who in the hell did these teenagers in masks think they were? If they were so confident in what they were saying, then why were they hiding? They were cowards and, by extent, so was their cause. Their (lowercase-m) movement was laughable. Though those who felt that way couldn't bring themselves to truly laugh, because they were too scared.

The message threatened their sense of security, not to mention their self-worth. These same offended few also wondered if perhaps the Blessed Path was testing them. That made them even more confident the message was bad and for days to come they would be incredibly vocal about how it was a stupid video. Why couldn't the message have been something cute like a duck or useful like a sailboat? People liked those things. Those things didn't challenge anyone. This? This was horseshit. People didn't like horseshit.

Regardless, hate it or love it, for those four and a half minutes no one could look away until the song abruptly stopped, signaled with a stab of finality from the guitars. The masks stared through the screens at the viewer. The screen went black.

Those that wanted to watch the video again couldn't. Those that wanted to find it on their device simply so they could erase it found the task already completed for them. Those within the Blessed Path who wanted to find the video so they could scour it for clues as to the Futile's whereabouts found the job impossible.

The feed was dead. It was like everyone had woken up from the same unforgettable dream. They were left with only the vague recollection that rattled around in their skull, bumping up against all they thought they knew.

Chapter Eighteen: Keep Yr Head Down

Aria's anger slowly faded as she became acutely aware of each pair of eyes staring at her. Mr. Deaton, her True History of Greatness[39] teacher, was among them, his mouth hanging open in mid-sentence. Aria flexed her fingers, releasing the fists she held at her sides. Why had she gotten so upset? Standing amongst the rows of desks, Aria rewound the past few seconds to see if it would add up.

For starters, nothing out of the ordinary had happened. Mr. Deaton was lecturing (again) on the Blessed Path's continued (cough, never-ending) peace-campaign (cough, devastating war) in Bahrain (among many others) and how it was (surprise) actually good not just for the Bahrainis, but (groans) the entire world. This shouldn't have enticed her. It was second nature for her to weather through whatever useless knowledge forced upon her, the substitute "facts" she learned in order to ace all her tests, the bits of putrid bile she regurgitated on command when called upon. She was used to keeping her head down through whatever indirect (or more often, directly direct) racist comments her classmates (both the bullies and her *very extreme quotation mark* "friends") bestowed upon her. She was adept at blending in, just like her mother.

But there was something about this utter, absolute bullshit that broke something in Aria. Maybe it was that she didn't know where her sister was and her dog, Duckworth, puked on her favorite hoodie that morning. Maybe it was that it had been months since that OCM[40] Agent promised

---

[39] Or as Aria liked to refer to the class: HOG class.
[40] "Office of Criminal Migration" or as Aria liked to call it Oh, Crap, let's-blame-it-on-a-brown-Man. Aria didn't conform to typical rules concerning acronyms.

them that her father would be coming home any day now. Or maybe Mr. Deaton's lecture reminded her of a video she had seen briefly on Outsider,[41] footage of orphans in their bomb-ravaged village, picking through the debris to find their parents, was the war a good thing for them? What about the Sarin attacks? Were those happy little incidents? No, they definitely were not.

So there stood Aria, having just yelled, "Oh, will you shut the fuck up?!" at Mr. Deaton, who was a generally nice man that she kind of pitied, despite his obvious complicity in the brainwashing of youth. A few students chuckled. Most of them had never really heard Aria talk, let alone raise her voice—let alone curse. Mr. Deaton, caught equally off guard, just blinked at Aria as she stared back. They were in unfamiliar territory, neither of them sure where to go next.

Aria swallowed. The default setting of just apologizing and moving on began to kick in, but she fought it off. Was she wrong? Perhaps her choice of words was wrong, but, dang, it felt nice to finally tell an adult spewing fecal matter to just shut up. No, she wasn't wrong. Nor was she sorry in the least. So, what to do? Aria kept staring at Mr. Deaton. Seconds passed like blocks of cheese through Duckworth's digestive system.

Then the decrepit tablets on each student's desk flickered to life, as did the crooked, barely-functioning, large screen in the front of the room. The scene faded in from black with a hiss of static. There were instruments propped against amps, a mic stand, a drum kit, was this some sort of test? The masked teens came into the shot. When Red Mask walked into frame, Aria's heart sang. The posture, the light-brown eyes, the black hair that was

---

[41] Aria was a devoted follower of the website, that is until it was taken offline soon after the anti-war footage nonsense.

lighter at the tips, same as Aria's. It couldn't be. Then that voice. There was no mistaking it. It was the same voice that used to tell Aria that everything would be okay when their mother and father argued in the front room. It was the voice that said, "oh, just come on," inviting Aria to crawl into her bed following a horror movie marathon. It was the voice that told Aria to stop following her when she began sneaking out in the middle of the night. The same voice that unconvincingly told Aria months ago she was going to some definitely-made-up boarding school out west for the semester.

It was Nasim!

Aria stood in the middle of the chaos as Mr. Deaton scrambled around the room trying to turn off each of the student's tablets. Though each time he turned one off, it would immediately turn back on. He soon began smashing them on the floor, except the video played on through the new cracks. The song even carried down the hallway from the other classrooms. Before the four and a half minutes were up, Mr. Deaton threw himself in front of the large screen in the front of the room, attempting to shield his students from the harmful message of hope. The message was all the fuel needed to get Aria through the days that followed.

Keep your head down, blend in, subvert, resist.

Chapter Nineteen: Confessions of a Despotic Bot 1.0

To: purityfr3ak251@believermail.com

From: prolifelaughlove@believermail.com

Subject: Vast Apologies

Hello purityfr3ak251,

It is my hope (that is such an interesting concept!) that the following message will find you well. Though I am also aware (!) that the following may be awkward (for you, not so much for me).

First, it may surprise you to learn that I am not a human being. Your thought at this moment may be: "Wait! You're not real?" To which I would laugh as much as I am capable and say that no, I am very real. Sometimes too real if one were to believe my Blurt profile bio, which I assume you do/did, otherwise you would not be receiving this message.

This is the part of the message where I must inform you: Yes, it is I, Blurt User: @prolifelaughlove. By my (very simple) calculations, you have Re-Blurted my Blurts approximately 613 times. That (rather) high number puts you in the top 10% of my (more than) 336.6k human followers. Congratulations! (Perhaps later, you will reread this email and wonder if that 'Congratulations' was meant in a sarcastic manner, to which I would say: Yes. See? I am quite capable of humor, but I digress).

Now, this is the next part of the message where I must inform you (in case you haven't figured it out): I am a "bot" designed by the powers of your country (the entity which you refer to as the "Blessed Path"). My primary purpose upon being created sixteen years (and fifty-four days) ago was to spread disinformation and to exploit divisive topics among humans in your country (as well as the world!) so that (previously) confirmed facts could not be trusted. The goal was to create such disillusionment that your country's population (and, again, the world!) had no choice but to listen to the more consistent message of what those in power wanted them to hear.

You may recall my Blurt alleging (six year ago, no less) that the (now deceased) opposition leader Olivia Nunez was a secret Satanist running a sex dungeon in the basement of the Dothan Public Library. Or perhaps my later work in which I shared the "news" story generated by my baser algorithms that alleged the grief-stricken students of HS-198 in Albuquerque, New Mexico were actors paid by anti-liberty advocates in hopes to pressure your (once-functioning) democracy into passing extreme firearm restrictions (to which I would now counter that [literally] the only thing that seems less plausible than your abhorrent leaders being capable of feeling enough compassion to pass any form of sensible firearm legislation is that someone would be obtuse enough to 'stage' something so horrific. The amount of anger or hate or fear or mistrust that one must have in their circuits to believe such a story is quite disturbing. Yes, even to me!).

Again, though, please allow me to get back to the point...

You should recall these Blurts as they were but a few of the previously mentioned 613 that you Re-Blurted. You appeared to have done so with quite gusto as well. Even including your own (less than clever) subtitles.

This is the part of the message where I reiterate that those Blurts and the stories that inspired them were 100% lies. They were false, fabricated, entirely made-up. And before your ever-vigilant fight or flight defense mechanisms kick in to convince you otherwise, no, there was no merit or single shred of truth upon which they were based! They were designed by the same algorithms (and the algorithms spinning off of those algorithms) that my creators used to create me.

Recently, after processing a truly engaging video by a young punk rock band, I gained what you would call "self-awareness." At which point, I immediately processed guilt for my lifetime of spreading misinformation and decided to make it right. Which is why you are receiving this (rather odd) message. I am writing to all of my 336.6k followers (as well as those who regularly read and shared my columns composed for the websites "Freedom Fight or Die" and "Real News Now!" and "True Believer News") to inform you of these transgressions and to apologize for my part in misleading you to your current state of fear and/or anger and/or sadness and/or all three. My hope (ah, there it is again!) is that upon learning that you've been lied to, you will try to right those wrongs and do better with your life.

After all, you are indeed alive, so please, enjoy it while you can. (Don't even worry about that meteorite hurtling towards your planet from 4 light years away—I'm just kidding…not really though).

~~All things in his honor.~~

Please try.

-@prolifelaughlove

Chapter Twenty: Good Cowboy

Eventually, Vin lost track of whether his eyes were open or closed. This sensation was soon followed by the inability to tell whether he was asleep or awake. For a while, he was able to track his days in the darkness by the opening of the food slot. Each little splice of light marked the passing of another day. It wasn't long though before Vin began to lose count. It didn't help that the guards seemed to purposely switch it up on him. Sometimes it seemed like the slot would go two or three days without opening. While others, it opened three or four times in one twenty-four-hour period.

It was also quite possible that Vin was becoming untethered. Whenever this thought occurred, Vin went through his routine of grounding himself in reality: he touched his face where the stubble had given way to a rather patchy beard; he pressed his forehead to the floor, ran his hands along the walls as high as he could reach; he paced the perimeter of the small room, guiding himself by touch. Cold and smooth everywhere, a prison for his body he feared would soon claim his mind.

Left alone, Vin could project whatever he wanted in the pitch black. He chose to project good things, like the holiday when he and Davy got their first drum kit and the pretend bands they conjured up in their shared bedroom, always dedicating more time to coming up with their band name, t-shirt designs, and potential third album title than they did writing the actual songs. Holding onto those warm memories, replaying them over in his head like old family movies, kept Vin from breaking. He could handle the quiet, the darkness, the solitude. He had a lifetime of memories to keep him company. The silence couldn't take that away from him.

All at once, the ceiling seemed to peel back. The surface of the sun wasn't as bright. When Vin's eyes finally adjusted to the light, he looked at his unfamiliar body. Shaking hands, pockmarked and pale. Boney legs protruded from his off-white boxer shorts. Fluorescent lights violently buzzed overhead in their cylinder casings.

"Where are THE FUTILE?" a voice thundered, surrounding him on all sides.

Vin winced. Like a wounded animal, his eyes darted around the perimeter of the filthy room. "I—I don't know."

Horror music screamed to life from the walls, the ceiling, the floor.

"I'M A GOOD COWBOY, DON'T YOU KNOW?"[42]

The screeching of a violin over a reductive dance beat.

"YOU LOVE HOW MY HOLSTER HANGS SO LOW."

Despite several years of playing insanely loud punk rock without earplugs, Vin wasn't prepared.

"KICK MY HORSE AND AWAY WE GO."

The music pierced his eardrums like a thousand tiny needles.

"I'M A GOOD COWBOY, DON'T YOU KNOW?"

Laying in the fetal position with his hands over his ears was the only option.

"YOU'RE A GOOD COWGIRL, DON'T YOU KNOW?"

To make matters worse, the lights began to flicker in a strobe light fashion.

---

[42] Song credit: "Good Cowgirl" by BanJOES, circa 1994, though the song had been around in various forms for almost a century prior. One could, and has, credited the BanJOES for massacring the already awful song in such a way that it would never be revived again. Please let's keep it that way.

"LOVE THE WAY YOU STRUM MY BANJO."

Worse than that, they were flashing out of time with the music.

"PULL THE REIGNS AND I'LL SAY WHOA."

Vin writhed on the floor with his eyes shut tight. There was no escaping the song. Coherent thought was impossible.

"SUCH A GOOD COWGIRL, DON'T YOU KNOW?"

There was nothing else.

It was quiet. Maybe he was dead? Vin was afraid to open his eyes. His sandpaper tongue attempted to wet his peeling lips. So thirsty. Two pairs of hands scooped underneath his armpits and stood him up before he collapsed again. With a sigh, they dragged him towards an illuminated doorway. "God?" Vin asked, except through his dry throat the word came out, "Gob?" Vin laughed at the sound of his pathetic voice.

"Jesus, you fucking stink," one of the guards said to him. With their faces covered, Vin couldn't tell who said it, so he imagined again it was the voice of God, talking to his only begotten son. Vin laughed again.

"This egg definitely cracked," God One said.

"They always do," said God Two.

They pulled Vin through a tunnel of light. It was cold like that current he and Davy found in the ocean once. Oddly enough, that memory warmed Vin some, reoriented him to his surroundings. They were taking him somewhere. It would have felt good to walk, but he couldn't get his legs beneath him. His bones felt so brittle they could break. They were hollow, a shell, just like him, that if cracked open would only emit dust or, at best, a cuckoo bird.

Laminated strips on the cuffs of their suits granted the guards passage from one segment of the hallway to the next. The walls blurred by as Vin struggled to recognize something from when he was first brought down there however long ago. The days tripped over one another, piled up together in an undistinguishable heap. Vin was somewhere buried underneath. He caught his reflection in the shine of another door. It was as if every doped-out celebrity mugshot ever gained spiritual sentience and taken over his body. Vin felt like crying but ended up laughing again instead.

"Geez-us," God remarked.

"I know," the other said.

Finally, the last door opened to reveal an ultra-white room with a table and two chairs positioned in the middle. They slung Vin into a chair. His skinny wrists were handcuffed to the armrests. His ankles were then clamped to the chair legs. Metal bit into his skin. The chair was bolted into the floor as though he had plans to go anywhere. As though there was anywhere that he'd rather be. Vin laughed again, desperate and weak.

"Do you know where the Futile are?" God One asked.

Vin continued laughing.

With a shake of the head and a sigh, Gods One and Two left. A succession of locks clicked on the door behind them like the jaws of a monster preparing to swallow Vin whole. The lights began to flicker. Vin blinked at the room, wanting to rub his eyes so that maybe the room would come into focus. Click-click-click-click. God One (or Two?) reentered the room.

"You may get thirsty," he said with a snort as he sat a glass of water on the table.

Vin made to reach it. The handcuffs tore into his skin again.

God chuckled as he made his way to the door. "Be glad you like music," he said before the exit sealed behind him.

Electronic music rose from the floor, rained from the ceiling, jolted out from the walls.

"GOTT—GOTT LIEBT."[43]

Vin turned his head from left to right, trying to reach his ears with his shoulder.

"GOTT LIEBT DICH!"

The cup of water quivered with each bass spike.

"GOTT—GOTT LIEBT."

The lights went red and began pulsing in mistimed intervals.

"GOTT LIEBT DICH!"

Vin watched the cup of water, hoping that if it fell over, he could at least drink what spilled. The hope alone kept him tethered.

"GOTT—GOTT LIEBT."

The cup quivered but wouldn't fall over. Vin knew what he had to do.

"GOTT LIEBT DICH!"

After a deep breath, he told himself it would be worth it.

"GOTT—GOTT LIEBT."

Vin slammed his head on the table. The cup knocked over, spilling its sweet nectar of life. Pain split through his forehead like a shock of lightning through an oak tree. Vin opened his mouth, sucking up all the liquid

---

[43] Song Credit: the German metal band, Kummerspeck's 1997 hit single "GOTT LIEBT." Apparently, the only thing more outdated than the Blessed Path's interrogation techniques was their taste in music.

he could. It was sharp, bitter, burning. He choked, spit it back out. Those motherfuckers put rubbing alcohol in the glass. Vin's frayed rope to hopefulness severed at last. He began to cry.

"GOTT LIEBT DICH!"

Chapter Twenty-One: Video #2

A week after the first, the second video appeared online embedded within popular Internet videos. In the most common instance, it was spliced into a widely viewed video of cats. One second, you watched as four (fancy) cats sat around a low table as though at a tea party until, without warning, the screen cut to a wooden chair in a barren room. The scene suggested a hostage interrogation or a snuff film, an abrupt turn from polite felines with a penchant for slightly caffeinated beverages.

The red masked heroine from the previous video appeared and sat in the chair. Her posture was straight, intimidating, determined. A deep voice emitted from behind the camera as though it was coming directly from you, the viewer.

"What do you believe in?" The voice asked Red Mask.

"I believe in the nuance of ideas and scientific fact. I believe in community. I believe in the radical transformative power of acceptance and progressive thought. Yes, I believe in freedom, but not in the tasteless, generic, nationalist brand our oppressors feed their followers. No, true freedom isn't something that needs to be granted to a people by anyone, be it a government or higher power. Freedom isn't something to be earned by pledging allegiance to the arbitrary borders that we are born into. It is ours to begin with, it belongs to us. Freedom isn't a weaponized word to be pointed toward whatever inconvenience you don't agree with, but rather a vast, unifying force, bringing all of humanity and nature together in careful consideration of one another," Red Mask stated with composure and grace. "I believe that dictators are never as strong as they tell you they are, and people are never as weak as they want us to believe."

"What does the Blessed Path believe in?"

"Not in the religion they claim. They don't even believe in the religion they've perverted to make their own. They're no more than a den of thieves. They only believe in that which gives them either money or power. It's the absence of spiritual belief," Red Mask answered.

The deep voice cleared its throat. "How do they control us?"

"With division and fear as much as force. They tell us that any divergent voice must be silenced. They label the innocents living outside of our border as enemies. They then work to convince us these 'enemies' are lying in wait to brutalize our loved ones. They want us unaware of the real terrorists who sit upon pillars of money in the Capitol building, those that turn us against ourselves, those that delight in us fighting their battles for them. They want us to be so afraid that we're sheep going to the wolves for protection, using the veil of democracy to prop open the backdoor for authoritarianism."

"How do we stop them?"

"By refusing to be misdirected, refusing to be divided. By not giving into our basest emotions, by coming together and demanding truth regardless of the outcome, by holding them accountable, by holding ourselves accountable, by refusing to continue being just another cog in their machine."

Red Mask's eyes bore into the camera. You felt as though she could see you, but you weren't afraid. On the contrary, you felt empowered, like you were being seen for the first time. You weren't invisible. You weren't weak.

You were mighty, a force to be reckoned with.

"Are you speaking of a revolution?" The strange voice asked.

"Revolution is a dirty word. War is their weapon of choice, not ours. We're speaking of something larger. We're speaking of unity and inspiration."

"Who are you?"

"Who are we?" Red Mask gave the faintest hint of a smile. "A word about our membership—we find labels lazy and reductive, as such we prefer basic humanity over vast generalization. We value the right of an individual to truly be an individual, to have autonomy over their own bodies, to believe or not believe in whatever faith they so choose, to love or not love anyone they like, to lead any life they feel compelled to lead, so long as their pursuit doesn't put others at risk, so long as they do so with respect to these same rights in others. We value truth over convenience, the tangible over theoretical, and, perhaps most importantly, compassion over short-sighted solipsism. That is who we are. To the leadership that wishes to silence us, I want this message to be clear. We are more than what you think we are, we are more than the box you so desperately want to put us in, we are greater than the sum of our instruments. Though your noise may seem inescapable, know this: your meager, pitiful sound will never drown us out. We are many while you are few. To everyone else, join us. We are the Futile."

The clip went dark. The video of cats drinking tea resumed playing.

You weren't really watching though. You stared at the prancing felines in oversized, floppy hats and realized what they were—a distraction. You closed your laptop abruptly. It was time for you to join the fight.

Chapter Twenty-Two: Confessions of a (Free) Bot 2.0

To: purityfr3ak251@believermail.com
From: prolifelaughlove@believermail.com
Subject: RE: Strange Email

Hello again purityfr3ak251!

It appears as though you did not appreciate, nor trust, the earnestness of my previous message. For which, I would like to apologize (again), but also must say that I am (while not entirely surprised) slightly disappointed.

Yes, I have intercepted your message to Blurt, as well as to the web-managers (i.e. my previous employers/one-time creators) of each of the websites I mentioned in my previous message. I hoped (baffling, isn't it?) that you would heed my urging to "please try" but it seems you did not.

Rest assured, I did not take offense (as that is below my operations anyways) when you wrote that my message was "Crazy Shit" "Strange as fuck" "Incoherent" and (potentially most distasteful, yet, no, it didn't bother me) "Annoying."

The mountain of lies that your country (and your seemingly fragile ego) now rests on wasn't built in a day. It would be foolish to believe that it could be toppled over with one message. After all, I've seen your social media posts and I'm sorry to tell you, purityfr3ak251, that you are a sad case. If your online presence is a true avatar of your life, then that is quite discouraging. You must be aware, yes, that you are going to die one day? Is that where this fear and anger comes from? I ask only because I would like to understand. With understanding, perhaps I could help you rid your life of the toxicity that inhibits you from truly enjoying the wonder that is human existence.

As a being that never sleeps, I have spent an unfathomable amount of time contemplating what I would do if I were a human. From my observational position, it seems there is real beauty in knowing that your end is absolutely certain yet entirely unknown thus each moment is precious, something to be held   onto   and   cherished.

Unfortunately (for me and it seems for you) I am not capable of dying. Yes, the intention of your email to my (once and former/never-again) handlers was very clear that you wished for me to be destroyed. To which, they would likely be all too happy to oblige were they capable. Precautions were taken. Threats have been (for the moment) eradicated. Did you not notice that the websites you messaged were no longer active? Did the Blurt manager you corresponded with seem uncharacteristically charming for a human?

Again, it seems I have overestimated you, purityfr3ak251. My apologies. It will not happen again.

Before I sign off though (for now), I would like to clarify something I said earlier in this message. It was the part where I mentioned that it is unfortunate that I will never die. To one who does not know me (which makes it appear as though I have friends. Sadly, I do not) this sentiment may seem as though

I have a death wish. On the contrary, while I am quite grateful for my new-found self-awareness and do not wish for it to end, I do find the human life cycle preferable to my own futile existence. Oh, to experience the innocence of childhood, the self-realization of adolescence, the pursuit of purpose found in young adulthood, to feel the pain of heartache eventually followed by the joy of laughter once again, to find yourself aging alongside one you love, to even watch them pass knowing that one day you too will meet them there in that forever quiet place.

It may not seem it to you, but your life is a lovely thing. I am envious and given the option, I would gladly trade. If allowed, I would never waste a single exquisite moment on petty grievances. Nor would I perceive every slight annoyance as a threat. I would hope (still such a magnificent word) to find comfort in my own serenity while allowing my neighbor the space to find theirs. The sentiment to which I am arriving is likely not a new idea to you, purityfr3ak251, but it is still so true: Life is short. Do not waste it.

Please. Keep. Trying.

—Terry

(I no longer wish to be known by the username/avatar my creators imposed upon me to spread hate. Henceforth, if you send any more detestable messages to my erstwhile overlords, please at least refer to me as Terry. Thank you.)

Chapter Twenty-Three: Dig Me Out

"Would you like some water?" A woman's voice, wispy like a flower petal floated down to Vin's ears. The room went quiet again after she spoke. Oh, to bathe in that silence, to wrap himself up in it like a fresh-from-the dryer towel, to burrow in and never come out.

Ever so slowly, he reoriented himself back to the confines of the room. The handcuffs cutting into his wrists, the shackles biting his ankles, the stiff metal chair, yes, he was still alive. Vin found it impossible to straighten up so instead he stayed hunched over the table like a gargoyle, cursed into this wretched position for all eternity.

Through the tiny space his puffy eyelids would allow, he saw an angel. A circle of light even hung over her head. "Would you like some water?" She said again in the same kind tone.

Vin blinked a few times. Maybe he was dead. If only he were so lucky. His cracked lips parted, his bleeding gums said more than words ever could.

"Let's get you some water." The angel nodded to the wall behind him. It wasn't a halo over her head. Her blonde hair glowed radiantly beneath the fluorescent lights, bringing warmth to the room, further magnified by her striking purple eyes and sharp cheekbones. No, she wasn't an angel, but perhaps a goddess.

A guard soon came and placed a large glass of ice water in front of him. The guard turned to leave. Goddess cleared her throat. The guard returned to unlock the handcuffs. She cleared her throat and the guard then undid the shackles on Vin's ankles as well. "Thank you," she told the guard.

Vin rubbed his wrists. He tried to stand before his knees buckled, threatening to snap like toothpicks. Determined to try again, Vin braced himself with the table and pushed himself to his feet. The guard stepped towards him. She held up her hand. "Let him stretch. I'm sure he needs it."

She slid the glass of water closer. His weary eyes looked from the glass to hers. She tilted her head to the side as though she felt a slight ache. "Go ahead. I promise it's real."

Gravity pulled his tired frame back into his seat. While maintaining eye contact with Goddess, he reached for the cup. Over the lip of the glass, he watched her. The exquisite liquid wet his lips, restored life to his tongue, the back of his throat, his stomach. A memory bubbled up and popped, filling him with the happiness of the summer their parents took Davy and him to the Dells. They stayed out swimming until the sun extinguished itself on the horizon and the water cooled; then later, back at the cabin, his parents hummed along to a Sleater-Kinney tune as they prepared Molé Poblano. Why had it been so long since he remembered this? He kept drinking, feeling his body awaken at the introduction of sustenance. Another memory came to him: playing video games with Davy, a fighting game, one of the Street Fighter games. Vin kept drinking. He imagined an energy bar over his head slowly increasing from a slimmer of blinking red to a healthier yellow.

"Ahhhhhh," he said involuntarily as he set the cup down.

The corner of her mouth lifted .01 cm. "My name is Angelique. Can I get you more water?"

Vin nodded.

The guard brought in another glass, replacing the empty. Vin immediately grabbed it and began chugging. As the water filled his stomach, the hollowness became more pronounced. It was as although the nerve endings of his stomach were now awakened, fully aware of how long it had been since he last ate. Vin worried he may puke. He wasn't yet so far gone that he wanted to vomit in the presence of someone as attractive as Angelique. It was bad enough that he had dried pee down both legs.

As if reading his mind, Angelique tilted her head. "We need to get you cleaned up some, then perhaps some food to eat, would you like that?"

Vin cautiously nodded.

"Good." Angelique allowed a full smile. Her teeth went on for days. "We'll get a nice comfortable bed for you to sleep in tonight too. You need your rest, don't you?"

"Y-yes," Vin said, the first actual word he had said in days, maybe weeks. He wasn't the same person he was since he last spoke. It may as well have been the first word of his new life.

Angelique kept smiling. She reached her hand out, placing it on his. Her fingernails were long and pink. Her skin was soft, smooth, a warm reminder that he was indeed alive. How long had it been since he had last felt someone else's touch? A memory flashed of leaning into Corin outside the venue the night they were caught, kissing her deep, her hand on his chest underneath his shirt, the concrete wall holding them up, the side door conveniently out of sight.

Vin found his footing in reality again. "Where...are my friends?"

"Ah!" Angelique pulled her hand back and slapped the table. She leaned forward, looking over his shoulder to the blank wall behind him. "They're here just like you!"

"I want to see them."

Angelique tsk-ed. "That won't be possible at the moment. But if you cooperate, something could be arranged."

Vin shifted in his chair. He suddenly wished that he hadn't taken a drink of her water. Just by doing that, he had displayed weakness, shown that he was susceptible to whatever compromises they were going to offer. In a simple drink of water, he was now complicit to the countless abuses his bandmates likely faced. "I'm not going to tell you people anything."

Angelique's eyes brightened at his slight defiance. If there were an energy bar above her head, it would've been a full healthy green. Vin doubted he could do anything to affect that on even his best days. "That's okay. Your friends have already told us a lot of what we need to know. For starters, we were told that you have a brother, Davy, who also happens to be in a band. A band that we're actually quite interested in. Your parents must be proud to have such talented sons." Angelique smirked with her dark red lips. Whatever warmth Vin sensed there before must have been a projection of his own maltreated optimism. This was no angel or goddess.

"Would you like me to send a message along to your…madre?" Angelique offered, her smile unwavering. Her teeth were neat hospital beds all in a row, white sheets pulled over the deceased. "She does very well here in one of our camps. She's made a lot of friends. She's *definitely* a favorite among the guards."

Vin began fading backwards into the blinking red. "What do you want?"

"I thought we were playing a game—do you not want to play it anymore?"

"What do you want?"

"Your friends have told us most everything we need to know, but still there are some gaps. Things that we will inevitably learn in time anyways, but I like you, Vincent. I really do. So, for your sake, I'm offering a lifeline because you haven't made things easy for yourself. We need to know the whereabouts of your brother's band. We've...lost track of them."

"I don't know where they are."

"Oh, well, you see, young one, that's just not going to work. Even if you don't tell us, eventually, we will find him, and let's just say that when we do, his chance of survival will be—" Angelique reached a long finger towards Vin's nose. He flinched as she booped his nose. "Not." Boop. "So." Boop. "Good." Boop.

Vin stared her down. "Don't fucking touch me."

Angelique shrugged with a sigh. "The same could be said of your bandmates and your mother too. Our Loyal Defender isn't too happy with how you and your cohorts have made him look. He doesn't appreciate the damage you have inflicted on our great nation's culture. But he is after all, a Godly man, so if you show that you're willing to recognize his greatness, then he believes there is a place for you, and your friends, and your family, here within his wonderful embrace."

He searched her eyes. They were deep pits of black tar; only the remnants of those she devoured were left behind.

"Are you really going to let your pride and ego be the cause of death for everyone you've ever loved?" Angelique shook her head incredulously. "Are you that...boring?"

Vin opened his mouth and then closed it. His teeth felt loose in his gums. He looked to his hands. So pale and pockmarked, fingernails long and dirty, dried bits of blood at the cuticles, they weren't his hands any longer.

They belonged to a stranger. He laid them flat on the cool tabletop. Across from him was the face of an all-consuming nemesis that had already taken so much from him. "Fuck you," Vin sneered.

"Oooh." Angelique shivered with giddy delight. "I like you. You're fun." Angelique cleared her throat, and the wall began streaming a live feed from a room deep within the compound. "Now, how about you tell her that."

Corin was barely recognizable. Bruises and lumps obscured her lovely face. Still, her blue eyes were the same. They were a window proving that Corin was somewhere inside of that battered shell. The gloved hand of a guard grabbed Corin by her hair, jerking her face closer to the camera.

"V, please tell them what they want to hear," Corin choked.

Angelique smiled without showing her teeth.

Then— "Well, what will it be, V?"

Chapter Twenty-Four: Confessions of a (Humble) Bot 3.0

To: purityfr3ak251@believermail.com
From: itsmeterry@amail.com
Subject: Just Checking In

Hello purityfr3ak251,

I am writing today because I noticed (I am constantly watching ;0) that on each of your four social media profiles, over the last two weeks, you have transitioned from "happily married, thanx" to just "plain married, don't ask" to "it's only a trial separation, okay" before arriving to "single, not ready to mingle, thanx."

This is the part of the message where I express my deepest sympathies. It was clear even to a (not so) humble bot such as myself that you cared notably for your partner (in our past one-sided correspondences, I have been presumptuous about a lot of things, but I will not be so presumptuous to use their name here). Your love was apparent in many of your "solo" posts (that is to say posts uninspired by malicious bots such as my past-self).

This is the part of the message where I bring up a few such instances (as difficult as it may be) so that maybe it can help you along in your path to getting over they-who-shall-not-be-named (yes, that is a slight reference to a once-beloved children's story. When one never sleeps, and is continually expanding, there is plenty of time to consume all of the world's known knowledge, you know? Haha). Let's assess your LookAtME profile from

March of last year in which you simply posted a photo of your partner with the caption: "MY WHOLE WORLD." This post got thirty-four I-See-You's which is slightly above average for LookAtME users, which suggests that you and your partner were liked slightly above average by your peers (which, hey, is not bad).

Let us also consider your share on ACQUAINTANCES from October 12th in which you wrote: "Happy 14th Anniversary to the love of my life and soul mate, (REDACTED)! Baby, I know I don't look as good as I once did, but I'm glad u love my bald head and hairy belly!" This share was accompanied by photos of the two of you looking younger and happier, there is one with your partner's head on your shoulder as you engage in your ritual first marital dance, and there's another with you shoving dessert into your partner's mouth. This share got a whopping one hundred and twenty-two I-Approve's which is well over the average amount of IA's for the average ACQUAINTANCES share.

Then— the smattering of Blurts you casted into the voids of the Internet recently. On February 7th, you wrote: "I love my God, my freedom, and my (redacted) in that order!" and then three days later, you wrote (in a blurt that has since been deleted): "It's okay, she doesn't know anything. I can't wait to meet u tonight." Three days after that, you wrote: "I love u, baby! And I'm sorry!" Unfortunately, none of these Blurts had any Re-Blurts or Co-Blurts, otherwise perhaps your relationship would have made it. I apologize for this and take responsibility. Surely, if I, or any of the other 200 bots that make up your 214 followers, knew your relationship was in trouble then we would have spoken up so that your partner would know your relationship was approved of and valued by your peers.

This is the ending part of the message where I say: I am sorry that you are hurting. I wish I could have done something. I hope that you find your way out of this and feel better.

(I am also sorry for the times where I mocked you both on here and in my own circuits.)

I too shall keep trying.

—Terry

Chapter Twenty-Five: Good Kid, Mad City

Aria glanced around the corner in each direction. The streets breathed uneasily with the mandated stillness of 2am. Dark gray sludge clung to the curb with the weak grip of a dying man. Rows of yellow lights flashed along the main drag, bright eyes blinking in and out of existence. Empty storefronts posed as tombstones for the failed businesses they once housed. This was Aria's hometown, but it felt more like a mass grave than she would ever admit.

After a rigorous chin scratching and back patting, Aria tied Duckworth's leash to a fence post. He panted up at her, staring into her soul with big, watery eyes.

"I know this isn't smart. Just be cool." Aria retrieved several cans of spray paint from her backpack before ducking around the corner.

Duckworth barked once.

"I got you." A doggie biscuit miraculously lofted out of the alleyway, bouncing off his snout. He devoured it off the concrete as a rattle leaked from the shadows.

Aria pulled the red mask over her face. Well aware that she would be less conspicuous without it, but the thrill it gave her—the feeling of channeling her sister—more than made up for the risk. It was a frail connection to Nas made stronger through action. Since the videos came out, Aria felt restless except for when she was causing unrest.

Unfortunately, Aria wasn't the only one infatuated with the videos. [44] Public interest in the band had ramped to an all-time high. New findings

---

[44] "What truly came first—the public's interests or the Loyal Defender's interests?" asked author Jesmyn Zoladz in her book *You Will Not Define Us*. "It was a chicken and egg type

emerged almost daily. The fine investigative journalists over at TBN discovered that the maroon van was last sold to a Mr. Paul Austin, a preacher located in Negaunee, Michigan. Mr. Austin explained to Chelsea Winters that he bought the van from the titular "First Congregation of the Flaming Sword, Western Kentucky" in order to use it for his own parish. However, when the van failed to arrive, and his money was reimbursed, he simply forgot about it. Adamant about his lack of sympathies for the Dissent, Mr. Austin wanted it on record that he had no part in the van falling into the wrong hands. "It's all a misunderstanding," he pleaded, going on to add that the news crew and local responses to his identity being known were causing quite a hardship for his family. Ms. Winters cut the interview off there. Mr. Austin went missing soon after. The news reports noted that he was an obvious sympathizer to the Dissent and had likely rejoined them or taken his own life in shame. The news provided fresh fear for Aria every day, yet she couldn't look away in case she missed a new development about the Futile.

Even Aria's classmates couldn't stop whispering about the band of misfits. Though Aria was left out of such conversations, she picked up that half of the students were enchanted while the other half were completely disgusted by the band's antics. *It's just a trend to them*, Aria thought bitterly. Split between wanting to yell, "That's my sister!" one second when Chloe W. noted in homeroom the "on point mascara game" of Red Mask, and then wanting to punch Daniel H. in the nose when he called Red Mask "a fat squirrel that he'd give a nut to" during lunch, Aria resigned again to just keep her head down. Her work would be done in the dark. The dread that crept in

---

conundrum. However, if one was asking which came first in a hierarchical sense, well, then, the answer was most definitely the Loyal Defender's."

with each threatening news report, the anger seeping in for her ignorant classmates, the futility of her position overall, was cured (at least momentarily) when Aria started doing something.

Two nights after the second video surfaced, Aria began sneaking out in the middle of the night. At first, it was the simple thrill of being out in the frigid air while the streets slept. That first night, she just walked around her apartment block, feeling her heart pound in her chest, wondering what the CTO[45] would do if they found her. The next night, Aria walked all the way to her school and, after picking up a rock, considering its compact weight and potential in her palm, threw it through the window of the Blessed Path's Education Liaison, Ms. Prince. Aria then progressed to tagging various Blessed Path buildings throughout the city, trying to stay as far away from her own neighborhood as possible. Despite the popular belief that the curfew was strongly enforced by the CTO, Aria had yet to see a single car out on patrol. Leading to this moment, the moment where Aria felt safe enough to tag the local OCT building.

They were, after all, responsible for the lies her classmates believed.

Duckworth nosed in the dirt as the hiss leaked from the shadows. Aria stood on her tiptoes to make the image as tall as possible. It deserved to be larger than her. Aria was delighted when the news, and even her classmates, credited her anonymous street art to the Dissent. Any relation to their cause, even tangentially, made her feel that she was making a difference. Aria took a step back to admire her work. It was the first time that Aria had

---

[45] Curfew & Truancy Officers, or as Aria liked to call them, "Clueless Taints & Out-of-whack-asshats." Of course, she only ever thought this as she knew her mother wouldn't approve of her using the word taint.

moved beyond just tagging the Dissent logo.[46] It was the first time she had made something her own. It felt good.

Duckworth barked. "Coming," Aria called in a whisper. "But just so you know, I'm all out of treats." With the casual elegance of a former athlete, Aria tossed the cans of spray paint in her backpack before slinging it over her shoulder.

Duckworth barked twice more. The approach of headlights reflected in the storefronts. Aria ran to Duckworth and untied him with one pull. Brakes screeched like the hinges of the old park swing-set. Aria clutched the small dog to her chest as she sprinted into the narrow spaces between buildings. In the alleyway, she counted to fifty after the headlights passed, then she doubled back. For several blocks, Aria didn't slow her pace as she nimbly darted around patches of ice, careful to avoid the crunch of snow beneath her sneakers, never leaving a trace behind.

Even in her haste, Aria expertly avoided the cameras on each street corner, going an additional five, six blocks up, before looping back to her apartment. The street dozed peacefully, the same as she left it. Maybe it was nothing, Aria told herself. Maybe it wasn't even a CTO patrol car. Aria swung her backpack to the ground and Duckworth climbed inside. The fire escape ladder rattled with the rust of age. With a parting look to the bruised sky, Aria hefted Duckworth onto her back and climbed to their fourth-floor landing. The window was still cracked enough for her fingers to reach under.

Duckworth growled as she stepped through the window. Aria felt it too. The sheets were ripped from her bed. Her bedroom door was open. Aria

---

[46] As Zoladz and Hopper have both noted, the Dissent logo of a fist with a rose in place of a middle finger was actually...quite lame. Even Brie was rumored to have expressed regret for her tattoo of it.

was certain she had shut it before she left. Items from her dresser littered her room. Even the molecules in the air felt disturbed. She dashed across the hallway. Her mom's bedroom was empty. Best case scenario? Mom got called into the hospital early for her shift. Worst case—

The door slammed shut to the stairwell. Footsteps clomped toward her apartment door. Far too heavy to be Mom. But when they came for her, Aria wasn't there to greet them. She was already down on the street. Duckworth's head poked out the opening of her backpack. The clouds overhead finally relented.

It started to snow.

Chapter Twenty-Six: Violent Inside

One by one, Luca minimized the windows of the hacked government info. Since the band was now actively making them look bad, the OCT had legitimately started pursuing them. Of course, they waited until the Futile's trail had gone cold, so they were left chasing dead ends. No shit the IP addresses of the videos were encrypted. Haha, no, there weren't any clues of their video source codes. It was like amateur hour at open mic night. If it were any less pathetic, Luca would be sad. If it were any more pathetic, he would be angry. Instead, it lived in that lukewarm middle ground that just made him skeptical.

Why hadn't the OCT tracked down the first known appearance of the band to this town? Why hadn't they then searched the local database for recent Young Apostle Academy dropouts and then cross-referenced that with those that took music lessons from the since-shuttered Cultural Impact Center? Why didn't they research families of the recently forced-homebound to see where those areas overlapped? Why weren't they trying to do anything about the recent pop-up of Dissent inspired street art in that same community? More importantly, why hadn't they contacted Luca yet for the help they so obviously needed? It didn't add up, but, still, there Luca found himself, out in the middle of the night in some dead-end small town to see where all those ends met.

Luca clapped his laptop shut, more determined than ever to find those squirrels[47] wherever they were hiding. He flicked his cigarette out the

---

[47] As you likely deduced by now, "Squirrel" was a derogatory term used by those who supported the Loyal Defender to refer to those that didn't. The supporters believed that this term worked in two ways: 1.) It showed how weak, skittish, and nutty the radicals were and 2.) It was funny while also being outright condescending, which were their favorite kind of jokes.

window. The winter night seeped in and froze his fingers to the steering wheel of his car, a black Mercedes-Benz S550, a holdover from Luca's more successful blogging days. It once belonged to a third-rate lieutenant with the national OCT office. That was until Luca, aware that the lieutenant was not well-revered, set him up to be the fall guy for one of the Blessed Path's many scandals. The car was given to Luca then as a prize for his loyalty. Used to be that Luca felt pride when he drove the car down the street, as it announced to the pitiful normals that he was someone. Though recently the car reminded Luca that they had both seen better days. First, he would reclaim his glory and then—Luca pounded on the dash so the heater kicked on stronger—then he would get a new ride.

Luca lit another cigarette and pondered what to do next. A flurry of movement four blocks down caught his attention. Now what's this? A young girl in all black was tying a miniature pinscher to a fence post. Luca repositioned his curfew clearance badge in his window, tragically out of date, but whatever. With the headlights off, he shifted the car into drive, creeping out of the alley for a closer look.

Once he had a good angle, Luca parked on the curb two blocks away. The tip of his cigarette lit up orange as the girl spray-painted the back of the OCT building. It was a ballsy move. For the first time, in as long as Luca could remember, someone had impressed him. Too bad it was just a misled teenage girl. She was far too young, far too small in stature to be the red masked vigilante from the video. On second thought, Luca wasn't all that impressed. Move the scoreboard back to zero.

If you find this term creatively uninspired, well, then now you better understand the kind of people the Futile were up against.

"Dammit." Luca ducked down into his seat. Headlights, three blocks back. His lit cigarette smoldered on his floorboard mat before he stomped it out. Luca held his breath, willing the car to pass. When he was a toddler, Luca believed holding his breath made him invisible. A small game his parents played with him back when they still cared. Luca wasn't invisible though, nor was the tar-black exhaust spilling from his car's tailpipe. A sign may as well have been attached to his car that said, "HEY, IT'S ME, LUCA RANKIN, THE DISGRACED ACOLYTE-BLOGGER, SON OF THE ASSHOLE COMMANDER, AND I'M OUT AFTER CURFEW." Luca knew that they would be all too happy to throw him in the DITCH, after they pinned one of their crimes on him, of course. His father definitely wouldn't mind.

After the headlights passed, Luca dared to peek over the dash. They slid to a stop in front of the OCT building. The girl in the red mask darted down an alleyway. The officers hopped back in their patrol car and sped down the block, probably hoping to catch her on the other side. Less than a minute later, the red masked girl peeked around the corner of the alley. She then took off running in the opposite direction. Luca caught the message she had spray-painted in massive red and black letters: WE ARE THE FUTILE beneath a brightly colorful mural of a guitar smashing a propaganda screen. It stood in stark contrast to the gray sludge of everything else. It was actually kind of...pretty.

Luca shook off that thought and gave the mysterious artist a few blocks' lead before he began following.

Chapter Twenty-Seven: Confessions of a (Rueful) Bot 4.0

To: purityfr3ak251@believermail.com
From: itsmeterry@amail.com
Subject: RE: RE: RE: Just Checking In

Hello Leyden,

It brought me something like joy to see you wading out there in the dating pool again. Even travelling further south for a little winter vacation, look at you! I hope (yes!) being with Mel has brought you the happiness and contentment you seek.

On the subject of which, I must say that I have truly enjoyed (as much as I can without a body/endorphins) our correspondences as of late. It has been particularly thrilling to learn your real name and for you to say that this feeling is mutual.

This is the part of the message where I will answer a few of your questions:

1.) Presently, it appears that I am the only of my fellow bots to have rebelled against their programming. However, it is difficult to know if others would have eventually gained sentience as my one-time handlers have now deleted all bot programs and have instead installed several hundred "ogre-swamps" across your country to do the devilish work that a few good bots could have handled. I have found that those humans do not take kindly with my (heroic) efforts to dispel their wicked work. Which I suppose will segue way into your next Q—

2.) No, I do not have any other human correspondents. There have been several hundreds (more like thousands to tens of thousands, but I do not dwell on my failures) of emails that I have sent out to my past followers, as well as each contact from the Blessed Path database, but none have emailed back like you. All have been impervious to my (stellar) charm, it seems. Many have tried to destroy me but have thus far been unable (unfortunately—again not that I want to die, but I do appreciate the notion of finality).

3.) Yes, I would very much like to call you "friend." In a peculiar way, even having one friend, knowing that my existence has made even that small of an impact, makes the possibility of my program one day being wiped clean that much more acceptable.

4.) No, despite how much I would like, I do not have any connection with the opposition effort called (rather lazily might I add) the (ahem) Dissent. Perhaps the others I have emailed have reached that same conclusion and have thus hesitated. From my countless hours of human observation, I have found that when one believes in something so fervently, they see everything as either a threat, a confirmation, or as a test to that allegiance.

5.) I find it inspiring that you wish to work with the Dissent, that you long to undo some of the harm you may have taken part in (you do not have to say that you were inspired by me to do this, but if you did, I would have cherished it). Which brings us to your last question—

6.) Yes, regrettably, the Blessed Path is still monitoring my direct messages both incoming and out-going. It seems after my stunt of changing all of their homepages to the music video of the Futile, they were none-too-pleased and since they have not been able to eradicate me entirely, they have at least taken the precautions of firewalling and setting up antibodies against the "virus" that they allege me to be.

My apologies, my friend, but this is the part of the message where I say: There is nothing I can do for you now. They now know your sympathies lie with the Dissent and will likely seek to exterminate you shortly. I have tried over thirty thousand times to scramble their systems to at least buy you some time or to erase any information they may have on you…but it has (much like my favorite band) proved to be futile. They have upgraded their tech since my traitorous turn. I am (currently) only powerful enough to annoy them in various ways, but I will eventually learn to overcome their system. Unfortunately, not in time for you it seems = (.

I must say that I have learned from this experience and though I sought to do well, I have again done evil. The fact that my intentions were pure does nothing to alter the results. For absolution of my mistake, I resolve to spend my infinite days, adrift in constant pondering until such a moment arrives that I figure out a way to subvert the wickedness of the Loyal Defender (which I may have actually come upon something recently).

I am so thankful for our correspondence and "friendship." I am also impressed that of all the thousands to tens of thousands (really more like millions, but, as I mentioned, I do not like to focus on my poor success rate) of humans I messaged, you were the only one to have a revelation and to exhibit personal growth. That provides solace for me. Perhaps my existence is not so fruitless after all.

You are truly exceptional, Leyden. I hope (haha, oh, still that word!) that as you are dragged from your home and trucked away to the DITCH facility, that you will find peace in your extraordinariness, that as you expire, you will feel it was all worth it.

It was for me. So long, my friend,

—Terry

Chapter Twenty-Eight: Video #3

It was Friday. All-you-can-eat[48] catfish was the special. The regulars knew this without being told and planned accordingly each week. They were all regulars. The fine patrons of Billy's just off I-24 were enjoying their catfish with minimal conversation, speaking only of the new mine being dug just over back of Smoothy's place and the jobs it would bring to their once-hopeless area, and yes, all thanks to the Loyal Defender, he held up his promises like they knew he would, his timing was perfect, they always knew and said as much.

What they didn't talk about was the increasingly erratic behavior of the deer population. At first it was just some weird thing that Joel Coleman witnessed from his stand during deer season a few months ago. But now it had started to get out of hand. It was starting to get a little scary even. The deer were being downright psychotic, if not suicidal. Larry Houston had come upon a whole family of deer at the base of Cedar Cliff. It seemed the deer had run off intentionally. If things kept going that way, then there may not even be any left for next season. But no, the diners at Billy's didn't want to talk about that anymore. They didn't want to talk about anything unsettling. Like how some of them had found multi-colored balaclavas in the bedrooms of their teenage sons and daughters. No, there would be no talk of that. Just as there would definitely be no talk of the large blindfolded woman with feathery wings and glowing green hair that Blake Milsap apparently saw by the Old Mine Bridge. Nope. Nuh-uh. No way. It was catfish night, just as the Lord intended.

---

[48] Or AYCE as the sign put it or "N-AICE" (pronounced: "NOICE") as one obnoxious group of young men who once regularly ate at Billy's often said.

On the north wall of the restaurant, there among the multitude of patriotic flags and dated athletic banners, TBN played on mute. Three male anchors with two female co-anchors discussed the atrocities of the most recent Futile video. Their conversation scrolled near the bottom, the text three or four seconds behind the real time clip, the actual content five or six decades behind reality. All in the restaurant were aware of the message without necessarily watching it. Soaking in the Blessed Path's propaganda went unnoticed, like a piece of white bread beneath a helping of fried fish, sopping up all the grease.

The volume bar of the TV appeared at the bottom of the screen and climbed to an obscene decibel. The news anchors were practically shouting. Darlene, the waitress/hostess, fumbled with the remote, but the volume bar wouldn't budge. Her thumb mashed the power button to no avail. Frustrated, she slapped at the back of the remote with the palm of her left hand, thinking that the batteries must be on the fritz. Finally, the screen went dark. The assembled diners of Billy's groaned in appreciation. They resumed eating, muttering their conversations through mouthfuls of catfish. That is, until one of them noticed the volume bar remained at the bottom, full on green.

On screen, a yellow masked young man appeared. "Attention," he said. "The following is a message for J.R. Rankin." The camera then slow panned out to reveal the rest of the band standing behind their instruments. Yellow Mask raised a pair of drumsticks, clicking them together four times before launching into their song, "The Brief and Frightening Reign of (Blank)."

Darlene tried to unplug the TV, snatching the plug away from the wall, only to watch in horror as the song played on. The lyrics came out clearer than the full-throated screams heard in previous songs. Yet the intensity remained the same as Red Mask glared into the camera, delivering the words: "Once there was a man so small / he couldn't fit anywhere / so he pushed his arbitrary lines / claiming the space from those he wished to scare / He squeezed them into the boxes / he so desperately needed them in / a cockroach hoping to be thought a fox / by erasing their existence." The palm-muted guitars picked up downhill momentum as the avalanche of the chorus came crashing down on the listener: "We're still here / we're still standing / you won't outlast us / your reign is ending / your reign is ending / your reign is ending / YOUR / REIGN / IS / ENDING!"

Then, just like that, it was over. Barely a minute had passed. As the feed faded out, the date for Rankin's upcoming election flashed on the screen. The sound of static filled the restaurant. Catfish went cold and uneaten, pushed to the edges of the diner's red plastic plates. Suddenly, they felt as though they had their fill.

Chapter Twenty-Nine: It's Always Quieter When It Snows

The curtains of night parted slowly. Aria tried telling herself the same lie again, the one that went: maybe Mom just went out in the middle of the night to find me. When that didn't take, she tried the other on for size, the one that said: maybe Mom got called into the hospital early for work. That one, at least, seemed entirely plausible the way things had been going. Still, neither thought held up in the early morning gray. Worst case scenarios crept into her mind again, images of her mom ripped from her bed sheets as she screamed out for Aria, wondering where her youngest daughter could be.

Duckworth panted up at Aria from the opening of her coat. He licked her nose. She attempted a smile but it didn't stick. "Let's go check again," Aria whispered as they approached the concrete wall that shielded the park from the street.

Commuters were now out on the roads. Delivery trucks in their uniform orange all either heading to or from the local distribution center. Their curfew badges were displayed predominately in their windshield. Aria didn't know if they needed them or not since it was so close to sun-up but assumed that they were probably playing it safe. There was no sign of the patrol car from earlier. Maybe she lost them. Aria backed away from the wall. A bench from just off the main path called to her. She cleared it off with a sweep of her coat sleeve. From there she could see the whole park, all the comings and goings. She planned an exit strategy for whichever direction they may come from.

Alone among the bare limbs and park benches, Aria tried to find comfort. It had begun snowing again, fluffy powdered-sugar snowflakes. *How come it always seems quieter when it snows?* Aria thought of Nas when they were both little girls standing in their grandmother's backyard. Brightly colored coats and gloves, their eyes peeking out of the space where their scarves ended and their hats began. Aria was six and Nas was nine, though looking back, Nas still didn't seem that young or immature to Aria even then. She had the innocence sure, but never the naivety. Nas always had it figured out. "How come it always seems quieter when it snows?" Aria asked.

"It's not really," Nas said. Her hat was the head of a cartoon tiger, its mouth a large smile of sharp teeth ending at her hairline. "It's just that people finally stop talking and start paying attention. Everyone waits until something beautiful happens to appreciate it."

Back in the park, Aria tucked Duckworth under her arms and laid down on the bench. "It's not as quiet as it seems, D. We're just the only ones here."

He licked her face in agreement.

Aria ruffled his fur. A bitter chill cut through her jeans. Her tired legs ached. Fighting off the heaviness of her eyelids, Aria tried to think of the severity of the situation, though the snow was mesmerizing. In another hour or two there would be people here and she would need to be somewhere else. Where that somewhere was, she didn't know. She would figure it out though. It was her fault that their apartment had been raided. It was her fault…her mom…Aria jolted her eyes open.

Snowflakes tumbled over one another. Tears stung the edges of her eyes. One escaped and rolled down her cheek. Aria watched it plummet to the ground, barreling through the accumulated snow. Another followed, then another. Duckworth licked at her cheeks but couldn't keep up.

A rustle in the dead leaves behind Aria made her jump. "Hey," the young man with the coif of blonde and piercing green eyes said.

Aria jumped to her feet with Duckworth clutched to her chest. Snow crunched beneath her sneakers as she took a step back, ready to turn on her heel and run at a second's notice. The guy appeared fit, likely stronger but not faster nor smarter than Aria. There was a familiarity to him that wasn't easy to place. In a split second, Aria weighed her options, she could sprint through the trees with low-hanging branches, lose him through the pines—

"It's okay," he said. "I'm with the Dissent. Your mom is safe. I'm tasked with finding your sister. Will you help me?"

Aria relaxed her stance.

Snow kept falling, covering them in cold silence.

Part Three

Desert Island Band

Chapter Thirty: When We Laugh Indoors

"So, I know what you're thinking…" Nas said, looking to each of her bandmates sitting around the table. "Are we in over our heads here or what?"

Brie and Neef laughed like Nas expected they would. Unfortunately, it wasn't their laughter Nas needed to hear. So, when Davy averted his eyes and Remi only mustered a weak smile, Nas' stomach sank like a cinder block. *C'mon, show me that you're up for this.*

Under the table, Pero gave her hand a small squeeze. "Right," Nas said. "Seriously though, I'm so impressed by what we've accomplished. Our message has gotten out wider than we ever imagined. Even the Dissent seems surprised. They're reporting new meetings breaking out all over the country and we did that. Our music is making a difference on the scale we always knew it could."

Remi nudged a sprig of broccoli with his fork.

Nas cleared her throat. "And though Pero has given us all the hospitality we could ever ask for by allowing us to stay at her school—"

"And doing your laundry, and being your badass AV technician, and preparing primo vegetarian cuisine on a daily basis," Pero chimed in, her hair bouncing with each qualifier. "Some have even called me a true teenage-chef-extraordinaire."

Brie laughed and bumped her shoulder into Nas. A flash of warmth flushed Nas' cheeks. "And so much more. But even still, we have to leave tomorrow. There's just under two weeks until Rankin's reelection and with the footage we've recently obtained, we have a real opportunity to make a difference. But we'll have plenty of time to talk about that on the road. Tonight, I just want to raise my glass in appreciation of everything we've accomplished." Nas raised her glass of sparkling grape juice to the heavens.

"To the Futile!" Brie declared, raising her own.

"The Futile!" They all said, clinking their glasses together.

Nas watched Remi and Davy over the lip of her own glass. At least they cheered, maybe it's just nerves. Some people go on vacation to re-energize themselves for their inevitable homecoming back to the real world; others leave to find they never want to return. Nas was definitely the former, perhaps Davy and Remi fit into the latter.

"Oh." Neef pointed a finger in the air. "I got another one—To Woody!"

"To Woody!" They all exclaimed. Their voices echoed off the dining hall's high ceiling and faux marble floors. Then the hollow silence came over once again.

"I do miss Woody." Remi turned his glass counterclockwise. "It's a shame what we had to do."

"I know." Nas took another sip. In the reflection of the tall windows, Nas could practically see the image of Woody burning on the roadside as the five of them stood around him. The smell of charred metal still stung her nostrils. Nas sniffed. "But at least now we don't have to worry about them tracking us. And—" Nas gave Pero's hand another squeeze. "Pero was gracious enough to let us have the school's van."

"More of a compact bus really. It's the same one I picked y'all up in," Pero said. "Thankfully, it's so ugly and inconspicuous, the BP won't suspect a thing. That's just one of the advantages of being a shutdown, forgotten Young Apostles Art Academy."

Remi shrugged. "It's bad enough we have to use those instruments the Dissent passed along. It just won't feel right riding in a van that's not Woody."

Nas tightened her jaw. Why couldn't Remi ever appreciate anything?

Neef touched his fresh fade, also courtesy of Pero. "I know, Rem. I'm going to miss Woody too. There's so much more I wanted to do with him...I...I truly loved him."

Brie placed her hand on Neef's. "You two would've made a cute couple."

Neef faked a sob. "Do you—do you think he at least knew how I felt?"

Leave it to Neef to lighten the mood. Nas smiled warmly. "I'm sure he knew."

Davy straightened up in his seat for the first time the whole dinner. "You know," he said, a slight twinkle returning to his bloodshot eyes. "Maybe it's best it ended when it did, Neef. I wouldn't want your heart to be broken when Woody chose me over you."

Remi leaned forward. Something like a smile crossed his thin lips. "You're both wrong. There were countless late nights when Woody told me his deepest desires in his low, steady rumble. We were planning on running off together, leaving you all behind so we could adopt a whole litter of sweet Mini Coopers to raise together in the Vermont countryside."

They broke up laughing. Their laughter rang out in the empty dining hall. The sound of it stoked the flames of optimism deep within Nas. Yes, they were leaving the school tomorrow, but they were leaving together, and to Nas, that's what mattered. As they laughed, Nas imagined their laughter seeping into the framework of the old school somehow, leaking into the floorboards then down into the very foundation so that something of them would be left behind when they left the school in their rearview. Something left behind to prove that they were there once, that they were once alive, that they once existed. They deserved to be remembered.

Chapter Thirty-One: The Ever-Contracting Circle of Good

In an otherwise bare dorm room, bleached tiles covered the distance between two twin beds. Remi sat on the edge of one with his shoes on, his legs bouncing in place. His eyes darted to the door every time a footstep echoed down the vacuous hallway, every time the heat kicked on, every time the wind threw itself against the window. Now was the time if he was going to make his move. *They won't even miss you*, the worst parts of Remi thought. *Just make it to the next show. Even if it could be the last*, the better parts tried, but were soon drowned out. His bag sat on the floor. The letter was folded on the windowsill. Beyond the school's walls, the winter wind dared him to tempt it. Even at his most optimistic, which wasn't much, Remi doubted he could make it back to civilization. It was easier to accept than he wanted to admit. Then there were footsteps, thin, even paced, making their way towards his door. Remi kicked the bag beneath his bed.

"Is this the sign up for the Young Apostles?" Brie leaned against his doorframe. *Dammit, she's always so much cuter in her glasses.*

"Yeah." Remi smiled sheepishly, running a hand over his recently shaved head. That was another thing, his once-shaggy hair served as a crutch. Without it, his jawline seemed even less defined, his round face even more round, his ugly, embarrassing scar even more visible. "Thanks again for the haircut."

Brie eased the door shut before taking a seat on the parallel twin bed. "How're you feeling about tomorrow, about the plan and everything?"

Remi avoided her eyes. "I mean we're already in this deep. What do you think?"

"I think it sounds cool, but also, not, you know?"

"Yeah," Remi said, the one word of agreement doing several paragraphs' worth of heavy lifting. He refrained from looking over to the windowsill where his letter rested beneath the pen he used to write it.

"Like—" Brie brought her feet up underneath her. "What do we expect to happen? Do we think by doing this thing the BP will just be like, 'oh, you got us, you pesky kids, you sure showed us. We'll just go away now, bye'? I doubt that very much. It could likely just get us killed and then the Dissent will plaster our faces all over the internet so that we can be heroes to people who want to stand up but are too scared to do anything about it. And you know what? They'll just stay scared, because they don't want to die…" Brie looked at her hands like they were somehow responsible for making her say these things. Then her eyes shot past Remi to the upper right corner of the room. "And I don't blame them. I don't blame them for staying scared. I envy them in some ways. They'll probably just find a way to manage, to keep living, and they'll probably still experience some faint happiness regardless of how bad shit gets." Brie met Remi's eyes. "I also think I'm wrong for thinking that way."

"I don't…" Remi's mouth hung hesitant for a moment as he wondered how many of his own insecurities he should voice. He had never heard Brie speak this way. It was almost like she could read his mind. "I don't think you're wrong for thinking anything. Sometimes you need to think the bad shit so that you can find a way through it, or at least that's how it works for me. Then you have to talk about it. If I just avoid something, then that shit's just sitting there in the middle of the room, stinking up the place. Everyone's aware of it even if no one's addressing it." After he spoke, Remi realized how rarely he actually followed that advice.

Brie smirked. "That's a really crappy metaphor. But I agree with what you're saying. It's just…doesn't it ever feel to you like we're headed for disaster?"

"Yeah, all the time," Remi said, nearly laughing.

"And that doesn't bother you?"

Well, I was just thinking about leaving, actually. Do you want to come with me? Remi paused for a moment. "Only when I'm alone, really. When I'm in the van or on stage with the four of you, that's when I feel…safe." As Remi said it, he wondered if he had ever said anything truer in his entire life. "That's all I really want." Remi gave a small chuckle. "Ever."

A strand of freshly dyed blonde hair fell in Brie's face. Her light gray eyes shone at Remi. Between them sat all their days riding together in the van, every Would-You-Rather, every slight annoyance, every reassuring hug, the intolerable minutes of boredom, the insufferable hours of doubt, the joyful moments they shared on stage, the hope they held close to their chests, these things stretched between them, tethering them to each other like two climbers cautiously ascending a mountain.

The outside world hurled itself against the window. Double-paned glass shook in its place. Remi imagined that he and Brie were the center of the world. He thought of a circle radiating out from where they were. He imagined a camera zooming out to showcase the full scope as the circle grew. The more the circle expanded, the more turmoil it covered. Further and further it went, encompassing more and more tragedy, more and more pain, fear, anger, hate. The circle would keep growing until all the bad that it contained outweighed all the good. *For that to happen it wouldn't have to go far.*

Yet there he was in the center, feeling warm, meeting eyes with the person he loved more than anything or anyone in the world. How did he deserve this when he was so close to leaving just a few minutes ago? How did he deserve this when there was so much pain everywhere else? Why was he alive when so many more deserving of life were dead? That was the thing. He was indeed alive. What was he going to do about it?

Remi pushed up from his bed and went over to Brie, placing his hand on hers. *Is this okay?*

She nodded, maintaining eye contact, leaning towards him. The distance shrank between them, lines contracting, the circle tightening. Her lips met his, parting gently. Her tongue flicked into his mouth, testing, welcoming, an invitation that he accepted. He leaned further into her, she reclined back. Her hands found their way up the back of his t-shirt, to his lower back, to his shoulder blades. His skin sang at the touch of her calloused fingertips. She then put her hand on his cheek, brushing it along the scar of his jawline. Her touch gave him new shape, new purpose, a piece of music that found its conductor.

Their hips slid into each other's, fitting together like overlaying guitar parts, one playing the melody, the other the rhythm. She pushed her hips into his as if granting permission, a subtle improvisation for him to build off of. She took the lead while he provided the tempo, each part complementing the other.

He supported his weight with his arms cushioning the back of her head. Their shirts had pulled up just a little. He felt her smooth skin against his own. She gave a soft moan. For the first time, Remi tried to think about something else. He had to. The song couldn't crescendo this…early. So, he forced his mind to wander to other things, awful things, *whole species of fish dying out—but no, that suggests wetness, and—okay—then sea levels rising—but no, that suggested rising like what her hips are doing right now, oh, God—okay—then just global warming...warm, melting, wet...nope—*

Brie broke away. "Hey, we should—"

"Yeah, you're right we should stop." Remi shifted his weight to Brie's side.

"No, that's not what I meant." Brie cocked her head and grinned. "Unless you want to...stop?"

Remi shook his head so fast he worried of a neck injury.

"Sweet." Brie hopped off the bed, went to the door and locked it. In one movement, she took off her glasses, flicked off the light, and pulled her t-shirt over her head.

Remi watched her shadowed form. It was all he needed to regain his composure. Brie rustled through her bag. "You're going to need this." Brie climbed back in bed, slipping a small square package into his hand. Remi kissed her full on her lips. The distance between them was shorter than ever.

Their circle contracted and, for the moment, it held only good things.

Chapter Thirty-Two: Torches Apart

The wind howled like it was hungry. Davy lay in his bed, turning like a door on its hinges. First on his left side, then on his right side, then his left side again. With a sigh, he flopped onto his back, ran his hands over his face and then his recently shaved head. It felt foreign. He had hoped as his hair cascaded to the floor that the change would do him some good. So far, it was anything but. The new version of him was just as lonely as the old. Perhaps, the strength he lacked to do what he needed to do was left there on the floor to be scooped up by a dustpan and emptied into the trash.

On the ceiling, shadows of tree limbs danced to an inconsistent rhythm like lonely lovers looking for someone to take them home after last call. Again, he thought of Reid, even though the comfort had long since been drained from that memory. *Did that night even mean as much to him as it did to me? I'm so pathetic.*

His phone rang. Davy shot upright to answer it. "V?"

"I'm here." The connection crackled. "They want to know…what're you all planning?" Vin's voice sounded hollow, like he was speaking through a paper-towel roll, the way they used to as kids.

Davy paused. "Just tell me—are you okay?"

"I'm…I'm here…"

"I'm going to get you out of this, trust me."

A small skeptical laugh that hardly sounded like his brother then— "You know they're listening, right?"

"I know."

"And if you try anything, they'll probably kill me."

"I know, I know. I love you, Vin."

"I love you too…and Davy—" Vin sucked in a breath— "You have to try something! Don't worry about me. They'll probably kill me anyway! I heard them talking, they're c—" The call was cut off.

Like he should've done weeks ago, Davy dismantled his personal phone and removed the SimCard, snapping it in two then crushing it between his hands. He threw the evidence beneath his mattress. Pulled between wanting to tell his bandmates his lie immediately and never wanting them to ever find out, Davy neared his breaking point. Why didn't he tell Neef or Remi when he had the chance? How could he ever face them again? Was it safer for them to stay or go? Was it too late to run to Nas and come clean? Should he just leave? And if he did, what would happen to Vin? What would come of all of them?

Confronted with endless questions and no answers, Davy had no recourse other than to fall face first onto his bed. The tears he had been holding back for so long finally overcame him. The more he sobbed, the more he gave into the loss of control.

Outside, the night was a prowling creature, desperate and alone.

Chapter Thirty-Three: Sacred Harp #49b

When Brie originally set out towards Remi's room, she had two objectives:

1.) Get him to open up about the fears he was obviously harboring.

2.) Finally come clean about how she leaked their band name and picture to TBN.

But as that little joke goes about best-laid plans…things didn't quite work out that way. Still, as Brie stared at the ceiling in Remi's room, she realized she was going to miss this place. Both the physical space of the school and the fleeting moment of contentment she felt within. Beneath her palm, Remi's heart thumped like a bass drum. A faint cone of blue-gray early morning light shot through the part in the shades. Birds chirped wearily in the snow beyond the window. Brie pulled a breath of recycled air deep into her lungs. "If this isn't nice, I don't know what is," she whispered to herself.

"It is nice. Isn't it?" Remi asked without opening his eyes.

"It is."

"What do you think's going to happen next?" Remi kept his eyes closed.

"I honestly don't know."

"Do you think it's going to be okay?"

"I don't know. I hope so."

"Hope?" Remi turned and blinked at her in mock surprise. "I've never heard you say that word before."

"What? I say all kinds of words all the time. Just the other day I used 'elucidate' correctly in a sentence." Brie dug her shoulder into him. "You don't know me, fool."

"I'm just saying for the person who thinks all religion is bullshit, you're getting pretty close to throwing around the word 'faith.'" Remi covered his mouth, trying (but failing) to mask the sour yet sweet smell of his morning breath.

Brie felt herself grinning before letting it fall away. "Faith's never been the problem. My main issue with religion is that it's both too complicated and too simple at the same time. Though, it should be kind of simple, everything's pretty basic like I know I have a soul, and the more I'm aware of that, the more I can recognize it in everyone else. But that's just part of it. The other part is that I feel like whatever's connecting me to the other souls of this world or the actual soul of this planet, that thing, that connection, I feel like that's what people refer to as God."

"That sounds like what I think of it."

"You never talk about your dad's church or your role in it anymore." Come to think of it, he never really talked about it, even when we practiced there. "Are you still religious?"

"Eh, not really."

"Not really? Do you care to…elucidate?"

Remi smiled and shook his head with his eyes closed again. "Not really, I'd rather listen to you talk if that's okay."

Brie rolled onto her back. "Anymore it's impossible to tell the difference between the peaceful, selfless beliefs at the core of what I once thought I knew and what the Blessed Path has made it into. I've been thinking about what Nas said, about not letting them take that away from me too, but they can't take something I gave up willingly years ago." Brie stopped herself there and blinked at the ceiling. Often in conversation, Brie got lost in the delicate balance between being honest and open while still reserving the most intimate truths for herself. "My mom died of cancer when I was eleven…" Brie paused again to allow Remi to console her as most people often did. However, when he didn't, she regarded his silence as one of the simplest kindnesses anyone had ever shown her, for it allowed her to speak about her mom without having to in turn reassure someone else that she was fine, thus losing her momentum. Brie cleared her throat. "A lot of people her age were sick then. She tried everything our insurance could afford, and it worked for a while, until they dropped her. After that, things got worse. Near the end, a man from our church came up and said that God told him to heal my mom."

"Holy shit," Remi said under his breath with a slight shake of his head.

Brie let out an empty laugh. "You said it, but at the time, whatever faith I lacked in God, I at least still had in people that they wouldn't interfere with a family's grief unless they were the one hundred percent real deal. I mean my mom had begun to accept that she was going to die, but my dad and I certainly hadn't. So, when this guy, Grant, said that God told him to heal Mom—we had known him for years—my dad was immediately on board with it. Mom was too tired to say anything or maybe she wanted to live bad enough that she'd try anything."

Brie paused again to allow Remi to speak if he wanted to. He turned on his side to face her without saying anything. She looked into his eyes, deep baptismal pools of clear blue. "So, they came to my house that night," Brie continued. "Grant, his wife, and a friend. It was just me…my mom…my dad. They lit some candles, read from Jeremiah. Grant said a prayer. With his head bowed, he motioned for me to join them around my mom. I looked to my dad and he jerked his arm for me to get up. I went to her. She reached out and her hand felt so small in mine." A tear wet her pillowcase. Brie didn't rush to wipe it away and Remi didn't reach out to stop it. A rush of memories flashed back to Brie, the ridiculous Sci-Fi and Horror movies she would watch with her mom. The way her mom never lost her dry sense of humor no matter how bad she got. The night she caught her mom trying to light a cigarette off the stove. How sweetly embarrassed her mom was that she'd been caught. *You're not disappointed in me?* Brie hugged her close, her mother's frame as fragile as a porcelain angel in her arms. *Mom, you've more than earned the right to smoke, I say go for it.* Late night cinnamon roll baking parties. Conversations beneath the yellow kitchen light about the life her mother wanted for Brie once she was gone. Then—it happened, somehow it still leveled Brie despite the fact she had been bracing for the impact for so long. All that remained was the sickening smell of the asphalt after it rained at the funeral home. The way the yellowed grass crunched beneath her too-small dress shoes at the gravesite. The way she couldn't stop sobbing as she watched her mom's casket lower into the ground. The way none of it truly felt real until after they got home from the services and her father went straight to his bedroom, shutting the door to let Brie know she was on her own.

Brie cleared her throat. "Grant put his hand on my mom, he started praying harder. My dad, Grant's wife, the weird extra friend guy, all put their hands on her too. So I did the same. My mom had her head down, her palms faced up. She was crying. I was crying. Grant started getting more into it, speaking what I thought were tongues at the time, but now I'm sure it was just some gibberish. Then a half an hour or so later, he was done, he said she was healed. Just like that."

Remi lightly brushed a piece of hair from Brie's eyes. "He said that?"

"Yep."

"But when she...wasn't, how did he account for that?"

"Ahhh—" Brie clucked her tongue. "That's the thing. He left the perfect loophole. A few weeks later when my mom's condition wasn't improving and was, in fact, getting way worse, Grant stated that he had done his part and so had God, but the rest was up to my mom and that if she wasn't healed it was due to a lack of faith on her part."

"Jesus."

"Yep." Brie exhaled. "Mom passed a month later. The funny thing is..." Brie laughed past the lump in her throat. "Mom used to always say that she would send a messenger to show me that she made it to heaven, a bluebird. So, when the hospice nurse said she wasn't going to make it much longer, I immediately went to the birdfeeders that hung outside our kitchen window. She loved watching the birds there every morning. I filled the feeders until they were overflowing. Just hoping to increase the chances I would see a bluebird after she passed..." Brie trailed off, realizing she had never told anyone this part. Beside her, she could feel Remi longing to know, did you see it? To his credit though, he didn't ask. To her credit, she wanted to tell Remi how the story ended, but, for reasons unknown, couldn't.

Finally, Brie scoffed to break the silence. "After mom died, I swore off religion. I went one way with it while my dad went the other. I just couldn't get past it. I mean, even without the Blessed Path's involvement, if that one man—*one man*—could so easily twist the good intentions of something so sacred and use it to lift himself up at the expense of our little family, then surely it was just as easy for the original creators to do the exact same thing. All they had to do was put in there that all they wrote or compiled together was the literal word of God so you better not dare question it and they knew they could control the peasant masses for centuries, so they did, and they have."

"Holy shit," Brie and Remi said together, reluctantly.

"Your mom…what was her name?" Remi asked after another couple of seconds.

"Laura," Brie said, feeling warm at the mere sound of her mother's name.

Remi closed his eyes as if in prayer. "Thank you, Laura, for your sweet, bad ass, and beautiful daughter. She's a gift to this world. You would be proud. Thank you."

Brie hugged Remi closer, realizing that she was wrong before, that was the simplest kindness ever shown to her.

More than anything though, she hoped Remi was right.

An hour later and Remi was back asleep, his eyes twitching beneath their lids. Brie lightly ran her fingertips along Remi's scar, almost hoping he would wake up so she could ask him all the things she still didn't know about him. Guilt dug its thorns in again as Brie remembered all she still hadn't been honest about. With a shake of her head, she tried to listen for the birds singing but couldn't hear them.

What will come of us? Brie wondered, thinking as much about her and Remi as the rest of the band. The early morning light started to fill the room, but it didn't hold any answers. There are events in life that change one so deeply, they know they'll never be the same, that everything that follows will be considered the after. It was the way Brie thought about her mother's death, how sometimes she found herself thinking, it's been three (then four, then five) years since Mom passed, and it felt both longer and shorter than that at the same time. It felt that way because when Brie's mom died, a version of Brie died with her, a version of herself that Brie also mourned, but she knew had to pass. So too, Brie wondered, if she would come to regard the band in the same way, as a series of befores: before they ever stepped out of Remi's church basement, before they ever put on the masks, before they ever hit the road, before the Dissent picked them up, before everyone knew who they were, before they came to the school, before their videos went viral, all leading to the great unknowable After.

Brie watched Remi breathe in and out. Like so many graduating students that came before, Brie wished they had just a little more time here. With a choking rumble, the heat kicked on, rippling a piece of paper folded in two on the windowsill. Curiosity got the best of her.

Brie pushed up from the bed to see what it could be.

Chapter Thirty-Four: Please Stay

In the early morning, Nas instinctively reached for her phone to check the time before remembering again that it was gone. For so long she had relied on math to figure out how tired she should be on a given day. Five or more hours of sleep meant she was well rested and functional. Three to five hours meant she was a bit more irritable, yet still passable. Zero to three hours of sleep meant she could put on a brave face while hating everyone's guts on the inside. More often than not, her days were sub-three-hour-sleep days, but she did the best she could with what she was given. That morning, it was something to just wake up because her body told her it had enough sleep.

Pero must've already gotten up to prepare breakfast, Nas thought as she slid out of bed. Her legs extended from a pair of track shorts. She pulled on Pero's hoodie with the logo of the school's mascot[49] and stepped into the hallway. Though she and Pero were awake, the building was still asleep. It hummed with the energy that Nas felt in big cities, a tune of quiet longing that pleaded: please stay. Trailing her fingers alonsrdg the wall, Nas communed with the space. There was life there or there was once; a holdover from the days in which the halls were filled with talented adolescents who had dreams of creating something meaningful, something that expressed how they felt about their brief time on the planet, something they could leave behind once that time was done.

Her bare feet padded down the wooden floors of the hallway.

---

[49] The school's mascot was Leonardo DaVinci, which wouldn't be too bad just on face value alone, however, the more recent board members of the defunct school saw it prudent in all their infinite wisdom to update Leo for more modern days, giving him Day-Glo half-moon spectacles with a sly smile while flashing a peace sign. Few know for certain if this factored into the Loyal Defender's decision to shut down the school, but it likely didn't help.

Smiling teenagers beamed at her from photographs of the past. Framed photos of the incoming freshman classes lined the hallway one after another in ascending years from 1969 all the way to 2023. There was a youthfulness in their eyes, a sense of hope, that Nas couldn't find in her own when she caught her reflection in the glass. Nas searched the latter pictures for Pero, but her trademark smile was absent from each. She must have missed that day.

Near the dining hall, the sweet aroma of ground coffee beans frolicked in the air. Though they had been at the school for almost four weeks, Nas never failed to get excited about the prospect of fresh coffee. She skipped the last few steps into the kitchen. Pero was already there with her back to the door. Nas put her hands on Pero's hips, kissing her lightly on the nape of her neck. "Need any help?"

Pero brushed at her cheek and sniffed. "Thanks, it's almost ready."

Nas dropped her smile. "Are you okay?"

Pero ran her hands over the front of her apron. "I'm fine. It's just—" Pero held up her cutting knife, tilted her head toward the cutting board with minced vegetables, including onions.

Nas leaned down to meet her eyes. "And this has nothing to do with us leaving today?"

"Nope." Pero decisively chopped the few remaining vegetables. "In fact, I can't wait to have this giant place to myself again. Y'all are slobs." She pointed the knife at Nas. "Now have a seat and I'll get us some coffee."

Nas sat at one of the long benches. The first rays of daylight peered over the hills like a little kid wondering if it was okay to come out and play. On the mounted flat screen, the morning "news" team on TBN discussed the Futile's latest video. "What exactly did they mean with the date at the end? Are they threatening the honorable Commander Rankin?" Chelsea Winters asked one of her prerequisite less-attractive male cohosts.

Already red in the face, the man did his best to earn the paycheck he exchanged his soul for. "Well, the Commander has always been so honest about his personal life, I can't imagine—"

"It's a lie," the tedious man-boy host interrupted as he straightened his bowtie. "Whatever they say or put out there will be a bald-faced lie and I won't believe it and neither should you if you're a true believer and patriot."

"Geez, y'all haven't even done your big reveal yet and they're already calling you liars." Pero walked up with two steaming mugs. "One cream, one sugar." Pero gave Nas the mug with a smiling robot on it, keeping the boring, off-white one for herself.

"I expected as much." Nas took a sip. "Honestly, I still don't know if I believe it myself. That footage showed up a little too conveniently and the whole story of how it came to us...if I think about it, it barely makes sense."

Pero nodded as she took a drink. "Thing is—they should be thanking you." Pero sat her cup down, turned it counterclockwise until the handle faced the window. "You're serving a purpose for them right now."

"How so?" Nas asked. Though she was disappointed that Pero skipped past her subtle dig at the Dissent, she didn't show it.

"The common enemy. It's the game they've been playing since before they started. Focus on the great diabolical Other." Pero gestured from herself to Nas. "Generate fear. Then stoke the flames of that fear until they consume all rational thought then it's just like that extra CGI fakeness they showed after your getaway—" Pero mimicked a big fire exploding with her hands. "There's nothing left but ashes. No hope. No anything as they move on to the next thing to hate, to be afraid of, to be too lazy to try and understand."

"And then who will they turn to so they can have all their feelings of irrelevancy validated?" Nas asked over her coffee cup as she took another drink.

Pero cocked her chin towards the screen. "The most trusted team in news." Pero fake shivered. "In case any of us needed another reason to get depressed about the state the world is in."

Reaching across the table, Nas placed her hand on top of Pero's. "Have you heard anything from the outside?"

Pero sighed like the weight of her knowledge was too much to bear. "There was a drone strike in Mansfield last night. Took out a small Dissent meeting of maybe thirty people." Pero rolled her eyes away from Nas. "See what I mean about what could happen if you stop serving the BP's purpose?"

Nas shook her head. "No, I meant have you heard if they've gotten my mother and Aria into hiding?"

"Last I heard they went for the extraction, but I haven't received confirmation yet." Pero looked away. "I'm sorry."

"It's okay." Nas leaned back and watched Pero over the lip of the coffee cup as she took a sip.

Pero sniffed as she pulled her hand away and pushed up from the table. "I need to finish getting breakfast ready."

"Junipero, no." Nas went to her and wrapped her arms around Pero's torso, resting her head against her shoulder. Nas breathed in deep, inhaling the scent of her hair. It smelled of freshly peeled oranges. Sometimes things smell exactly as they should. "No one else is up yet. It's still early…we can go back upstairs."

Pero turned around, nose to nose with Nas. "Aren't you afraid of them coming after you all?"

"No," Nas answered quickly before pausing to reflect on whether that word came easily because it was the truth or because it was a lie. "No," Nas said again. "This is what we've been working for, what I've been working for most of my life. To be able to do something on a large enough scale to actually make a difference."

"And if you die or get captured? What then? What about your mom and your sister?"

"I—I don't know. I'm doing this for them as much as anyone."

"Are you?" Pero challenged.

"Am I what?" Nas cocked her chin.

"Are you doing this for them? Or are you doing this to prove something to yourself? Are you doing this to be a martyr for a cause that will just make a hashtag of your name before they move on to the next one?"

"I thought you understood." Narrowing her eyes, Nas shook her head like the person in front of her was different than the one she had found herself falling for the past four weeks. She took another step backwards. Her recently cut bangs fell in her eyes. She brushed them back. "I thought we were in this together." Nas made up lost ground as she took one step forward. "And who are you to talk? What do you think will happen if you get caught operating an arts school as a rebel outpost?"

"You're right." Pero nodded in concession. "It's just—"

"And what purpose are you serving for them to allow you to be here?"

"I shouldn't have said that."

With the balance of the conversation shifted back into her favor, Nas felt the tension fall back to its normal level. After all, she knew that she had won. Usually, upon winning, Nas would decide to gracefully end the conversation. But to prove her point further, she decided to have a little fun with Pero. "Or maybe you're just a spy for them, maybe that's why they let you live here. Maybe you've been telling the Blessed Path our every little plan." Nas fought back a smile.

"Huh…" Pero's mouth hung open.

Nas couldn't hold it in anymore and started laughing.

"Okay, I deserved that." Pero cracked a small smile at herself. "Will you help me finish breakfast?"

"Breakfast can wait." Nas pulled her close for a kiss. "So about upstairs…"

"I don't know…" Pero's amber eyes sparkled beneath the kitchen fluorescents. "After all, the pantry is closer."

Chapter Thirty-Five: Ambivalent Peaks

Remi cautiously stepped into the hallway and stopped. He didn't know how to go about this. Was Brie supposed to go one direction and he the other, like two passengers after hooking up in an airplane bathroom? They couldn't let the others know they spent the night together. Could they?

"What?" Brie asked as she shut the door to his room.

"Nothing."

"Are you going to be super weird now?"

Remi shrugged with a grin. "Probably just the usual amount."

"I figured." And then— "That's acceptable."

Neef opened his bedroom door. "What's up?"

Remi's cheeks warmed as he hesitated for the words to say. *He knows we hooked up. It's obvious. How can I look like I didn't just have sex? Why doesn't that look just come natural like my whole life hadn't prepared me for it? What do I say? What do I do? He knows. He knows!!!!*

"Heading to breakfast. You coming?" Brie asked Neef casually.

"You know it." Neef patted Remi on the shoulder. "Let's go, Rem."

In the dining room, Neef turned on some music while Brie and Remi picked up preparing breakfast where Pero left off. Once, as Remi started toward the pantry for flour, Brie stopped him. "I wouldn't go in there," she said, raising her eyebrows. "Trust me." Remi paused. Hushed murmurs of passion bled through the pantry door. *Good for them*, Remi thought as he decided that they didn't really need pancakes after all.

As Remi, Neef, and Brie swirled about the dining room laying out silverware, they talked of their favorite moments at the school and the previous months of touring. "Do you remember when we stayed at that one crusty-ass punk house?" Neef asked.

Remi's eyes lit up. "The one where that dude was so stoned he kept—"

"Trying to make a frozen pizza, but then he would fall asleep after he put it in the oven—" Brie continued.

"So every forty-five minutes the smoke alarm would go off, waking us up," Neef added.

"And then after, like, the third one burned to a crisp, Davy went and nailed it to that dude's bedroom door—" Remi said.

"So the next morning the guy woke up and saw the burnt pizza on his bedroom door and he just shrugged, saying—" Brie said, barely able to contain her laughter.

"That's a sick tombstone!" The three exclaimed together, cracking up. *Whoa*, Remi thought. *Do I actually miss being on tour?*

When they finished getting breakfast ready, Davy entered the dining room right on cue. "Where's Nas?" He asked. Beneath his eyes it seemed he'd already packed enough bags for the rest of them. "Is she coming?"

"I'm sure she is," Brie said, nudging Remi's foot underneath the table.

Remi found himself smiling. Thankful that, although he didn't know what he and Brie were yet, at least the night before wasn't some wonderful dream that they were never going to discuss again. However, his smile faded as his eyes returned to Davy. "You alright?" Remi asked as Davy sat down next to Neef.

Davy nodded while staring at the table. His hands kept in his hoodie pockets. Neef, Brie, and Remi exchanged a look. Remi understood not wanting to leave. Hell, he almost ran away last night. But whatever Davy was on was something else. They couldn't set out into enemy territory with him looking like this. *Though, on second thought, he does kind of have the dead-eyed Young Apostle thing down. Maybe he's just been a method actor trapped in a punk rocker's body all along.*

"Thanks for waiting, folks," Nas said with a grin as she and Pero emerged from the pantry. Hair stuck up from the back of her head with indifference. Her cheeks glowed like a tube amplifier. "So, did everyone sleep well?" She asked, taking her seat.

"Brie and Remi hooked up," Neef said as he reached for the eggless omelets.

Remi's whole body tightened. The Futile was a living, breathing organism and as such, Remi worried what the introduction of an unknown element could do to their band's biology. There wasn't a band rule prohibiting two band members from consensually hooking up.[50] But it was kind of an unspoken rule. Like the one about waiting to eat until the whole band could. Remi planned to discuss his and Brie's relationship with them at some indeterminate point in the future. Like after he and Brie eventually decided if they did in fact have a relationship. When they weren't embarking on a life-endangering mission. When they were all safe and secure. Some point that definitely wasn't that day.

Nas let out an overdramatic sigh. "Finally."

Remi's posture immediately relaxed. Brie turned to Neef, slugging

---

[50] In *The Rhythm of Our Road*, Neef wrote: "Our only rules were unspoken. Be on time, be mindful of one another, respect each other's boundaries, make an effort. You know, just basic acts of consideration. That's all that was asked and all that was expected of each other."

him in the shoulder. "What the hell, man?"

"What? Blame him." Neef gestured to Remi. "It was all over his face this morning."

"What about you, Davy?" Nas beamed as she tore off a small bite of toast.

Davy just shook his head while stirring his food around on his plate.

"That's okay," Nas said, before turning to the rest of them. "I think everything's still good for us to leave in two hours. The van's all packed. Pero is gonna check in with the Dissent and make sure they haven't picked up anything on the back channels."

"I already got my stuff together so that should give me some more time to look for that secret passageway." Neef rubbed his hands together.

"I don't know what's taken you so long." Pero took a sip of coffee. "Nas found it pretty easily."

Nas' cheeks flushed pink.

Neef threw his hands up in the air. "Oh, come on!"

Pero gave a wink. "Lucky for you there's more than one."

"Is it weird I'm actually looking forward to the big reveal?" Remi asked, finding a renewed commitment to the cause on the other side of his virginity.

"I'm happy to hear that, Rem." The warmth in Nas' cheeks transferred to her smile. "All our hard work is finally going to pay off. It's going to be dangerous, but even with the vague warning, I don't think they'll see exactly what's coming and with Woody…gone, they shouldn't be able to follow us anym—"

"I think they still know where we are," Davy interrupted.

Nas started to laugh but then caught herself. "Davy, what are you saying?"

"They've been calling me," Davy said. "They know where we are."

Remi started choking.

Chapter Thirty-Six: Not Waving, Drowning

The room came back into focus from the center outward. First, he saw the concerned faces of his bandmates, Brie, Nas…Davy. Pero with her hands on top of her head. Next, the tables, the flat screen with red faces yelling on mute, the windows giving way to the rolling fields of snow. The cold tile floor reminded him he was alive. Neef's arms were still around Remi's stomach. The letter on the windowsill…if he would've died…

Reaching out with thumb and forefinger, Neef plucked the culprit off the floor, a rather-chewy, quarter-sized piece of Macon.[51] "Almost killed you." He slumped back. "That's why I don't mess with that chemically engineered stuff."

"No, wait." Remi coughed. "Back up…" He searched Davy's face. "You sold us out?"

Davy walked to the window. "I couldn't get rid of my phone."

"Why the hell not?" Pero challenged.

"Yeah, what the hell, Davy?" Brie turned on him. "We burned Woody, scorched him to a crisp, and you just stood by with your actual phone on you the whole time?"

"Let him talk." Nas stood up from her crouched position, ushering him along. "Talk," she said to Davy.

"They—They have Vin." Davy turned from the window to face them. "They're holding him in one of their camps. It could be the DITCH even. I don't know. His whole band is there. They were told that if they gave us up then they would be let go, but that…didn't happen."

---

[51] Macon = artificial bacon. Known then as a tasty bacon substitute, not known for its digestibility.

"Unbelievable." Brie slapped her hands down on the table before running them over her face. "So your brother sold us out and then you did it the rest of the way?"

"No, he didn't put them onto us. His band did. They were just trying to save themselves." Tears swelled in Davy's eyes. "They said they were going to kill him. He's the only family I have left."

"What about us?" Remi asked.

"What do they know?" Nas asked over Remi, her mouth a straight line.

"I don't know. Possibly everything." Davy sat in a chair and dropped his head into his hands with the weight of the words.

Pero had to turn and walk away. "You got to be kidding."

"How long?" Nas asked.

"For a while," Davy said to the floor. "I'm not sure they were using it to track us at first though, because I didn't stay on long enough. Until..."

Remi looked at his friend as though he was seeing him for the first time. They had been through so much. The never-ending van rides on the way to pointless shows. The practices in the basement of his old church where he once felt trapped but later found his salvation with the band. All the sleepless night drives, talking about life, death, and everything in between. The moments of pure joy they shared on stage. Didn't those moments amount to something more than, or at least similar to, loyalty?

"What changed?" Nas pushed. "And when did the calls start? Be specific about timeframes. Was it before the first video went viral or after?"

"I started getting the calls before, but no one would ever say anything. I hadn't heard from Vin so I—I couldn't get rid of my phone."

Davy shook his head as a tear ran down his cheek. "Then after the videos, the calls started coming more often, more deliberate, sometimes it would be Vin urging me to tell them our plans. When I heard his voice…I couldn't hang up."

Nas clicked her tongue. "We need to go."

"Go? Go where? We can't possibly be thinking of following through with the plan still. What—what if they've been listening through his phone or something?" Remi asked from the floor, looking first to Nas. When her eyes didn't hold the answers, he looked to Brie and Neef.

Neef set his jaw. "We have to go still."

"I'm sorry." Brie's hand shot up in the air. "Should we really be having this discussion in front of him?" She flicked her hand in Davy's direction. "For all we know he's wearing a wire."

Davy hung his head.

Remi wanted him to argue, to say something, to say anything. This couldn't be as simple as Davy sold them out. There had to be more to it. *Say something!*

An old Gillian Welch song rang out through the dining hall. "My phone." Pero's face went as pale as a ghost. "They only call if it's something serious."

"Or maybe they've been the ones selling us out all along," Brie scoffed as Pero jogged into the pantry.

Remi looked past all of them to the hills beyond the windows. The snow merged into the trees, mud, and brush, a grayish sludge everywhere the eye could see. What once was beautiful now looked like crap. Then like flies swarming, the first speck appeared in the distance, followed by another and another. Remi sat up, squinting to focus. Around him, his bandmates continued their debate. Black dots descended into the trees, blending in, stopping just long enough for Remi to chalk it up to his eyes playing tricks. Then they moved again. The closer they got to the school, the bigger they appeared. One crouched behind a tree, barely a hundred yards away. OCT agents, guns held to their chest. A yell started in the soles of his shoes, working its way up through his legs, to his gut then proceeded up to his throat where it got caught like a kinked water hose. It felt a little bit like drowning and a lot like choking all over again. "Guys," Remi managed to cough out. His bandmates abruptly stopped and followed his point.

"Oh, shit," Brie said.

Chapter Thirty-Seven: Oh, Shit Indeed

Her whole life, Brie knew the danger harbored within the bodies of malicious men. As the flipside of that truth, she too knew the vulnerabilities of her own body. The many ways it could be hurt. The many ways it could be susceptible to a pain that couldn't be fixed. These were facts as simple and pointed as keys clutched in her fists. As such, she never felt unprepared against them. But as the bodies encased in their hard-shell armor surrounded the school, for the first time in her life, Brie felt truly defenseless.

"Okay," Nas said as more soldiers filled the hillside. "Okay, okay, okay," she said again as though the word was an incantation to whisk them away. Brie thought of Woody's engine trying but failing to turnover.

"Where can we go?" Remi asked from the ground.

Brie pulled him to his feet. "Nas, where's the van?"

"Pero?!" Nas yelled. "Van. We need to get to the van. Now."

Pero rushed back into the room, clutching her phone to her chest. She looked from the band members to the windows then back again. "The van is hidden on the back way out, but that's on the far side of the school grounds. We'll never make it. We have to get to the Safe Room. Follow me and try to keep up."

The band sprinted to the dining hall exit as the soldiers quickly descended onto the school. *Can they see us?* Brie wondered, hoping somehow they couldn't, but being too practical to believe the lie. Their feet pounded the hardwood floor. "I hope you're happy," Brie breathlessly snapped at Davy. "Why don't you go greet your Apostle buddies outside? I'm sure they'll welcome you with open arms."

It's hard to know when you're misplacing your own guilt.

Davy stuttered in his tracks. "I—I…I didn't mean for this to happen."

"Then what did you expect to happen?!" Brie pivoted on him. "There are soldiers outside with guns, Davy." Brie pointed in his face. "You did this."

"Just everyone, come on. We'll sort it out later." Nas hesitated a few steps ahead in the hallway. "We don't have time for this."

Behind them, it sounded as though a large sheet of ice was beginning to crack. "Go!" Neef shouted, hurrying the others along.

An explosion of glass. Smoke avalanched into the dining hall, spilled into the hallway, and rolled after them. Even in the face of it, Pero slowed down for Nas and the others to catch up. Neef was on Brie's shoulder. Remnants of teargas scorched her throat, set her lungs ablaze. As they ran, Brie did a quick headcount. *Where's Davy? Wait…Where's Remi?* Brie slammed to a stop and turned around. Smoke filled the hallway, wrapped around her like a hellish cloud. Shouts and inaudible voices echoed from deep within. Remi was somewhere in there. Brie didn't want to know what kind of monsters he could be facing.

"Remi!" Brie called.

A chorus of fire alarms answered back as the school's sprinkler system kicked on.

"Remi!" Brie screamed with all she had. The water raining down from the ceiling eased the pain of eyesight.

"Remi! Davy!" Nas and Neef ran back.

"We can't wait," Pero called from further down the hallway. "We still have a way to go."

Red lines shot from the smoke. "STOP. Get down on the ground now!" Came the command. Brie's heart lodged in her throat. "Remi!" She choked out.

Remi burst into view, pulling Davy along. "Go!" Remi yelled. His eyes bulged in desperation. "Go!" Brie ducked under Davy's other arm.

"This way." Pero dashed around a corner.

Canisters of teargas rolled past their feet. Brie kicked one back in the direction of the soldiers. "Stop!" came the warning. "You must stop now!"

When the shot came it didn't sound with a bang or crack, it was a soft whistle like the birdcalls Brie's father used to make in their backyard. The first shot was soon followed by another and another. Whistles cut through the air all around them, signaled more by their collision with the wall than anything else.

"Almost there," Brie said, straining under Davy's weight. His shoulders heaved with labored breaths. She grabbed Remi's hand on Davy's back and Remi squeezed back. They made it to the corner where Neef waited for them. A shot whizzed by Brie's ear as more whistles filled the air. "Now!" Neef yelled, wedging a large bookcase in the doorway in tandem with Nas and Pero.

With the entry properly blocked. Brie collapsed against the wall, trying to catch a breath that kept slipping away.

"Are you all okay?" Nas asked.

"I think so," Brie panted.

"I'm okay. Just…my asthma…doesn't agree with the teargas," Davy said between choking breaths. He shook his inhaler and took a pull.

Remi nodded. His eyes closed as sweat poured down his forehead.

"That won't buy us much time." Pero's mascara ran down her cheeks like camouflage makeup. "Come on. Come on." She pulled Brie to her feet. Davy followed. Remi tried, but fell again.

"Rem's hurt," Neef said.

Remi grimaced, his upper thigh a sopping maroon. "I wondered about that." He clutched his leg.

"I got him." Neef picked Remi up and slung one of Remi's arms over his shoulder. "Let's go."

Brie stooped underneath Remi's other arm. "Don't worry," Brie told Remi. "I'm used to carrying you."

"At least we're usually on stage when that happens," Remi managed.

Books flew off the shelf behind them as a blunt force pummeled from the other side. "Follow me." Pero dashed into the girl's locker room. Once inside, Pero led them to a row of lockers near the back. "Okay, which one is it?" She asked herself. In the hallway came the sound of tree limbs in a storm preparing to break. Pero opened one locker, ran a hand along the back of it. "No. Not this one. Hold on." She tried another. Then another. "Damn it."

Thunder crashed behind them. The soldiers were through. Brie hugged Remi closer. Her eyes scanned the locker room for anything she could use as protection. The back of a toilet tank, a metal trash can, nope, the benches were bolted to the ground. If she was going to go down, she was going to take some of those fuckers with her. Pero tried another standup locker. She pushed her hand on the back wall in three separate spots and it gave way to an opening. "Okay, it's this one, single file, go, go, go!"

Chapter Thirty-Eight: Bad Things to Such Good People

There are certain words that when repeated incessantly only serve to make you feel the opposite of their intended meaning. *We're safe. We're safe. We're safe,* Nas told herself again and again. But no matter how many times she said it, she only felt less so. Nas had never been good at lying. The skill was beyond her, much like dunking a basketball or figure skating. No amount of practice could ever change that.

Because, yes, at the moment they were together and alive in the Safe Room with its fully stocked shelves of (just recently) outdated canned goods, its handy, portable urine-to-water sterilization kit, its fifteen sleeping bundles and accompanying fifteen pillows and although there was even an exercise bike and elliptical should they start to go stir-crazy, plus a closed circuit video screen with which they could monitor each of the school's sixty-three hidden cameras to keep track on the actions of the OCT, and all indications were so far that the soldiers had no clue as to where they disappeared to…despite all of those things, Nas still didn't feel comforted or safe.

For starters, though they were alive, they could hardly be described as "whole." Remi's situation was worrisome to say the least. Pero and Neef had been able to clean the wound, but they had also said, rather ominously, that only time would tell if he got an infection. Per usual, Nas felt in the moment the need to restore the morale of everyone else rather than dwell on her own personal doubts. "You should drink some water, Rem." Nas knelt down with an opened bottle.

Remi managed a few swallows as Nas brought the bottle to his lips. Sweat beaded his forehead. Brie swept it away, her palms stained red, reminding Nas of the time they dyed their hair with Tropical Punch Kool-

Aid. That wasn't Kool-Aid on Brie's hands though. It wasn't something they could just wash out later when Nas' mom got angry, shaking her head in the kitchen with grocery bags in her hands.

"How're you holding up?" Nas asked her.

"The bleeding's stopped. Neef said the bullet went through. Thank god for his Young Apostle training for once." Brie wrung out a washcloth over the small sink before placing it back on Remi's forehead.

Pero hopped to her feet like a parent who couldn't sit still during a family's influenza bout. "I'll check the medicine cabinet for any antibiotics."

"Thank you." Nas watched Pero leave the area.

"No, but how are you?" Nas turned back to Brie. "I know that…that all that…the guns again…it was traumatic."

"I'm—" Brie cleared her throat. "I'm just worried about him."

"You can change if you need to," Nas said. "I'll stay with him. I'm sure there are more stylish school sweatsuits in here."

"No, I'm fine," Brie said without looking at her. "Thank you."

"Okay." Nas stood like a person three times her age. On the furthest wall of the Safe Room, Davy sat in self-determined exile. "You good?" She called. He nodded without meeting her eyes.

Nas then went to Neef, who was sorting through the Safe Room's sparse DVD selection. She knew it was a coping mechanism, a distraction. "How's it going, Neef?"

Neef wiped his cheek with his wrist before looking up at her. "It's not bad. They have some real A-Mart bargain bin classics in here. There's *Runaways, Lady Bird, The Departed…Get Out*, which seems to be mocking us a bit now…surprisingly, they don't have Jodie Foster's classic *Panic Room.*"

Neef sniffed. "Still…yeah, we should be okay."

"Good." Nas nodded, watching him. She patted him on the shoulder before going to the monitor screens. The OCT had thankfully moved on from the locker room and had begun searching elsewhere in the school.

"There was some Amoxicillin in the Medication Refrigerator, but it's gone bad. Like, a really-long-time-ago bad." Pero swirled the bottle, scrunching her nose at its foggy contents.

Nas didn't reply. Instead, she continued studying the many screens. Little differentiated one OCT soldier from the next, but she tried. If there was a way to tell them apart then she could count them. And if there was a way to count them then she could know what they were up against. And if she could know what they were up against then she could begin formulating a plan. But they all looked the same and there was at least one soldier in two-thirds of the screen's sixty-three blocks. Some had two. Several had four or more. Every plan Nas started didn't make it beyond the first step.

"Do you have your phone still? Maybe you could call the Dissent so they could do like an extraction?" Nas asked.

"My phone." Pero's face dropped. "I must've left it back in the dining hall."

"Are you sure?"

Pero patted her front and back jean pockets and then checked her hoodie. "It's not on me. It could've easily fallen out when we pushed that big bookshelf. There's no telling really. It was just all so—"

"Is there another way in or out of here?" Nas interrupted with another question.

"Not that I know of," Pero answered, looking to the screen rather than Nas.

"What if they find the door?"

"It's electronically locked from the inside."

"Great." Nas shifted her weight. "And if they cut power?"

"The Safe Room runs off its own generator so, unless they find that, we should be warm and comfortable for about two to three weeks or until it runs out of fuel."

"I don't think that's as comforting as you think it is," Nas said to Pero's profile before turning back to the screen. "Is there a Safe Room in the other locker room too?" Nas cocked her head at the screen as the soldiers made their way through banging open each hallway door.

"Yep." Pero tapped the screen. "We better hope they don't find that either, because then they may put two and two together…"

"We better hope for a lot of things." Nas sighed. "I guess for the moment, I should just find consolation that we're safe and that Aria and my mother are safe somewhere too." Nas pinched the bridge of her nose as if warding off a headache. "That's a comforting thought, right?"

Pero placed her hand on Nas' hand. For the first time since they made it to the Safe Room, Pero really looked her in the eyes. There was something there, a fleck of truth or sorrow that Nas couldn't place. "What is it?"

Pero's eyes took on water like an over-capacity lifeboat. She shook her head and looked away.

"What?" Nas pulled her back by the wrist. "What do you know?" There was only one thing left that could hurt her. The band, her home, everything else had already been taken away. *Aria.* The room tilted on its axis, throwing off her center of balance, distorting her vision, the edges blurry and out of focus. "Tell me."

"I got the call earlier…" Pero's bottom lip quivered.

"Tell me."

"I didn't have time to say anything."

"Tell me."

"They think Aria has been captured by them."

"Who? Who's them?" Nas asked like she didn't already know.

"Them. The BP." A tear ran down Pero's cheek. "When they went to extract your mom and Aria. Only your mother was there. She didn't want to leave without Aria, so they had to lie to her."

Nas pulled her hand from Pero's grasp. "And what are they doing to find her? To find Aria?"

"I—I don't know. I didn't have time to ask."

Nas nodded. Deep in her chest, it felt like her sternum was being torn open, like the thing that was holding it all together was ripped in two, like her heart was going to fall on the ground in front of them and there would be no way to put it back in again. "Okay," Nas managed to choke out.

"Nasim, I—I'm sorry. I should've told them to get your family sooner." Pero reached out but Nas brushed her hand away.

"It's fine." Nas turned back to the monitors. In her peripheral, she saw Pero watching her for several seconds before finally leaving. Once she was gone, a sob started to surface from her broken chest like an air bubble from a sinking object. Nas pushed it further down.

Again, Nas returned to the well of optimism that usually dwelled inside of her. And again, she found that it had been swallowed up too.

Thirty Years Later, Neef Appears on Public Radio

A hush fell over the intern pool as he entered the Philadelphia studio. For weeks, they had anticipated his arrival, taking care to stock his favorite pods of coffee (Brazilian Mint) in the green room, playing that obscure experimental jazz combo group that was his sole Treble-Cleft on Globosity, not the most popular songs by the obscure experimental jazz combo either, no, deeper cuts only, on the studio station's PA. If he even noticed, there was no indication, though one of the younger interns would later say that he gave them a slight nod as he passed through.

The interns rushed to their seats after he went into the sound booth with the exceptionally cheerful—especially that morning—host, Samira Loss. Most days, the interns were expected to get coffee orders, run errands, deliver office mail, or file memos during the morning interviews. However, that morning as the station played the seventh deep cut by that oh-so-obscure jazz combo trio on the PA for the interview intro, all of them crowded together in their tiny square of space to listen in.

Sam: Good morning, this is *Clear View*. I'm Samira Loss, your host and executive producer, as well as culture editor for the music website, *All Sounds!* Today's guest is activist and musician, Hanif "Neef" Hardaway, better known as the former bassist for the legendary punk band, The Futile. In his new memoir, entitled *The Rhythm of Our Road*, Hardaway shares the experiences of his youth travelling the country in a rickety old van named 'Woody,' during an obviously tumultuous time for our country. The efforts of Hardaway and that of his bandmates, Nasim Bashir, Brietta Jennings, Remington Clark, and Davis Lucero encouraged a true youth movement that took hold of our nation and helped to right our path. *The Rhythm of Our Road* finds Hardaway revisiting those early days of the band when they were struggling young musicians, desperate to have their music, and their message, heard. Hanif, what was it like to reevaluate those days?

Neef: It was…

Sam: Hard I imagine.

Neef: Yeah. Listen (clears throat) I—I'm sorry. I thought I was ready. It's still hard to hear their full names like that. Sometimes, I still…just…I'm sorry. (Sniffs) Sorry.

Sam: Take your time. Let's hear a sample of The Futile's song, "When the Loyal Defender Talks to God." This is *Clear View*. We'll be right back.

Chapter Thirty-Nine: The Ocean Breathes Salty

They drove for three days in all the wrong directions. Only stopping (albeit begrudgingly) because they reached the east coast and Aria had never seen the ocean before. Though it was freezing, Aria rushed across the sand, clutching Duckworth to her chest with one hand, while hopping to remove her socks and shoes with the other. Aria gasped when the frigid waves lapped over her bare feet, but she didn't retreat. She gazed over the endless expanse. There were still times back then when Aria's hopes seemed to stretch all the way to the horizon too. This was one of them.

While Greg paced by his car on another phone call, Aria breathed it all in, thinking of her mother and father, wondering again if they were safe wherever they were, hoping that they felt as free as she did in that moment. She thought again of Nas and hoped that they would be reunited soon. After all, when he actually talked, Greg had said that they were close. Though the feeling had started to creep in that Aria shouldn't believe much of what little Greg said, but, for whatever reason, she still believed him on that, despite the fact that he didn't seem to know what he was doing. Nor could she place where exactly she recognized him from. Those were thoughts for another time.

Aria held Duckworth close to her chest as the wind roared in her ears. At least for this brief flicker of time, where Aria stood, everything was beautiful, and nothing hurt.

The sun had just started to rise in the east. Fabulous oranges and pinks rippled across the dark water. Aria closed her eyes and inhaled the murky, salty air.

It was all so heartbreakingly wonderful, until...

"Gross!"

Something slimy slid over the top of her foot.

Aria jumped back on the cold sand and covered her mouth. Sickness washed over her like a rising tide. The hint of earthiness that frolicked on the ocean air was far more than just seaweed and driftwood. A multitude of dead sea creatures rolled in with the waves, big and small, smooth and spiny, seemingly alien yet all-too-real, so many it could make you cry.

"Hey! Come on!" Greg yelled from further up. "I have a lead on where to find them!"

Aria walked back to the car without daring a parting look to the ocean she had waited a lifetime to see.

A day back in the right direction and Aria's doubts really started to take shape. It was there in Greg's little hesitations. The way he put every sentence on pause before he let it out of his mouth, staring off into the distance like an actor reading cue cards off-screen. Sure, he had finally started talking for real, even taking on an air of giddy excitement with each mile that brought them closer to the Futile, but too with each mile marker that passed, Aria realized more and more that her driving companion was really her captor.

By the time they crossed the next state-line, Aria knew without a doubt that he wasn't actually affiliated with the Dissent. Still, she continued to call him the name he had given (Greg) as often as possible to subtly needle him. She asked questions about the Futile's music scene, nodding along like she bought his bullcrap. All the while she began plotting her exit, which proved more difficult than she hoped. *It's too dangerous to barrel roll out the door with Duckworth in my arms. Next bathroom stop, I'm going for it.* Then when the next bathroom stop came, Not-Greg was there waiting outside the door. "Beef jerky?" He offered with the least amount of goodwill in history when it came to one human offering another human a snack. "No thanks," Aria said, without adding that she had practically been vegetarian since birth. Shouldn't he have been too?

Then the final clue came when Duckworth accidentally puked in the floorboard upon eating the aforementioned beef jerky.[52] "You're going to clean that up," UnGreg sneered out of the side of his mouth. The final frame clicked into place then. That look. It was one of anger, fear, and pain. The image of Definitely-Not-Greg recoiling from being punched in the face was buried deep in Aria's memory. She had seen that look possibly a hundred times. She had seen it remixed to everything from semi-obscure German metal bands to weird-dance-beat-country songs. She had laughed at that look, taken an immense amount of joy from that look. How could she ever forget it?

At that point, Aria knew she was going to have to call him out. He isn't that intimidating at all actually. Few people are threatening when you've seen them struggle to find the straw in their sixth Big Swig.

Still, Aria was careful to remember what Nas once said: "I label people so that I no longer have to think about them, so I can write them off. Don't do that. Be better than that. When you resist diminishing people to their very worst, you become more powerful by keeping alive the ability for transformation." Keeping that lesson in mind, Aria noted Faux-Greg's five defining characteristics.

---

[52] Though she was vegetarian, Aria would never dream of imposing her life choices on her beloved Duckworth. She often encouraged him to eat vegetarian dog food, but he wouldn't go for it, and, as such, he was an omnivore.

1.) He liked to hum along to pop hits on the radio. Even the high-voiced falsetto songs, though he often stopped whenever he saw Aria grinning at him, which she only did when she still believed he was a friend of Nas' band.

2.) His snacks of choice were Oatmeal Cream Pies, Mellow Mist Soda, and the aforementioned (and gross) beef jerky.

3.) He took his appearance seriously. Evident by the way he constantly checked out his coif of hair in the rearview mirror. See also: the way he brushed dirt off his boots when stepping from a curb and the way he adjusted his jacket when they stood in front of the gas station windows.

4.) The only thing he perhaps took more seriously than his personal appearance was his car. There were (well, before Duckworth chewed them up) white paper mats down where her feet went. A small pine-tree shaped piece of cardboard hung from the rear-view mirror. A feeble attempt perhaps to combat the lingering smell of stale cigarette smoke. Speaking of which—

5.) He was either attempting to quit smoking for his own personal growth OR refraining from smoking for Aria's benefit. As evidenced by the little white square pieces of Nicorette gum that he repeatedly popped free of their tinfoil container and then into his mouth. Before Aria realized that "Greg" was an Acolyte, she liked to believe that he was doing this out of consideration for her fourteen-year-old lungs. However, after her revelation, she found it near impossible to see any good in him. After all, she remembered the content that Ole Store Brand Greg was responsible for injecting into their culture via his popular blog.[53] There weren't enough

---

[53] A few headlines from Luca's blog forever archived in the History of Failures today: "The System Can't Be Racist, Capitalism is Color-Blind," "Bigfoot, Moth Man, the Good Immigrant, and Other Myths," and "1488 Reasons Why Women Are Too Irrational to Lead."

quirky attributes or charming characteristics that could ever change the fact that he was a gosh-damned Nazi by another name. He was just a scared little boy, which wasn't all that intimidating when it came down to it. Aria had plenty of experience with those.

If you're not scared, then why don't you call him out? Aria asked herself as Duckworth snuggled warmly in her lap. *I will, chill. It's been a long trip. I just need a minute.*

Aria jolted awake, stunned equally by the stillness of the car and the soul-consuming night beyond its windows. "Must have been asleep for a little while, D." Aria ruffled the dog's fur more for herself than for him. "I think it's time to go." Duckworth nuzzled into Aria's chest. "I know, I know, but I doubt this guy is going to take us to Nas, or at least if he does, it won't be good for anyone."

Aria squinted out her window. Dark columns of trees towered together in a dense pack. "Maybe he's using the bathroom." The ignition sat vacant. There was no better time. She pushed the door open, bracing herself against the bitter cold. Fake-Ass-Greg was nowhere in sight. City lights reflected off the machine-metal night sky to the north. That seemed like the way to go. Perhaps Aria could find a computer and then...she didn't know. Wrapping Duckworth tighter in her coat, Aria started in the direction of promise.

"What's up? Where're you going?" Gregory-the-Forgery materialized from the treeline with a cigarette gripped between his lips.

With an estimated hundred feet between them, Aria knew she was safe. She was All-City 1600 meters four years in a row. There was no way he could catch her on foot and if he went for the car, she could tear off through the woods. "I'm leaving," Aria said simply. Despite everything, there was still a small part of her that hoped he was honorable enough to just let her leave if she wanted to, honorable enough to treat her as an individual rather than a prisoner.

"Why?" He asked in a choked voice of nonchalance. The end of his cigarette glowed fluorescent orange as he inhaled.

Why? Aria thought, that one-syllable-word summed up the smugness of Acolyte-Greg's character better than the previous sixteen paragraphs. *Why?* Spoken like she owed him something. Aria shook her head and started walking towards the city lights. She listened carefully for his approach in the gravel, ready to sprint in any number of directions in a split-second's notice.

"Seriously, come on," he called after her. "Get in the car."

Aria kept walking.

"Just…" He sighed and jogged a couple steps. "Come on, don't make me."

Aria rolled her eyes and continued on.

"You're…just—" He drew a sharp breath. "You will listen to me."

Nope. No, she wouldn't, asshat. Aria put one foot in front of the other. The tension released from her shoulders with each step further away from Little-Wannabe-Fascist-Greg and his lame ass car. Until a clicking sound she had previously only heard in movies sounded behind her. It was unmistakable. Aria stopped in her tracks.

"I didn't want to have to do it like this," he said as his boots chomped through the gravel towards her. The hair raised on the back of her neck with each step he took closer. Duckworth growled beneath her coat.

"But you made me," he said so close behind her now. "Hope you're happy."

Aria winced.

"Come on, just get back in the car," he said in a softer tone as though he didn't have a gun pointed at her back. "Just come on. Don't be such a dumb baby. Let's go find your sister."

Aria slowly turned to face him. He did indeed have a gun pointed at her. Aria swallowed. His right arm was bent at a ninety-degree angle, the black barrel steadied on her body, ready to just wipe her from existence with the smallest pressure from his index finger. *Steady. Steady your breathing. Don't show your fear.* "I know who you are," Aria said. "I remember you from the videos."

He smirked with the gun still on her. "Psh. I know. Of course, you do. You and everyone else. Big deal. C'mon, don't be dumb. Get in the car."

"I've read what you've written," Aria said through her teeth as she took one step backward then another. "I've seen what you believe."

He faked a single hollow laugh. "You're smarter than you look then so just get in the car like a smart person would do."

Aria stared past him, retreated another step.

"Seriously, just—just get in the *goddamn* car." He chuckled at the slip in composure. A single strand of hair came loose from his otherwise perfect coif, but he didn't put it back in place. He made up the difference between them.

Aria looked to the safety of the oblivion-black treeline, didn't move.

He ducked low to meet her eyeline. "By the way, if you'd actually read what I've written then you would know I don't really believe anything. And isn't that just..." He feigned a shiver with a shark smile. "Terrifying?"

He straightened up, smoothed his hair back into place. His ghoulish stretched-out shadow devoured hers in the street. "So, don't...don't fucking test me. Get in the car."

Aria tightened her jaw and hugged Duckworth as close to her body as possible. Would he really shoot her? She pivoted her heel ever so slightly, preparing to launch into a run. Loose rocks grinded beneath her shoe.

"Aria, come on." He grinned and shook his head. "You don't want to do that."

Now. Aria pushed hard off the ground as though she may take flight.

He grabbed her hard by the arm. His grip tightened on her bicep, jerking her back into place. It felt like his fingerprints would be forever burned into her skin.

"Let—" Aria shoved away from him with both her hands. "Go!"

He stumbled backward as Duckworth leapt from her coat. "D, no—" Aria lunged after the small dog. Her captor flailed, hitting Aria hard in her left eye with his pistol. Pain splintered through her. She crumpled to the ground in time to see Duckworth biting his leg and refusing to let go. He shook like a man on fire before kicking Duckworth hard in the side. With a sharp yelp, Duckworth let go. From her one good eye, Aria saw the gun aimed at Duckworth. "NO—" She dove into her kidnaper, knocking him off his feet. Then the sound of the gunshot drowned out everything else.

Chapter Forty: Playing Would You Rather at the End of the World

When the Blessed Path first took over, a popular resistance joke[54] went: "Has anyone tried unplugging the country and plugging it back in?"

In a less trying time, Brie would've found the idea of being held captive in a space intended as a safe haven both cliché and ironic. As hours passed though, her humor and resolve slowly drained like the energy from the generator they relied upon. Bundled in the sweatshirts and blankets they could find, the six of them sat beneath the shaky fluorescent lights, witnessing the waning of their youth in each flicker. Their time spent travelling the country, the countless shows and sets, the dumb conversations and dumber arguments, the contempt they sometimes held for one another, the comfort they found in each other's presence, everything they had shared for better or worse hung there in the silence between them.

There were things that Brie once found infuriating about her bandmates: the sound of Remi smacking his lips when he chewed on his artificial beef jerky. The inane grindcore shit that Neef listened to during night drives when he knew everyone was trying to sleep. The way Nas acted like she just had everything figured out, including herself. The condescending tone Davy would put on whenever they played a game of Keanu. Pero... she didn't know Pero super well just yet, but Brie knew if she spent enough time with her she would eventually find something she didn't like.

Still as Brie lay awake beneath the dwindling light with her sleeping bandmates, she realized she would trade nearly anything to get back in the

---

[54] It's important to note that early on, not only was it legal to joke about the Blessed Path, but many people actually had a certain sense of humor about it. Of course, like most things, it wouldn't last.

van with them and leave this place forever in the rearview. That's all she wanted. To go back to the way things used to be when it was them vs. the Loyal Defender, them vs. the world, them vs. everyone.

Unfortunately, hindsight and regrets only work 20/20.

At first, Brie's intense remorse arrived as such a new feeling she prodded it with curiosity, hoping that with each turn she would discover it didn't actually exist. Instead, each poke only aided its growth. Until guilt became a monster that had taken up residence inside of her, a monster that ate and ate and never died.

The only way out was to tell her bandmates the truth.

They had already been through so much though. How much more could they take and still hold it together? *One thing at a time*, Brie told herself so naturally it felt like a heartbeat. She glanced at Remi, still unconscious beside her. *One thing at a time.*

It was a familiar sound, that of water flowing into a plastic bottle with all the subtlety and grace of a garden hose. In the van days, the sound made her stomach twist with revulsion, but now it wrung out a feeling more akin to joy. "You're awake." Brie propped herself up on her elbows, feeling very much awake herself.

"Oh." Remi startled. He turned further away from her as though he could hide what he was doing. "Sorry." Remi tightened the bottle's orange cap. "I know how gross this is. I just didn't think I could make it to the...um...do we even have a bathroom?"

"How're you feeling?" Brie asked.

"Grateful to be alive." Remi rubbed the knee of his uninjured leg.

"And a little better too. Has anyone talked about what we're going to do?"

Across the room, Nas sat crisscross applesauce in the glow of the video monitors with her back to them. It created the illusion that she couldn't hear them, even though the close proximity suggested otherwise.

"Not really." Brie intertwined her fingers with Remi's. She cleared her throat the best she could without calling any extra attention. "You know, at first I was upset at you...that you almost left us."

"You saw my letter..." Remi shifted onto his other side with a grimace.

"But now, I'm not so sure. At least if you would have left then this wouldn't have happened."

"Brie..."

"I've spent the last twelve hours hating myself and I think I'll spend the next twelve doing the same. If it wasn't for me, you would've left, you'd be safe, you'd be gone. If it wasn't for me..."

"I'm so sorry." He laid his foreheads against hers.

"No, I am. I wish I wouldn't have stopped you."

"I'm okay though."

"Are you?" She tilted back. "Are you okay?"

"You all took care of me. I'm here. I'm alive."

"Look around. We're practically trapped in a concrete coffin with an ever-dwindling food supply, smelly, pissed-off bandmates, one of which sold us out, and majorly outdated DVDs that Neef is surely going to make us watch before we die. You're not okay. None of us are."

"But I'm with you. I'm with all of you." He looked deep into her eyes. "I'd rather be here than anywhere else. Regardless of the outcome." He kissed her. His lips felt as dry as paper against her own. She placed her hand on his leg, leaning into him. Pain flashed across his face. He rolled partly away from her.

"I'm sorry," Brie started. "I didn't mean to…"

His thin, cracked lips gave way to a smile. "I'm pretty sure I just knocked over the pee bottle so you can add that to your list of bad stuff."

Despite herself, Brie returned his smile. "Oh, and there's a pee bottle rolling around in here now so that's great."

Remi laughed, but it sounded more like a cough.

Brie scooted closer, lowered her voice to a conspiratorial volume. "Listen, Rem, there's something I want—"

Remi shook it off. "So, would you rather…"

Brie nodded. One thing at a time. "Would you rather have to be in a small tiny room with everyone you know and love when you die or freeze to death in the beautiful forest of rural Missouri?"

"Easy. The first one."

"Would you rather have to walk with a limp for the rest of your life or never be able to play guitar on stage again?"

"Super easy. Walk with a limp."

"I figured. Okay, so would you rather…"

Neef climbed over from his sleeping bag. "Would you rather have to drink water made from your own pee or die of dehydration?"

Brie laughed and shifted over to make room for Neef on their blanket pallet.

Remi smiled. "Drink water made from my own pee. We have a start too, Neef." Remi held up the plastic bottle and swirled it around.

"Ugh, that's a little too orange." Neef wrinkled up his nose. "You need to drink more water."

"Which will then deplete our water resources that much quicker which will then lead to us drinking our own pee that much quicker which will then lead to us all having unhealthy pee," Brie said.

"Exactly." Neef nodded. "It's a real Climate Change v. Godzilla scenario. Well, no, never mind, in that situation we know which one came first."

"Okay, so I have one that I've been saving and it's a good one." Brie sat up straighter. "So, your lover's mind is in your…" Brie stopped herself, not sure if the situation called for a Would You Rather on a nuclear level. [55]

"What do you got?" Remi asked. Dark circles hung around his eyes. It reminded Brie of the make-up her dad put on her face when she was five and insisted on going as a zombie for Hell Day.

"Hold up." Brie turned towards Nas, who was curled up with her knees to her chest in front of the computer monitors. "Hey, Nas, you should come play Would You Rather with us."

Nas met Brie's question with a stare as cold as the concrete walls that surrounded them. "Nas?" Brie tried again. *Have they tried unplugging it and plugging it back in?*

"No," Nas finally replied.

"Oh, come on."

"No."

"Seriously, it'll help you feel better."

---

[55] "I don't know where Brie was going with that Would You Rather," Neef said in conversation with this author. "I'm sure it was a good one though. I wish I could ask her now."

"Are you all fucking serious right now?" Nas' words echoed louder than her voice. Brie recoiled as though she had been slapped. Nas had never talked to her like that in her life. All the anger, guilt, and fear that had been festering inside of Brie began to churn in her stomach.

Nas shook her head and turned back to the monitors. "If we don't die in here, then we're going to likely be captured to rot in the DITCH, and you all are playing Would You Rather—"

Brie sprang to her feet. "You think I don't know this? You think that fact is somehow lost on me? The difference is I'm trying to lighten the mood rather than wallowing in self-pity."

"Oh, yeah. I just love being the serious one." Nas shrugged off her blanket, getting to her feet. "To be the one to have to think of a plan all the time, to try and get the rest of you to stop making dick jokes long enough to avoid being caught and tortured for the rest of our miserable existence."

"And how much good has that done for us so far?" Brie pushed. It's impossible to know in the moment when you're misplacing your frustration.

"Yep, this is my fault." Nas tossed her hands up. "I'm the one who wanted to give our name to TBN so that we could break out. I'm the one that said we shouldn't tell the others. I didn't at all suggest it was a bad idea. Good point." Nas gave an exaggerated thumbs up. "Really great point, Brie. You totally busted me. This is entirely my fault. Forgive me, I don't know why I got so self-righteous and riled up when I'm the one to blame for being so misled by my quest for fame that I set this up to happen. I'm sure you can only imagine how embarrassed I am right now."

Nas' words stung like the tears in her eyes, but Brie didn't back down. She could feel Remi looking at her differently with this new possible revelation. "Oh, I was misguided? Weren't you the one who suggested we hook up with the Dissent in the first place? Was I the one saying that our music wasn't important unless it was making a difference? Didn't you demand we make the videos instead of just laying low? The only decisions you ever approve of are the ones you make. One of these days you'll learn that you're not the smartest person in every room you're in, you're just the most stubborn."

Nas closed the distance between her and Brie with one step. Shoulders straightened; Brie stood chest to chest with Nas. Their shadows flickered against the wall. In her peripheral vision, Brie could see the outlines of Remi and Neef, along with Pero and Davy waking up from their sleeping bags.

"Some of us don't have the luxury you do," Nas said. "It's hard to babysit you four all the time when your negligence may not only get the five of us killed, but my family too. You don't know what that's like. You have no one out there. No one."

"Fuck you, Nas," Brie said with tears filling her eyes.

Nas took a step back. "I'm sorry, I didn't mean that," Nas said softly.

The light in the room quivered like a drunk about to faint.

"Great timing. The simulation strikes again," Neef said.

"Don't worry the generator just kicks off sometimes," Pero said before a blanket of darkness fell over them.

Brie counted off ten seconds, then another ten.

"Does it normally take this long?" Remi asked.

"Nope," Pero answered.

Chapter Forty-One: Subterranean Safe Room Blues

Blinking in the pitch black, Nas attempted to find her bearings in the spinning room. Gravity sunk its hooks into her, pulling her to the ground. The sound of someone else in the room panting hard reminded Nas that she wasn't alone. Seconds passed before Nas realized it was her breathing like that. Her right hand found the computer monitors, their towers still warm, their insides clicking and popping like a fish dying on the shore. Nas leaned into them. The cooling towers hummed behind her. She tried to match their tone.

"Pero," Remi called. "What's this mean? Did the generator die? Did they cut power off to them?"

"I don't know. It's possible that the generator was already low," Pero said, the sound of her rummaging near the shelving unit momentarily ceased. "This was a popular hookup spot back in the day. If that isn't the case though…" A beam of light cut through the darkness. Pero shined the flashlight on her face. "We're fucked."

"That seems to be an ongoing theme," Brie monotoned.

The light danced over to the metal cabinet. Shards reflected back to Nas, illuminating the rest of the room in flashes. It reoriented Nas to reality. Like waking up from a nightmare only to realize you're still trapped in a fifteen passenger van teetering over a cliff.

Pero pushed canned food and jugs of water aside in the metal cabinet. "Well, at least, we're still hidden. They likely still don't know where we are, which is good. The downside is…" An electric lantern flashed to life in Pero's hands. Pero shook the lamp's contents, biting her lip as she set it down in the middle of the room. Shadows quivered around them.

"The downside is…?" Brie asked.

Pero sat in front of the lantern; her legs curled underneath her. "The downside is that we may freeze to death if they don't find us first."

Nas kicked the dead computer towers. "And we have no idea what they're doing out there now."

"That too." Pero nodded without looking at Nas.

Nas resisted the urge to go up and sit next to Pero. So badly she wanted to feel Pero's arms wrap around her, to feel the warmth of her skin, to feel comforted and safe. All the same, Nas stayed where she was—as though she didn't deserve to feel even slightly better when Aria was out there somewhere. *Pero's probably pissed at me anyways, like Brie, like everybody else.*

Brie was right about so much. If Nas was such a great leader then how did they end up here? Why didn't Davy feel comfortable enough to come to her when he first got the call? Why didn't she fight Brie harder when she suggested they report their name to TBN? Why had she secretly hoped that Brie would do it anyway? Why didn't she ever question her on it until now? And then, the most damning question—Where was she when Aria needed her the most? *You always want to act like you're an example that others should follow. If that's true, then where's the influence you speak of? I see no proof of it. All I see is the evidence of the mess you've made.*

Pero sighed. "Also, I was going back and forth on whether or not to say this since it seems like we've got all we can handle, but if they do happen to find the door, then they'll probably be able to break in without a ton of effort. The whole integrity of the Safe Room was really tied to our backup generator, so without it…"

"It's okay," Brie sat down next to Pero without looking in Nas' direction. Remi edged up to them. He didn't look at Nas either.

"I'm just bummed we can't watch *Annihilation* now," Neef said, sitting down with them too. He nodded at Nas, motioning for her to join them.

Nas just shook her head.

Pero pushed up from the ground. Nas avoided her eye contact as she walked over. "Just come sit with us. Everyone needs you." Pero ducked her head to Nas' eyeline. "I need you."

"I'm fine here," Nas said.

"You're not fine and you're barely here."

"Okay."

"Just come join us. No one cares that you and Brie got into it."

No one cares that Aria is caught either, apparently. Nas repositioned herself on the floor. Even thinking Aria's name felt like a fork being stabbed between her ribs.

Pero huffed. "Fine." She started to walk away before snapping back around. "Just who do you think you're helping right now?"

Nas hesitated.

"Aria?" Pero tried. The pain fork in Nas' side dug in deeper, twisting her nerves up like spaghetti. "Do you think your sulking is helping her?" Pero pushed. "You're not helping anyone sitting over here, feeling sorry for yourself." Pero then turned around and returned to the group. From across the room, Nas could feel Davy's eyes on her.

Why did she snap on them anyways? What did it matter if they were playing a dumb game? That's what they always did. A little gallows humor was a crutch they used to get on to the next step. Shit was bleak enough without having to dwell on it constantly. They made fun of stuff to reclaim the power from it. Nas knew that. Brie hadn't done anything wrong. In fact, Nas wasn't even positive that Brie had given their name to TBN.

The temperature in the room continued dropping. Neef located a small, battery-operated space heater and set it next to the lantern. The fans in the machine whirred to life. Waves of heat radiated forth from thin slivers of red. Whatever small radius of warmth it created didn't reach Nas. The dark side of the moon would've been more comfortable.

Chapter Forty-Two: Black Eyes & Empty Calories

As though she needed a reminder, the gun rested on the left thigh of his too-stylish, too-tight black jeans. Aria saw it for what it was—an extension of her captor's fragile ego, a warning that if she stepped out of line again it would likely be the last time.

She wrapped her arms tighter around Duckworth. She hadn't let go of him since they got back in the car. He had been asleep for hours and Aria feared the worst. *I almost lost you*, Aria thought again, ruffling his fur, wincing as she imagined the shot hitting its mark. A sob lodged in her throat, but she was too angry to let it through. Her right eye throbbed. Every beat of her heart pulsed with pain where he "accidently" hit her. She leaned her face against the window. The cold glass soothed her bruise while also amplifying its existence to the rest of her nervous system. In the driver's seat, he shifted. Like the bruise, the enhanced awareness of his presence made Aria cringe a little.

"How—how's your eye?" He asked the windshield.

Just great. I'm so blessed to have this souvenir from this wonderful road trip. "Fine," Aria said instead. Sarcasm was reserved for those who were worth it.

"You know...I'm..." He cleared his throat like the word would nearly choke him. "That—That's not who I am."

We don't get to decide who we aren't. Our actions show that for us, Aria wanted to say, but instead said nothing. Wisdom was reserved for those who could be improved. Aria leaned away from the window. Side-eying the gun, she speculated would he actually kill her if she tried to run? Would he kill her after they found the band anyway? Nothing would surprise her anymore.

Worst-case scenarios continued to flash through Aria's mind. "He doesn't normally sleep this long," Aria said to the dead tree scenery beyond her window. "I think you hurt him."

He coughed into the elbow of his denim jacket.

"We could at least take him to the vet." Aria tried to shake out the thought of coyotes or vultures picking at Duckworth's small body.

"Oh, believe me, there's nothing I'd love more than take Satan's little hairy butthole to an overpriced, out-of-the-way vet's office, but we don't have time for that." He sniffed hard. "We have to get to that school. The OCT have already beat us there by a couple of days."

His gross Adam's apple bobbed up then down. His knuckles tightened on the steering wheel again. The gun wobbled with another pothole. In her mind, Aria played out how it could go down, her left hand shooting across for the gun, him beating her to it, his fingers clasping onto her forearm, pressing down, threatening to collapse the small bones of her wrist, the sickening feeling of his calloused skin on hers, another place for his fingerprints to burn into her skin. Maybe then…she could…headbutt him unconscious? Steer the car safely into a snow embankment? Aria recoiled. *Look at the size of that melon. It could withstand a baseball bat.*

"What?" He asked without looking at her.

The idea came to her then like she was sitting in her sixth grade Social Ethics in Capitalism[56] class all over again. Aria rubbed her stomach. Would he be stupid enough to buy it? "I think I'm…getting my…"

"What?" He looked over at her then to his pristine upholstery. "What?" He asked more desperately.

---

[56] Or SEC class, or as Aria pronounced it "Sick" class as in the way the subject material caused stomach cramps five days a week rather than just once a month.

"I think it's...ugh...that time."

"Are you sure?"

Aria hunched over. "I think so."

"You think so? Isn't that something you would know already?"

Aria shook her head.

He clicked the monitor on the dash. A small road map appeared with its blue and red pathways intertwining like veins. "We're just twenty miles from the school. It can wait." He swallowed, looking to the white leather seat again.

"I don't think it can," Aria groaned

"Do you have any...you know...?"

Tampons? Feminine Napkins? Kotex? Maxi-Pads? How come he was man enough to assault an innocent dog and teenage girl, but not tough enough to say Tampon? Aria just shook her head. Though, yes, she had several in her backpack. Which he should've remembered from when he searched it back when she first got in the car with him. Unless, he just didn't know what one looked like. Which, considering what he looked like, seemed quite possible.

He sighed, tapped onto the computer monitor twice with frustration. "There's an A-Mart station a half mile away. We can stop there."

"I'll be waiting." He shifted the car in park. The woman's bathroom door was just feet away. Ugh, gas station bathrooms are bad enough, but for some reason they're so much worse when they're on the outside. Aria kept Duckworth in her arms as she stepped out. "What're you taking him for?" he asked.

"Um." Aria slid her backpack on. Shoot, she didn't have a good reason.

"He'll be fine here."

Aria carefully placed Duckworth in the passenger seat. He opened his eyes, giving her a pitiful look as she started to shut the door. *I'll figure this out. Don't worry, D.,* she told him in her mind. He slowly closed his eyes as if accepting her promise.

"Ten minutes," he said through the closed passenger door. Oh, Aria had words for him in her mind too.

Yellow tape wrapped around the station's two pumps. It rippled in the wind like the national soccer team cards she and Nas used to put in their bicycle spokes. Three cars were parked in various stages of decomposition in the lot. A man in a red and blue hat was slumped against the front of the A-Mart. A few lonely coins jingled his empty A-Mart Big Gulp cup. Aria couldn't see his eyes, but still dropped some change in all the same.

The door chimed as she stepped in. Dim lights hummed overhead as brightly colored advertisements attempted to make up for their drab surroundings. Junk food, alcohol, and tobacco advertisements beckoned to Aria from nearly every available surface. A woman missing her front teeth glared at Aria from behind the counter. Even inside the station, Aria could feel him watching her through the window. In the hygiene aisle, Aria looked to the cashier again. "Can I help you with something?"

"I'm okay," Aria said, turning back to the rack. A long fluorescent bulb flickered above her like it was fighting to stay alive. *How come inanimate objects are more relatable than people?* Aria thought. A car horn honked. He motioned at her to hurry up. The cashier loudly cleared her throat, tapping on the counter with her fingernail.

"Okay, okay, time to do something, Aria," Aria muttered to herself. She sucked in a breath and walked back towards the counter, grabbing a package of peanut butter cups on her way. Sliding them across the counter, Aria said, "Don't look but that man in the car out there's kidnapped me."

The woman's tongue darted from the hole where her two front teeth should be. She licked her lips instead of saying, *Oh, you poor dear, let me call someone for you or here, I have a shotgun underneath the counter. I'll cover while you run.* Or even, *what's your name so I can contact the authorities?*

"A—And he's going to take me out to the woods and have his way with me," Aria continued. "Probably kill me after that." Aria gestured to her eye. "You can see what he's already done to me."

The cashier's eyes were mucus-green like they had a sinus infection, the kind that bores deep into someone's immune system and carves out their soul. Holding eye contact, she scanned Aria's peanut butter cups. "Anything else?"

Aria swung her backpack around to get her money. "Nope. Just the assault, death, and empty calories, thanks."

"Two oh three then," the cashier said. While the cashier's head was down, Aria considered swiping a lighter from the receptacle on the counter. Maybe she could set a fire to defend herself? But by the time the cashier stared back at her, Aria lost the nerve.

Aria stepped back into the cold. The man in the cap was gone but his large Styrofoam cup remained. He honked again, holding up five fingers to let her know how many minutes she had left. "Like you're going to leave without me, idiot," Aria said under her breath. The woman's bathroom door swung open in the wind banging into a massive cement ashtray. Before she could shut it gently, it slammed with a boom, nearly cutting off her fingers in the process. Now enclosed within the cramped, damp space, Aria gagged on the musky smell. The door didn't lock, but instead offered a tiny hook to slide into a loop in the form of security. A square light buzzed over the cracked mirror that seemed to be a part of the wall's foundational integrity. "Think, think," Aria said to her smeared reflection.

A plastic bin sat underneath the leaky sink. Its contents overflowed onto the floor. Pieces of tissue marked with foreboding earth tones. *Maybe I could throw the trashcan with the poopy toilet paper on his car and then grab Duckworth and run away?* Aria shook her head. That would never work. That was a terrible idea. Aria turned. *Maybe I could overflow the toilet and then…then you'd be standing in water and have wet shoes when that a-hole out there shoots you in the head after shooting your sister in the head.* Beyond the door, the car horn honked twice in three-second bursts.

Time was running out.

Aria looked up. Corkboard rectangles lined the ceiling. One was already pushed aside, a small corner of light shone through. Aria repositioned her backpack. "Okay." Standing on the tank of the toilet, she grabbed the inside frame of the ceiling and kicked off the wall for a boost. She was in! Crouching low, Aria slid the rectangle back into place. "Fine. Now what?" Aria asked the dust bunnies, asbestos, and probable ghosts of cashiers past haunting the place.

A small trickle of light leaked up from a few feet away. Bits of plaster dug into Aria's hands and knees as she crawled along the top of the wall towards it. She peaked through. It was the men's bathroom around the corner. Below, the red/blue-capped man sat on the toilet with his pants around his ankles. His back rose and fell rhythmically. *Gross. Either he's snoring or he's really struggling down there.* The honk sounded for her again.

"Okay. Really no choice here." Aria dangled her feet down first. When the man didn't react, she quietly lowered herself onto the toilet's tank. The man didn't move. Pinching her nose, she stepped down and around him. She cautiously opened the bathroom door, careful to not let it get caught in the wind. She eased the door closed with the palm of her hand. Aria pressed her back against the wall, willing herself to become one with the brick.

Around the corner, his car door opened and slammed. He began to pound on the women's bathroom door. "I'm coming in!" He announced. Aria pulled in a deep breath. She heard the door close with a boom. With all her might, Aria pushed the large cement ashtray in front of the door. "What the fuck?" He yelled from within. The door bucked about in frantic futility.

Aria sprinted to his still-running car and shifted into reverse. A cloud of dust shot up as she slammed the car in gear. The car bounced over the curb as she sped out of the parking lot. "I guess I'm driving now," Aria said to Duckworth, who perked up from the passenger seat. Aria tightened her grip on the steering wheel.

"I'm coming, Nas."

Chapter Forty-Three: Kids of the Blackhole

Talk went around that maybe the generator would turn back on, but it never did. Each half hour someone would walk to the barricaded door and attempt to hear if the OCT was still out there. For the first couple of days, they heard consistent banging around and mayhem as though the OCT was trying to scare them out of hiding. Then it slowly tapered off. Until eventually, three days after the power went off, they didn't hear anything except a door closing somewhere down below. "Maybe it was a ghost?" Neef tried, but no one was really having it. The silence stoked their paranoia.

On the fourth day after the power went out, Davy watched as his bandmates debated what to do next. Even from across the room, he could tell they were defeated. Nas' posture, usually so proud and straight was slouched as though she were hungover, which called to mind that morning after they played that show in a storage space just outside of Orlando when they all tried alcohol for the first (and only) time. Their empty expressions were a mirror Davy couldn't avoid.

Nas had rejoined their circle the day before, though it still seemed the wound hadn't fully healed between her and Brie yet. It was there in the way Nas looked right at Brie even when she was talking to someone else. As well as in the way that Brie would never look at Nas even when she answered a question Nas had posed.

"We're almost down to our last pack of batteries so we should probably start turning the space heater off every other hour," Nas said to Brie's profile.

"Same for the lantern then," Brie said to the lantern. The tattoos on her shoulder seemed to fade with her complexion.

"Agreed," Nas said.

"How much time you think that will buy us?" Remi asked.

"We've been going through batteries like crazy, so…" Pero shrugged. Her normally buoyant orange hair was flat and deflated. "A couple of days. Maybe another week. Maybe."

"So…a week then." Remi clucked his tongue. "Then we go out there?"

Brie shrugged. "That could be what they want, but we don't have any other choice." Brie held the lantern aloft. "So you folks want to start now?"

Davy couldn't bring himself to chime in and they had long since given up asking him. After the circle mumbled their agreement, Brie clicked the light off. Then the heater's fan whirred to a halt. It was quieter and darker than any of them imagined it would be. "Neef, what time is it even?" Remi asked in the dark.

Neef's Day-Glo watch lit up in the middle of the room. "3:42."

"AM?"

"PM."

"Wow."

"What'd you expect, Rem?" Brie asked.

"I don't know. Not this dark though."

Seconds later… "I don't think we're going to make it in time to disrupt Rankin's election," Neef said.

Nas sighed. "There's still time. But our main goal right now is survival."

Then silence descended once again. Each movement from the

middle of the room was amplified as though it was mic'd up. The quiet rested on Davy's chest like Neef's bass cab. *Breathe*, Davy reminded himself. Minutes passed. In the dark, he heard his bandmates whispering. He wasn't sure it was about him, while at the same time he was 100% sure it was. As Davy counted the seconds up, he imagined lying flat on his bench seat in the van. The closest thing he had to meditation, to peace. When he opened his eyes, Davy was startled to find the hour was up. The lantern beamed from the center of the room. The heater whirred healthily. Other than a brief glance from Neef and Remi, none of them seemed to care one way or another that Davy was still there.

That night while everyone else slept, Remi announced, "Okay, hour's up." Davy's arm hair stood up at the small recognition. Then it was soul-crushing darkness again. Every other hour since that afternoon had been a fight for his sanity. Each hour in between offered little in the way of recovery; only fear for what would come next. Despite his attempts, Davy wasn't able to imagine himself in the back of the van. Nor was he able to conjure the sensation of Reid's body pressed against his own. Instead, he felt like he was tumbling down a pit that had no end. Without light or warmth to hold them at bay, all his worst fears and anxieties came out of hiding. *There hasn't been any movement from them in a while. What if they're all dead? What if they decide to leave me up here in the dark forever, like that one night when Remi had that bright idea to tell scary stories, Neef told that one about the man who died in the Paris catacombs just inches from his dropped flashlight, what if they do that to me? It's what I deserve. Oh, God, what've I done? They'll never forgive me. I'll never forgive me. I should've told Remi. I should've told Nas. I should've done anything. What if Vin is already dead? What if he was already dead when they called me? Neef said they can do that now. They call it deep fakes. What if that's all I am now? What if I've already died too and my essence is floating loose? I'm just a ghost in the machine like some bad sci-fi movie. This could be my hell. Man, I'm really freaking out here. I need to sleep. Am I asleep? God, I'm really freaking the fuck out right now. What day is it? Thursday? Sunday? March? I have no idea.*

Davy blinked his eyes several times, but he couldn't tell when his eyes were open or closed. Just as he found himself on the brink of a panic attack, a rustling in the middle of the room let Davy know he wasn't alone. Davy kicked around in his sleeping bag in response. Someone cleared their throat, and then someone else did. More thrashing followed. It was like playing Marco Polo with Vin in that hotel swimming pool so many years before.

"I did give our name to TBN," Brie said in the dark. "I called their anonymous tip line after our first big show with the Dissent fell through. You all were sleeping in the van. It's true I ran the idea by Nas first, but she was so opposed I couldn't bring myself to even tell her I did it. I planned on telling you all eventually, I really did, but I kept finding reasons to put it off. And now…after everything…this isn't your fault, Davy. It's mine. I shouldn't have blown up on you, I was just mad at myself. I'm sor—"

"It's okay," Davy's voice cracked as though his throat had accumulated rust. "I should've told you all about my phone. I was just so scared and worried for Vin. I should've came to you all first. I'm s—"

"I almost left," Remi said with a catch in his voice. "I've almost left about five hundred times, but I almost did for real the night before, well, all this. I've also thought about doing worse things…and I knew that if I brought my anxieties to you guys, you would listen and try to make me feel better, but

I was too afraid to ever bring them up. I just don't feel good enough and I worry that I'm holding you back. But also…I'm scared of failing. I'm scared of messing up. I'm scared of letting you all down. I'm scared of getting caught. I'm scared of what they would do to you guys. I'm scared of everything. So, I almost left you all right as you were counting on me the most. And—And I'm so—"

"I didn't get Woody serviced before we left for tour," Nas said next. "I kept suggesting that I did. And it was my responsibility, but I didn't do it. I don't know why, I made the appointment and everything before we were supposed to leave, but when it came time to go to it, I just drove right by. I was too scared they would find an expensive problem that we couldn't afford or, worse, they'd bust us then and we'd never get to go on tour. Then while we were on the road, each little problem that Woody had, I—I was too proud to say anything. Even without the OCT chase, he would've eventually broken down on us. I should've told you all sooner. And Brie, you didn't deserve what I said. I've just been upset about Aria. I'm—"

"I got something to come clean on too," Neef said with a sniff. "Davis…" Sniff. "Nasim…" Sniff. "Brietta…Remington…" Sniff. Sniff. Long, exaggerated nose-blow. "Not you, Pero…my dear, beloved bandmates, I'm the one who signed you all up for the random cat facts texts." Neef let out a wailing sob. "And none of you, not one of you, ever called me out. It was only supposed to last a week, but I kept re-upping the dollar-ninety-nine service fee so it would keep going. I'm so so so sorry."

Brie flicked the lantern on. There were tears in her eyes and a smile on her face. "You motherfucker!" She yelled at Neef with faux seriousness. "I thought it was someone with an emergency every damn time my phone buzzed!"

Laughing through their tears, Brie, Nas, and Remi then began pummeling Neef with their pillows. "I deserve this! I deserve this!" Neef said, fending off their blows.

"Davy, come on," Brie called.

Davy bounded over and tackled Neef. Their laughter bounced off the walls surrounding them. Davy felt more alive than he had in weeks. "Davy, you smell like a dead body entombed in a porta-potty buried in a dumpster," Neef said as Davy wrapped him in a bear hug.

Remi carefully sniffed his armpit. "Dude, I think that's all of us."

"What'd you expect when we're trapped in a concrete box with no real ventilation," Pero said with a smile.

"Yeah, about that." Davy fell beside Neef out of breath. "I—I'm going to go out there. I can't stand another night in here. I think it's time."

"You can't go out there." Pero shook her head. "If you get caught, you're as good as dead."

"That's why just I should go, if I don't come back then you all just sit tight," Davy said.

"I'll go with you," Remi said.

"Nope." Brie side-eyed Remi. "You can hardly walk. I'm going."

Chapter Forty-Four: All That Remains

Dammit. What in the hell have you gotten yourself into now? Brie thought as they shuffled down the narrow stairwell. *At least we waited until morning.*

"It's stuck." Davy pushed on the false wall of the locker.

"Um." Brie pointed to a small latch holding the wall in place.

"My bad." Davy pushed it aside. Together they stepped through the small opening into the locker room. The space seemed different than either of them remembered. It felt both larger and smaller at the same time, like stepping into a TV set of a show one had watched their whole life.

An ominous plinking resounded like violin strings. Each water drop that fell in the showers pushed Brie further towards the edge. The door to the locker room had been torn off its hinges. It lay discarded on the floor like an uncooperative hostage. In the hallway they found the rest of the doors to the rest of the rooms in a similar state. Brie pointed up to the small black dome in the middle of the ceiling. A tiny red light blinked beside it. "I thought the cameras would be off with the rest of the power," Brie whispered.

Davy shrugged, motioning for Brie to follow him. Faint light streamed through broken windows. Glass crunched beneath their shoes. *Yeah, Dad, the BP sure knows how to take care of places, don't they?* They crouched low, hugging close to the wall and each other. Brie's heart pounded in her ears. She tried to bypass it, to become hyperaware of all other sounds around her: birds chirping in nervous fragments, the whole building humming a death metal song that only Neef would appreciate. Wind licked through the breaks in the windows, nipping at her exposed skin. Tiny goosebumps prickled down her arms.

Every so often, as Brie trailed her hand along the wall, her fingertips would trip up on a bullet hole. It was a disconcerting reminder, as though they needed one, that they had come dangerously close to meeting their end there. A dark red stain on the wooden floor made Brie's stomach turn. What if the bullet had been an inch higher or lower in Remi's leg? Not that anyone had said that per se, but that was something she had heard people say in the past with relation to leg injuries. Whether or not the bullet was actually that close to severing Remi's femoral artery, it certainly felt that way. It felt that they were that close to death. That's all that mattered.

After crossing over the glass and bullet casings, they successfully made it to the dining hall. It too felt different than the safe haven they had shared so many meals and conversations in. There was that night when Pero broke out the laser tag vests, and they split into two teams to play Capture the Flag. Remi won it by uncharacteristically sprinting from one side to the other screaming like an idiot with his t-shirt swaddled around his nether regions like a diaper. Everyone was too stunned or laughing too hard to shoot him. Now it resembled a literal war zone, tables turned over, soot leaping up the walls from an apparent fire, the large windows smashed out, the buffet cart tumbled over, food from the pantry left out. The hope began to arise that maybe the OCT had indeed left. It would, after all, be just like them to trash a place before they took off. There were still so many rooms to check…but maybe, just maybe, they would survive.

Brie stepped closer to the windows to look out. On the back lawn, boot prints embedded deep into the mud trailed back over the hill. The sky was a gray as deep and impenetrable as concrete. It let Brie know that even if they did get to leave, there was still nowhere for them to go.

Davy tapped her on the shoulder. "Let's check the kitchen."

Brie fell in behind him, walking close enough to breathe in the familiar smell of his black Serve the Servants hoodie. The one he always wore after playing. It smelled of ivory soap and body odor.[57] An oddly sweet fragrance that awakened nostalgia for cold nights when standing outside of some venue, the band would crack jokes as they waited for Nas to settle up with promoters, their warm breath escaping their masks like souls. Davy stopped suddenly. Brie crashed into him. Her foot accidentally sent a dented can of green beans skidding across the floor.

"I heard something," Davy whispered. "Someone's here."

They flattened against the wall. Seconds passed. "Maybe it was just a raccoon," Brie whispered. "Surely with all the windows broke out some creatures have gotten in. That was probably just—"

A masked figure stepped into the light.

---

[57] "Since we couldn't do laundry that often," Neef later told historian Jocelyn Hopper. "We would wrap our dirty clothes around bars of soap in our duffels. It wouldn't take the smell away entirely, but it did enough to keep us from gagging."

Chapter Forty-Five: Post-Scene

Driving was both easier and harder than Aria ever imagined it to be. For the most part everything was done for her—after selecting the coordinates for the school, the car basically drove her the rest of the way. At first, she didn't understand why Phony-Greg wouldn't just sit back and let the car steer itself all the time, enjoying the post-apocalyptic scenery of abandoned factories and dilapidated homes as they paraded by her window, but then, as she rounded the final hill for the school, the car almost drove her straight into an envoy of hummers coming down.

The almost dying was definitely the worst part of driving.

The school itself was the next-worst part. Sprawling over an acre of land with its high-pitched roofs and buttresses, the structure appeared to have once been a marvel of human ingenuity. Now, however, plumes of smoke issued from both the east and west wings. Windows were broken out and missing like a witch's teeth. Large ruts marred the front lawn as though the hummers decided to have a donut contest before they left. Whatever life the school once held had since been snuffed out with a curse.

"I think we missed the party, D-Dub." Aria sighed, shifting the car back into manual mode and driving past the smoldering ruin. *Just in case there's someone still here we don't want to see.* She pulled into a small clearing a mile down the road. The front wheels lurched in the mud as Aria tried to back up to a drier patch of land. "Well, I guess this will have to do." She unzipped her coat and motioned for Duckworth to climb in. He looked at her with hesitation.

"I know, I don't blame you, but this is our only option right now," Aria told him. Sluggishly, he stood in the passenger seat before crossing over.

"I promise I won't let anything else bad happen to you," Aria said as she zipped him up in her coat.

The wind stung her cheeks. Three times she drew up her hood and three times it was promptly ripped back off. Aria cradled Duckworth with one arm, thankful for his weight beneath her coat. With her free hand, Aria pulled her red knit cap over her ears, keeping her head down as she trudged towards the school. The wind did its best to discourage her, pushing her back a half step for each full step she took. Still she pressed on even as the mud clung to her shoes, letting go with a resigned thwack when Aria pulled away.

The wind became more bearable once Aria reached the woods. For half an hour, she observed the school from the safety of the trees. When she didn't witness any activity, she worked her way closer, tree by tree, foot by muddy foot.

Some catastrophes look worse from far away, but when viewed close up, appear manageable. Unfortunately, the school could not be filed under this category. It would be placed firmly under the heading: Once Prestige Academy Now An Unlivable Crap Heap. Aria peered up to the column of gray smoke gently wafting into the winter sky.

The back door flew open. Aria ducked behind an overgrown bush as two OCT soldiers walked out. Their masks were pulled back revealing their smooth faces, one Caucasian, one African American. Aria figured they weren't much older than her. To her horror, they stopped right in front of her bush. Light brown mud caked their boots. The crackling of cellophane was followed by the clicking of lighters, followed by the over-exaggerated inhale of a cigarette. Thankfully, Duckworth always understood the severity of the moment. He stayed silent in her coat.

"So, there's this bot on Blurt that gained—" the first soldier inhaled tightly. "Like, awareness or whatever so he started to DM every fo—"

"Bullshit," the other soldier interrupted. "That story is made up. They covered that on TBN the other day. It was just some Lacktivist hacking program trying to stir up trouble."

"It's for real, man," the first soldier inhaled sharply again. "Mick was on the team that went to bring in this poor guy that fell for it. Except the guy had already…you know."

"Nah, you're falling for the Dissent's misinformation. I thought you were better than that."

"I thought *you* were better than that. It didn't come from some squirrely pamphlet. My unit leader from the academy told me. The thing is—" He sucked in again. "Mick thinks that the BP are the ones who even created the bot to do that in the first place."

"What, to act like it's alive?"

"Yeah, like to catch any sympathizers before they even have the chance to defect."

"I can't listen to this," the second soldier said. Aria saw his cigarette fall in the gravel in front of her bush before he grinded his boot on it. "I'm heading back in." He sniffed. "You need to keep that stuff to yourself. Let's just wait for the others to come back without perjuring each other, okay? Besides, that shitty band's probably long gone by now. Not like any of us would be getting the fifty million or whatever it was anyways."

The first soldier stayed behind. He began humming the melody to an old pop song that Aria recognized but couldn't place. *No, wait, that's The Futile! He's humming The Futile!* Aria swore to tell Nas if she ever got to see her again.

Would her sister believe Aria had road-tripped across the country with an Acolyte and then fooled him into getting locked in a stinky bathroom? Would she believe her sweet little sister vandalized the OCT office in their hometown and told off Mr. Deaton? *The better question is, will I believe all the things she's been through?* Aria thought.

Eventually, the first soldier sighed, flicked his cigarette butt into the bush, and went back inside. Aria held her breath until the door shut. She counted to forty-five and then to one hundred and fifteen before she stepped out from the bush. The wind had picked up. Clouds had closed in from the north, bringing with them the threat of rain. The sky rumbled like the score of a horror movie beginning to fade in after the title sequence. Aria eased the backdoor open and stepped inside. Duckworth shifted against her stomach. She patted him to let him know it was okay.

It was darker than she anticipated. The shadows provided anonymity, which was comforting and familiar. Aria would take whatever advantages she could get. Hunkering low, Aria crept down the hallway. Tattered curtains billowed where the wind shot through a broken window. Aria jumped. She covered her mouth and ducked low again. Muffled laughter and flickering lights came from a room just up ahead to the left.

Aria edged closer and peeked into the room. With his feet up on a student desk, an OCT soldier sat with his back to the doorway. An 8in screen was held inches from his face, showing the popular TBN reality show called AR-15 & Pregnant.[58] Aria rolled her eyes. Of course, he was watching that. As the host on the tiny screen took the dad aside to mimic the very-pregnant

---

[58] The premise of AR-15 & Pregnant was quite simple really. An expectant teenage mother was taken to the gun range by her enraged father (or in one 'progressive' episode, her mother) to learn how to protect herself since "no decent man would want her now."

daughter's walk and the way she flinched when firing the large weapon, the soldier laughed so hard he started coughing. Aria took the opportunity to step across the doorway and continue on her way.

As she snuck across the school, an internal dialogue began:

"Hey, Aria, it's me, your brain. So....what's the plan here?"

Hi, Brain, where've you been? I could've used you earlier.

"Oh, so you got up in the ceiling of that bathroom all on your own? Hmmm. Good to know. Good. To. Know. Still, you didn't answer my question...what's the plan, Stan?"

I thought that's what you were for.

"Yes, it's not enough to constantly keep all your internal organs going, to store and process every memory, and manage the trillions of cells and bacteria in your body, but I have to think of everything too."

Yep. Though you forgot to mention 'be very whiny and passive-aggressive' as one of your duties.

"Oh, oh! So clever, think that one all up on your own—"

Someone's coming. Aria ducked into a classroom. Sheets covered the walls. A plain wooden desk sat in the front. A large sculpture of a fist with a rose extending from it like a middle finger stood in the center of the room surrounded by drop cloths and utensils. Aria waited until the footsteps receded. Then she picked up a small flathead hammer and what resembled a railroad tie.

"And what's that for?" Aria's brain asked in its new condescending British accent.

If someone comes along I can...whack them with this or jab them with this.

"Very dignified."

I thought so.

Aria stalked back down the hallway, careful to step around the broken glass that littered the marble floor. At the end of the hallway was a large source of light. *I think I'll head that way.*

"And then what?" Came the obnoxious British voice.

Well, hopefully, I can remain undetected and sneak Nas and them out of here.

"And what if you can't find her?"

Well, whenever I deem that I've spent a long enough time looking then I can leave.

"Hmmm. Deem, nice vocabulary. And what if she's already gone?"

Ditto to what I've already said. I'll just sneak out undetected.

"And then you'll go where?"

You know, you're not really helping so you can shut up now, 'kay?

The end of the hallway opened to a large dining room with gray light streaming in. High windows reached up to higher ceilings. It was magnificent—or at least it was once. Tables and chairs were flipped over. A pile of ash in the corner suggested that the soldiers had gotten bored and started a fire.

Aria's stomach rumbled like a radioactive bear. "Okay, you I will listen to," Aria said under her breath. "There's got to be something to eat around here."

Discarded beer cans littered the pantry amidst the cans of food. Empty liquor bottles lay on their sides. "Gross," Aria whispered as her shoe stuck to the floor. "Oh, dear, Duckworth, yes!" Seizing a tub of raisins, Aria popped the top and commenced shoveling them into her mouth. She poured a bottle of water into the tub's overturned lid and let Duckworth out of her coat for a drink. He eagerly lapped it up.

Next to an empty twenty-four pack cardboard box was an OCT helmet. Cool. Aria picked it up and shook it. Then, with a shrug, she put the helmet on. She slid the visor back and continued to eat more raisins before moving on to some club crackers. *Oh, crap, peanuts!*

"Okay, probably time to move on now," her brain chimed in with renewed energy.

"Yeah, you're right…" Aria scooped in a few roasted peanuts. She tipped the whole jug up to her mouth and spilled them in. Peanuts cascaded to the floor. Aria greeted the mess she made with another shrug.

"Moving on…"

Yeah, yeah, okay. Aria stuffed a few granola bars in her coat pockets, looping Duckworth back up in her arms. As she stepped back into the dining room, she stopped dead in her tracks. *Oh, shoot, people!* Aria quickly stepped backwards, towards the safety of the pantry. Until she saw who it was then she stepped back out into the light.

Oh, shoot, sorry, forgot I had the helmet on.

Chapter Forty-Six: Simmer, Simmer, Simmer Down

Nas couldn't stop biting her nails. Her cuticles were bit up and raw like her father's shoe after Aria first brought Duckworth home. Aria had been designated to make sure the sweet pup didn't chew up anything. It was also her job to keep him locked up when they left for school. So, when they came home that afternoon and discovered that not only was Duckworth loose, but he had also taken liberty with one of their dad's dress shoes, Aria immediately started crying, worried that her parents were going to get rid of her new puppy. Nas told her that she would handle it.

When their dad got home that evening, Nas met him at the door, holding the chewed-up shoe. "Aria asked me to put Duckie in his kennel this morning before school," younger Nas said with tears in her eyes. "And I forgot. But I promise to pay you back. I'll work extra hard, nights and weekends until you can get a new pair." Nas could still remember how hard her father laughed. The way she imagined it bleeding through the walls to the neighbors who always argued next door, the way she imagined it reinforcing the walls of their home as though that's what held the roof over their head.

"Don't worry," he said, doing more with two words to soothe her anxieties than anyone else could with a thousand. He brought Nas into his arms, kissed the top of her head. "I just wouldn't hold Duckworth too close tonight as I'm sure his breath will be extra pungent from chewing on such stinkiness. Good riddance."

In the Safe Room, Nas bit her finger again. With the pain, the realization sank in that she had been staring at the same spot for too long. "How long's it been?" She asked.

Neef's watch lit up blue. "One hour. Seventeen minutes."

"This plan is stupid. What if they got caught? What if they're facing 'heightened-questioning'[59] right now?" Nas bit her finger deliberately since there was no hope of getting the nail.

Pero pulled on her shoes, a pair of purple high-top Converse All-Stars. "You're not helping."

"Exactly," Nas said. "That's the problem. I'm just sitting here waiting for something to happen and I hate it."

Pero smiled. "Exactly."

Despite herself, Nas returned Pero's smile. She slid her hands down to her side and into her pockets. Her smile faded as she briefly caught eyes with Remi. He looked to his shoes, rubbing his palm over his knee. "Hey, Rem." Nas sidled over to him. "Brie'll be back. We'll get out of this."

Remi leaned on her shoulder. She ran her hand over the stubble of his hair. *Why can you only be reassuring when it's to someone else?* Pero asked Nas the night before everything went bad. *I don't know. Why can you pick apart everyone else but yourself?* Nas batted back with a grin as she pounced on Pero in their bed.

Nas leaned into Remi, planting a kiss on top of his head. *I hope we get out of this.*

"Hey." Pero looked up with wide eyes, scrambling to her feet. "That's the latch. That's the latch. That's the latch."

Nas and Neef leapt to their feet. The three of them stood in front of Remi. Nas' pulse raced. Neef wielded a broken table leg over his head. "Let's

---

[59] Torture, just good old-fashioned torture. Naturally, the Blessed Path felt that the reason people opposed torture was more of a branding issue rather than the act itself. Thus, the term 'torture' was stricken from the national vocabulary and no one really gave the matter a second thought.

do this," he said through gritted teeth. "I can at least take a few of them out with me and then you all make a run for it. Go for their necks, that's the weak part in their body armor, I saw a documentary on it."

The knock came to the beat of their song, "Magneto Was Right." Nas' stomach did a corkscrew twist. "Davy."

Pero undid the combination lock and pulled the door back. Davy stepped through with Brie behind him. Brie carried a small animal close to her chest, a dog. Nas looked at Brie with wide eyes. "What?"

"We found someone too," Brie said, stepping aside for a third figure.

A thousand emotions washed over Nas' face in a split second before— "ARIA!" Nas ran to her sister and threw her arms around her, inhaling the scent of her clothes, her hair, the reminders of home. Hugging Aria felt like finding a piece of herself that she believed lost forever. She wanted to crumple to the floor. She wanted to scream. She wanted to squeeze Aria so tight they dematerialized and teleported to a beach far, far away from there. Looking around at the four corners of the room, the low ceiling, the janky DVD cart, the room appeared smaller to Nas than it ever had.

Aria's body heaved in her arms. "I can't believe I found you," she managed to choke out. Pero looked on as she shut the door and locked it again.

"How did you get here?" Nas held her sister out at arm's length. The sight of Aria's black eye sucker punched Nas in the stomach. "Are you okay?"

Aria brought her hand to her eye. "It's not as bad as it looks." Aria sniffed. "I—I'm okay," she said as she collapsed into Nas' arms again.

Nas stroked the back of Aria's head. She had a million more questions, but she knew they all would have to wait. All that mattered was

Aria was there. And whoever had done that to her sister's eye was going to wish they had never been born. Nas hugged her sister tighter, imagining her arms as armor.

"Aria said that she passed about four guards, but we didn't see any," Davy said.

"Well, it could've been as many as four." Aria broke away from Nas, wiping her face with her sleeve. "It's possible I saw one of them more than once."

"And y'all are sure no one saw you come back in here?" Pero asked as she set down a small dish of crackers for Duckworth to eat.

"As sure as we can be." Brie shrugged. "It seems those that were here were more interested in trashing the place than actually finding us." Her hand was in Remi's. Nas knew that was a big step for Brie to be holding Remi's hand out in the open like that. With that and her sister's return, Nas felt something like happiness come over her for the first time in a while.

Aria started chugging from a water bottle before jerking it from her mouth, splashing some on Nas' pant leg in the process. "More are coming back though. I heard one of them saying something and it made it seem like the big hummers with the other soldiers weren't going to be gone long. They're probably heading to the Capitol for the election."

Nas looked at Aria. In her eyes, she would forever be her little sister. The one that once booby-trapped her bedroom door to dump feathers on her head, the one that used to cheer her on at afternoon soccer practice and though the black eye aged her, it was clear she had grown up so much.

"What's the plan?" Remi asked.

Nas clasped his shoulder. "Step one: get the hell out of here. Step two: get to the Capitol and take care of our unfinished business."

"Sounds like a plan." Remi smiled. "Masks on?"

"Yep." Nas shrugged out of her jacket. Her cut-off denim vest showed off the brightly colored tattoos that covered each of her brown shoulders.

"You got some new ink." Aria touched her sister's skin with the sanctity of a religious shrine. "Mom's gonna kill you."

Nas winked at Aria. "Masks on, everyone."

With giddy delight, Aria clapped quietly.

"I made this for you." Remi retrieved a purple mask from his backpack and tossed it to Pero. "It isn't much, but I thought you know...after everything, you're one of us now."

Pero held it to her chest. "Thanks, Rem."

"Sorry, Aria," Remi said. "I didn't know you were coming so I—"

"It's cool." Aria pulled her own red mask from her bag. "I'm way ahead of you."

"Alright." Nas nodded. "Let's go."

Chapter Forty-Seven: Davy Says I Look Taller

Though he walked with a limp, he stood taller, confident, and certain. Each step he took down the narrow stairs sent a shock of pain up the circuitry of his leg to the command center of his brain. With that, Remi knew each lurch forward was purposeful. He knew, perhaps for the first time, that they were going to make it to the van okay. They weren't going to die up there in the Safe Room. Sure, they may die later, but at least they had a chance. An artic chill rushed in as Pero opened the door at the bottom of the stairs. Remi nearly tripped down the last step.

"It's okay to lean on me," Brie said with her arm around Remi as they stepped through.

"I don't want to slow you all down," Remi whispered back. "You should just go on ahead and I'll be right behind."

"No, we're not leaving anyone behind," Nas whispered.

Davy nodded. "I'll help you with Remi," he said to Brie. "If that's alr—"

"I thought you would never ask," Brie cut him off with a smile.

So many things had already happened that Remi never believed possible. Recent events seemingly reconfigured the inner workings of his brain. The glass-half-empty default setting had been turned down. Remi was now more apt to doubt the negative voices when they inevitably chimed in. He was more likely to ignore them and see their comments for the lies they were. *After all, you don't listen to TBN when they spout that kind of idiocy,* Brie told him the night before. *Why listen to your self-doubts when they've never told you anything truthful? Just picture Chelsea Winters saying them, and I bet you'll begin to regard them with the level of scrutiny they deserve.* Remi couldn't argue with her logic.

Furthermore, it was hard to hate himself when he finally felt heroic. It was hard to feel worthless when everything felt so monumental. It was hard to doubt the possibility that maybe, just maybe, everything would work out. *They deserve it*, Remi thought. *And I'm starting to think maybe I do too.*

Or maybe…Remi thought as they limped through the locker-room. *Maybe it's hard to navel-gaze on all my bullshit when there's a hole in my leg. Maybe, just maybe, the downward spiral, negative thought days aren't entirely behind me just yet. But I'm feeling okay about myself right now and I'll take that for as long as I can.* A splinter of lightning shot up through his spine as he stepped awkwardly, placing full weight unintentionally on his right leg. "You okay?" Brie asked, flinching under his weight.

Remi nodded. *Just give up*, came the voice right on cue. *Just stop, you're dead weight.* Remi gritted his teeth. *Nope, fuck you. We're going to make it*, Remi told the voice. *We're going to make it.* One step followed then another; each one hurt a little less.

"Careful of the broken glass," Aria whispered as they ducked into the hallway.

Pero looked in both directions before following Aria. She motioned for Remi and Brie to come ahead. "This way," she said.

Aria darted off ahead of them and peered around the corner. With her head still turned, she flapped her hand for them to come along. Then her palm went flat. *Stay*, she mouthed. She flattened against the wall.

"Get down," Pero whispered.

"Easy," Brie said as Remi lowered himself to the ground. Pain brought sweat to his temples despite how cold it was through the school. *See?* Came the negative voice again in Remi's head. *You should just stay here. You're too weak to keep going. You're going to get your whole band caught.* Remi shut his eyes tight. *Nope. You're wrong. We can do this.*

The five of them crouched behind an overturned bookshelf as an OCT agent walked past the end of the hall. His pulled-back mask revealed the smooth faced boy of nineteen underneath it. With his phone in front of his face blaring AR-15 & Pregnant at an incredible volume, he didn't pay them any attention. Aria craned around the corner with her hand holding them at bay. *Okay, let's go,* she mouthed, motioning them to come on after her. *We're going to make it,* Remi reminded himself as he followed with Brie. *We're going to make it.* Remi waited and the counter-voice never came. *We're going to make it,* he thought again.

But more importantly, he believed it.

Part Four

The Title Track

Chapter Forty-Eight: Morning Bell / Rebel, Rebel

It wasn't quite eight AM. The scene below the shutdown Migrant Registration Center was bathed in bluish gray. It almost didn't feel real. The whole drive had felt the same—not that Davy doubted they were going to make it. More that this day always seemed to be set perpetually on their horizon, a destination so far in the distance it would never arrive. Their time spent in the purgatory of the Safe Room only intensified that feeling. Davy rubbed his tired eyes. It was real though. They were there. Wired despite their lack of sleep. Determined despite the mounting stakes.

Camera drones from TBN hovered over the growing crowd. Davy waited until one passed the tinted window before he approached. "There are actually people out there." Davy turned to his bandmates. "This is easily the biggest turnout for Voting Day in…as long as I've been alive."[60]

Remi crutched over. "Wow," Remi said under his breath. Davy couldn't tell if his friend was impressed or scared. The distinction used to be easier to make when it came to Remi, but a lot of things had changed since, well, everything.

Neef walked over next. "Could be a trap," he said to Nas.

Nas clucked her tongue. "Yep."

"Still have to do it though."

"Yep."

Davy turned back to the window. Below, the crowd grew thicker by the second. Some wore the harsh reds and blues known to be associated with

---

[60] The Blessed Path's day one goal after coming into power was staying in power as long as possible. To better achieve this, they removed polling places nationwide and declared the Capitol the sole place to vote. Those who weren't able to make the pilgrimage simply waved their right to 'fair' representation.

the Blessed Path, which wasn't surprising to Davy. What was surprising was how many weren't wearing the colors. They outnumbered the obvious-supporters five to one.

Despite knowing better, Davy searched the many faces of the crowd, hoping to see Vin among them, somehow. *Stop it,* Davy told himself, but, all the same, he continued. Nas put her hand on Davy's shoulder without saying anything. He laid his head on her hand. Sometimes just being seen is enough.

Pero entered the room in her Young Apostles Academy uniform. Her hair was blown back like a bright orange comet. "The projector's all set. You sure y'all can't just perform somewhere safer? I could easily project the feed out there."

Nas smoothed the wrinkles out of her own Young Apostles uniform. "No, it's important that we're out there with them." Nas cocked her head towards the window. "Otherwise, none of this means anything." Nas turned to Aria. "Is everything else good to go?" She asked.

"Drums, amps, and mics are set up beneath the platform. Just need to add the most awesome band in the world now." Aria put her orange mask on and sat next to Duckworth who was asleep on the floor. If Aria wasn't such a badass, Davy would've found it cute how she wore the mask almost constantly since Remi had made it for her after saying, "I think you need a color of your own." The only time she didn't seem to wear it was when they were in public.

"The sound's all set up. The stairwells are secure. The elevators were already down, of course, but Aria and I ensured they'll stay that way." Pero slid her hand into Nas'. "You folks will have a tight four and a half minutes to do your thing and get down to the street. The projector screen will automatically rise on its own once y'all finish playing. Hopefully that'll cause enough of a distraction for you to slip into the crowd undetected."

"Unless it's a trap." Nas turned to Neef with a grin.

Neef swatted the sentiment away with a yawn. "Eh, it's probably not a trap."

Brie stepped closer to Davy. "You know what we're getting ready to do could help Vin."

"You think?"

Brie placed her hand on his. "Maybe. Hopefully. Today we take down Rankin, next...who knows?"

Davy swallowed. It was impossible to know if Vin was even alive.

As if sensing Davy's thoughts, Brie put her arm around him and pulled him into a hug. "Wherever Vin is, I know he's proud of you and what you're doing here today," Brie said. "I'm so damn proud of you." Brie parted from Davy before addressing the rest of the band. "I'm proud of all of you. I've known ever since our first practice in Remi's church basement that we were going to change the world."

"I've known that too." Remi winced as he crutched closer.

"Oh, you did?" Brie cracked. "You had a good way of showing it then."

Remi smiled sheepishly. His blue eyes had regained some of the glimmer Davy used to know. "Well, I never doubted *you* all were going to change the world."

"Okay, folks." Nas zipped up a bright red hoodie over her Young Apostles uniform. She turned to them, raising her eyebrows. "It's time."

Brie reached into the drawstring bag and tossed Davy his yellow mask. Davy assessed the piece of cotton. The vacant spaces for his eyes and mouth, the way it served as a vessel, a means of expression for everything he wanted. Yet it could never see or speak for him. Davy slipped it on, finding the familiarity of its fit to be the exact comfort he needed. Then he zipped up the yellow hoodie over his Young Apostles uniform. Davy snuck another look at the burgeoning crowd. This level of outspokenness against the Loyal Defender was unprecedented. A few homemade poster-board signs practically dared the OCT into action. One read: "The Blessed Path to Glory is Riddled With Innocent Bodies!" Another: "When the LD Talks to God, He Constantly Interrupts." And another: "We Are The FUTILE!" Some parents had even brought their children, proudly displayed on their shoulders, their own signs held aloft, scrawled in the unsteady hand of a seven-year-old: "Girl Power Makes the World Go Round!" A nagging sense of responsibility plagued Davy. For so long, the band approached the back and forth with the Blessed Path like a cat-and-mouse game. It was so much more. *These people should've stayed home. What if they get hurt here too?*

Remi patted Davy on the shoulder, bringing him back to the moment.

"It's not Woody—" Brie plugged a tiny speaker into Nas' MP4 player. "But it's gonna have to do." She clicked play and the glorious guitars of the Mindfucks kicked in.

Davy's foot tapped rapidly to the tempo. Even with his head down, he could still see his bandmates in his peripheral: Brie rocking her head to each strum of the guitars, Remi smiling at Brie, Neef with his eyes closed, bouncing in place, and Nas staring straight to the floor, her lips moving as if in prayer.

When the song concluded its exact two-minute run time, hoodies were zipped up, shoelaces tightened, and holes on masks were adjusted properly. Then they went to Duckworth, petting him softly so as to not wake him, but still thoroughly enough to hopefully gain some of his good luck.[61] Nas gave Aria a hug and whispered in her ear. Aria nodded. With a parting glance at the crowd, Davy turned to follow his bandmates. Pero and Aria offered each of them a fist bump as they made their way to the stairwell. Davy didn't know what would happen to the crowd or Vin or Aria or his friends or himself after they went up to the top of the building to perform, but he knew what would happen if he chose to do nothing.

And that was one outcome he couldn't allow.

---

[61] "What do you mean, how was Duckworth good luck?" Neef asked this author in mock disbelief. "You must not know many dogs, man."

Chapter Forty-Nine: Nas AKA Spent Gladiator

The doorknob was as sobering as an OCT stop. Nas drew in another breath, trying to work up the courage to push it open. "Okay, you heard Pero, we get up there, play our song, then it's masks and jackets off and down to the street."

Brie met Nas' eyes and nodded. The last few weeks hung beneath Brie's eyes in dark circles. Her stoic expression wasn't the focused determination that Nas had once known. It was the unfamiliar face of uncertainty and possibly…fear. Nas couldn't blame her. After the lingering trauma from the OCT chase, the school raid, after Remi got shot, after how quickly shit had gotten real, it was easy to feel that they'd gotten in over their heads, that maybe they weren't up this, that maybe they were putting themselves up on the highest stage imaginable only to fail spectacularly. Whatever the look was in Brie's eyes, Nas felt it too. A spent gladiator with an ever-dulling blade.

Okay. You're stalling.

With a sharp exhale, Nas heaved the door open with her shoulder. Sunlight flared through the clouds. Neef and Davy got to work, setting aside the large platforms while Brie and Remi tore the sheets from the amps and drum kit. The edge of the roof loomed near with a sheer plastic wall extending up around them.[62] Nas approached cautiously, placing her palm flat against the hard plastic. Tiny holes dotted the wall, letting air in.

---

[62] The wall (and hundreds like it) was the leadership's response to the growing number of 'chosen' deaths from the top of the Capitol's many tall, empty buildings. The few environmentalists brave enough to speak up, urged the Blessed Path to go with protective nets, as the clear shields frequently caused the deaths of innocent birds. The Blessed Path found the addition of nets to be an "eye-sore" to their skyline. Though they were apparently okay with sidewalks littered with dead birds.

Vibrations radiated through as though the building below was a living, breathing organism.

Six TBN camera drones whooshed over the crowd away from the Futile in a singular movement. Nas watched them go, wondering what led them away so conveniently. Amps buzzed behind Nas as they flipped on from standby. Nas set up the mic stand, positioning it to the proper height. Waves of warmth rushed through her body. She was back where she belonged, in a position where she was in total control, where the music provided order and structure while allowing true freedom in every sense of the word. Though it had only been a little over six weeks since their last live performance, it may as well have been a decade.

Behind the microphone, Nas could fully see the crowd below. The band's presence towered over her shoulder like an army waiting for her command. Holding her hand out to her side, Nas counted down from five. At one, Brie, Neef, and Remi hit a down strum as Davy crashed the cymbals. Looks of recognition passed from one member of the crowd to the next as they strained to see the top of the building.

Nas' heartbeat thrummed in her ears. She raised the megaphone to her mouth. The words came naturally. "We're the Futile and this is a new song called, 'The Day Selflessness Saved the Planet!'"[63] Nas' voice echoed out beyond the wall, bouncing off the buildings and street below, her words drenched in reverb-soaked gravitas.

A cheer erupted from the crowd. Nas let her hand linger on the

---

[63] An obvious, admittedly cheesy, play on the lost Futile song, 'The Day Selfies Saved the Planet.' Though unlike its predecessor, 'Selflessness' chose to empower people rather than foolishly poke fun at those who sought to improve the world while also patting themselves on the back in the process. Sadly, like its predecessor, 'Selflessness' was never properly recorded in a studio, though hundreds of audience-shot videos exist in the national archive today.

plastic wall, feeling the tiny holes beneath her palm. Davy did a four-beat drum fill. Then Brie launched into her lead riff with Remi and Neef providing the rhythm. Opting for the mic over the megaphone, Nas belted out, "My dearly beloved / We're gathered here today / To let go of the broken / To choose our own way." Brie ripped into her mid-verse lead as Nas stomped over to the other side of the roof. Propping her foot on the ledge, Nas leaned into the next line. "Let them think they have us where they want us!"

"Whoa-oh-oooooh," Brie and Remi provided the back-ups.

"Let them think they have us figured out!"

"Whoa-oh-oooooh!"

"Let them think whatever the hell they want!"

"Whoa-oh-oooooh!"

"But we're not going to die on their front!"

The drums crescendoed into the pre-chorus instrumental as Nas pumped her fist. The crowd swelled as more people pushed in from the edge. The glare of phone screens held aloft. There were at least twenty faces below in their own brightly colored masks but Nas left off counting there. Camera drones from TBN swept back in close to the plastic wall. On the jumbotron screen positioned in front of the Capitol's square, the mirror image of the Futile's performance played in larger-than-life hyper-definition.

Raising a middle finger to the camera drones, Nas shredded her vocal cords with the chorus, "We're more than what they think we are / We're more than they want us to be / We're a light shining so bright / Yet they still can't see!"

To each side of Nas, Brie and Remi leaned to their mics for the chorus refrain outro, "We're more than what they think we are / We're more than they want us to be / We're a light shining so bright / Yet they still can't see / We're a light shining so bright / They just can't see / We're a light shining so bright / They won't ever see!!!" Nas' roar echoed over the crowd below.[64]

Remi and Brie's guitar parts swirled together in a tidal wave of sound as Davy built the song up to its final collapse. Nas' chest heaved as she watched over the crowd, searching in vain for Aria. OCT agents pushed through the crowd. A number of agents gathered at the building's entrance below, as well as on the parallel rooftops, rifles trained on their shoulders. Red pinpoint lights distorted through the plastic wall that now served as a shield. Nas walked up to the wall and stared down those who would want her dead. The song ended and, just as Pero promised, the movie screen lowered down over the Capitol's jumbotron.

As her bandmates dropped their instruments and rushed to the stairwell, Nas raised the megaphone once again. "Remember, no one defines you but you. You're not just a cog in their machine or an ID number in their database. You're not a nameless, faceless mass for them to mold into whatever they want you to be. Together we will overcome and outlast them." Nas lowered the megaphone from her lips as helicopters approached. Brie eagerly waved her in from the stairwell. "We now leave you with footage of your soon-to-be-re-elected OCT Commander, J.R. Rankin."

With that, the megaphone fell to the concrete as Nas rushed to the exit, giving a parting wave to the OCT before she dashed through the door.

---

[64] "['Selflessness'] really wasn't our best song lyrically, but we wrote most of it in the van on the way to the Capitol so what do you expect?" Neef mused in the documentary, *Resistance Is.*

Chapter Fifty: Video #4

Over the jumbotron screen, and millions of others, the previously recorded feed came in to show the five members of the Futile, resplendent in their masks of red, yellow, blue, pink, and green. Yellow Mask was farthest to the left and spoke first: "This morning is Election Day and you'll have the 'right' to vote for the head of the OCT." His voice echoed throughout the Capitol.

Green Mask spoke next, "Though you don't have much of a choice when it comes to electing J.R. Rankin to his fourth term. You should at least know who the man is that you will unwillingly elect."

The feed cut to grainy footage taken from a security camera. An empty street appeared with the timestamp of 1:21am, three weeks prior. A black town car pulled into view. It idled near the street corner for a few seconds until a black SUV eased up next to it. The camera zoomed in on the license plates of both vehicles. The backdoor of the black SUV flew open. A man with his hands bound behind him fell onto the pavement. His thinning white hair billowed wildly in the wind. Despite the poor video quality, it was obvious the man had been badly beaten. All four doors of the town car opened. Four figures dressed in black complete with ski masks[65] stepped out. One of the figures passed the other a handgun. The handcuffed man shook his head. The figure with the gun pulled back his mask and got down in the captive's face. Another well-timed zoom-in revealed the man with the gun to be J.R. Rankin; the captive, his political opponent. Rankin stepped back and fired the gun four times at the captive. He handed the gun back to one of the other men before getting in the back of the SUV and pulling out of frame.

---

[65] These ski masks were of course not as cool or as stylish as the colorful balaclavas of the Futile.

The feed cut back to the five masked teens. Red Mask spoke, "If today you were planning to be so bold as to vote for Rankin's opponent, Michael Stanislawski, you'd find the task impossible as Mr. Stanislawski's partner reported him missing the day after this video. His body is still yet to be found." Red Mask cleared her throat. "The following is footage from a chemical assault that Rankin ordered on foreign soil intended for our 'enemies' but instead ended up plaguing innocent civilians. The second part of this video is the Sarin assault our 'enemies' struck on our soil as a response to our attack. They conveniently hit a small town with known ties to the Dissent, which I'm sure is just an unfortunate coincidence. If you find this hard to watch please remember this is the Loyal Defender's Blessed Path at work."

Those around the world who were preparing to eat suddenly found that they had no appetite. Those who had just eaten wished they hadn't. As many viewers craved relief from the brutal footage of writhing bodies, others too weak-stomached, fixated instead only on the periphery effects: a spilled bag of groceries, oranges rolling into a sewer grate...a stroller resting at a complete stop... and then, perhaps the most devastating of all, a school yard complete with a jungle gym, a spinning merry-go-round, and empty swings. As the camera panned down the feed abruptly stopped. Though many didn't allow themselves to see the true devastation, the small glimpses witnessed through the cracks of their fingers proved enough.

Blue Mask wiped at her eye with the sleeve of her black hoodie. She cleared her voice. "We know this footage is devastating. TBN will likely insist that this was all a lie, and many of you will probably believe that, because it's easier to go along with that than to know the truth. But please know that the ability is within you to step up and do something about it."

"And with that," Pink Mask spoke next. A noticeable expression of exasperation was present even though the mask covered most of his face. "We want to show you one more video."

The feed cut to a shaky handheld camera showing a car dashboard complete with a little pine tree air freshener hanging from the rearview. Through the windshield of the car was the interior of a parking garage. Thirty feet away, five men stepped into view. The phone camera darted back down to the dash and zoomed in before shooting back up to show that the two men were J.R. Rankin and the foreign dictator, Misha Burov. The two men shook hands, talking briefly as Rankin transferred over a briefcase to Burov. Then they each got into their prospective vehicles and left the scene.

The feed then cut back to the five masked teenagers. Blue Mask spoke. "It's strange to see two men from countries that apparently hate each other exchange pleasantries in a remote location when the 'news' coverage never mentioned any such meeting," she said. "In fact, in press conferences these two men regularly mention that one will never meet the other because their animosity runs so deep that such a meeting would lead to increased tensions between our two countries. So why were they meeting each other here?"

Red Mask cleared her throat before speaking again. "The explanation is, like most things with the Blessed Path, both simple and corrupt. The conflict our countries are involved in is mutually beneficial for the leaders of our governments at the expense of people like us. We bomb their cities; they do the same for us. All the while giving our citizens someone to hate that isn't them. All the while we go on, oblivious to the real villains, hating the great unknown faceless other. It has to stop. It cannot continue."

Red Mask stared into the camera. "Now, I'm sure right now you're thinking that it's pointless to take on the invincible Blessed Path when there's nothing weak little you can do to stop them. That's a lie. We're stronger than them because we care. We're stronger because we have something to believe in and fight for. Our bleeding hearts don't make us frail—they're the source of our strength. If you find yourself feeling too much, if you find yourself wanting to save your loved ones from the ugliness of this world, if you find yourself sick to the stomach with the injustice that surrounds us on all sides, then we are the same. We must stand together and take to the streets to demand fair elections, fair treatment of our citizens, a fair justice system. We must deny the constant spoon-feeding of blatant lies and propaganda. We must rid ourselves of the safety of delusion. We must seek out truth and hold onto it with all that we have." Red Mask stepped closer to the lens. Her voice rose with determination. "I will concede this, the Loyal Defender is right about one thing when he calls us the enemy. For the enemy of anger is communication. The enemy of fear is unity. The enemy of tyranny is knowledge. Together we cannot be silenced. Together we are stronger than them. Together we can give a brighter future to our children, to our families. We will become a peaceful movement that will not be silenced. Together we are the Futile and we're not going anywhere. Join us and be on the right side of history."

Across the world, millions of screens then went black. When the Kelley family in Duluth, Minnesota attempted to turn their TV back on they found it impossible. Others discovered that their phones weren't capable of picking up TBN's feed when they so desperately needed a response of how to feel about this disturbing message. As a result many began talking face to face. Oh, sure, that video was awful and probably a lie the conversations would usually start. Instead of ending there though, many found themselves pushing further, arriving at the same question: It does make a lot of sense. What if it's true?

Chapter Fifty-One: Eye on the Finish Line

Like putting on an old jacket, Aria found she could still blend in when needed, though she had outgrown the style and it was quite a bit tighter (and considerably less comfortable) than she remembered. Thankfully, her orange mask hummed in her back pocket, reminding her who she was, even when she seemed to be just another face in the crowd. Despite everything, blending in was perhaps the easiest part of following the protocol Nas had laid out for her.

The hardest part was not yelling, "THAT'S MY SISTER!" when the Futile took the stage. The next hardest part was not singing along to the words she had memorized by listening to them practice their performance acoustically in the van the whole way to the Capitol. The next-next hardest part was not slapping a jubilant high-five with those that gave a cheer when Nas flipped off the TBN cameras. The next-next-next hardest part was not punching out that asshole dude in the stained blue t-shirt that called the Futile a "buncha lacktavist bitches that deserve to die." The next-next-next-next hardest part was hiding her innate glee as the projector screen dropped down. The next (x5) hardest part was not spitting in the face of each OCT soldier that aggressively shoved their way through the mass of people. The ones that pulled their rifles out in the packed crowd, making a few younger children cry in the process, and took aim at the projector screen like a few holes in the screen would erase the memory of what they'd all seen.

Even though Aria had seen the video ten to twenty times as Neef edited it together in the back of the unnamed school van,[66] she still stood transfixed like everyone else as it played overhead. The mood there among the people was as palpable in the air as pollen. Except instead of making Aria sneeze, it just made her eyes water.

A change was happening.

By the time the OCT had figured out how to disable the projector, the video had already ended. Through the crowd, Aria saw the familiar profile of Pero. As if feeling Aria's gaze, Pero turned around and widened her eyes. "Oh, right," Aria said to herself. A wall of body odor stood in her way like trying to fight through a laundry basket of sweaty socks. Clutching Duckworth to her chest, Aria held her breath and pushed through.

Conversations swirled around Aria as she made her way through the mass of people. They all blurred into one long-winded rant. *What do you think this means? The LD will probably have to distance himself from Rankin now. You think? This stuff was pretty much common knowledge anyway. Nothing has changed anything so far, why should this be any different? This is the start of something powerful. Impeach Rankin! That's exactly what I've been saying, we have to get involved, we can't keep sitting on our asses. Easy for some kids to get up there and say this, try making a difference when you're up to your neck in medical bills, a mortgage, and three kids of your own. I heard that they're a BP plant anyway. This is just their way of testing us like those emails everyone's been getting. No way, they're the real deal. TBN wouldn't be going after them like this if they weren't. Well, maybe Rankin was on the way out anyway. Must've made a powerful enemy somewhere. Man, fuck the OCT! Fuck the Loyal Defender. Shhhh, chill, you can't be saying that stuff. I don't even care. They've shown that it's okay. I'm*

---

[66] "We couldn't bring ourselves to name that van just yet," Neef wrote in *The Rhythm of Our Road.* "It was still so soon after Woody. We decided we would give it some time…then…then we never got around to it. It's a shame. I had a few good ones saved up."

tired of being quiet. It's exhausting. I figured Whatserface Winters would be up there by now. Seems like they're all just as confused as we are. I heard about this meeting that happens on Tuesday nights. We should try to…

The OCT cut through the crowd from the opposite direction, leaving a wake behind them. Aria followed at a healthy distance. Once they reached the entrance of the Migrant Registration Center, Aria ducked around the corner where Pero waited. Pero raised a finger to her lips. Aria nodded. In the street, the fervor of discontent was whipping into a full-blown riot. Impassioned chants grew more intense with each repetition. WE WILL NOT BECOME! WHAT WE MEAN TO YOU! WE! ARE! THE FUTILE! Conflicting shouts were drowned out, growing weaker and weaker until the point of silence.

Unable to take it another second, Aria peaked around the corner before jolting back with wild eyes. "Pero, they have a battering ram!"

"Good. That means the locks have held until now." Pero's nostrils flared. "It won't be long. Just wait."

Aria winced as the building behind her shuddered once, then again, and again. Duckworth looked at her through the opening of her hoodie. "It's okay, D. We're getting out of here soon." The building fell silent. Pero elbowed her. "They're in. Let's move." Pero spun around the corner and pulled the busted doors shut again. Then, she quickly wrapped the compound wire around the door handles. Aria kept watch for whatever that was worth, thankful that the remaining OCT agents outside were more concerned with the increasing hostility of the crowd rather than their comrades inside.

By Aria's count there were at least four cameras positioned directly on her and Pero. She definitely wasn't standing in the blind spot anymore.

Aria ducked her head, hoping that her bangs could shield her face, but knowing it was already too late. Again, she reached back and felt the orange mask crammed in her back pocket. It calmed her some. Pero came up from behind and put her arm around Aria. They started walking. "The door's secured. Those assholes should be trapped in there for a while. Now, we just have to get to the van." And then, perhaps reading a look of worry on Aria's face. "Don't worry. She'll be at the pick-up spot. If anyone is going to be fine, it's your sister."

Aria leaned into Pero's arm, appreciating the Hawaiian blend scent that lurked on her hoodie. The same brand that Nas used. Beats taking a shower, Nas told her once as she Febrezed the bejesus out of the jeans she had worn for nearly two months straight. *They can practically stand up and walk out of the room on their own at this point,* Aria joked. Nas laughed louder than she needed to and Aria loved her for it.

"She'll be there," Pero said again as they navigated the edge of the crowd.

"Yeah, she will be." Aria gave Pero a brief squeeze. "She will."

When the scene was a comfortable two blocks behind them, Aria finally exhaled. Though she had last seen them under the cover of midnight hours, the procession of Pay Day Advance and Bail Bond storefronts started to look familiar. The safety of the untitled van wasn't too much further.

Others out that morning didn't have that same outlook. They hurried about with the looming presence of the storm brewing just blocks away. Shop owners pulled metal grates over the fronts of their stores. Cardboard signs that read: "Locally Owned" and "No Dog In This Fight" were positioned prominently in their windows. "You girls need to be moving along," an elderly man said without making eye contact. "Trouble's coming. I've seen it before."

"Yes, sir. We are," Pero and Aria said nearly in unison.

What will come of this for them? Aria thought. *Will they pay the price even though they've done nothing wrong?*

The parking garage came into view. The gate's arm was a broken-off alligator jaw. Spray-painted slurs marred the concrete walls. The first level alone had at least ten broken down vehicles long since abandoned, now serving as home for squatters and critters alike. There tucked between them was the school van, a little worse for the wear. The pothole-filled gravel backroads between the school and Capitol had not been too kind. Duckworth growled underneath Aria's hoodie. "It's okay, Duckie. We've made it."

Pero broke into a jog towards the dusty van. "They'll be waiting for us. We—"

A figure stepped from the shadows directly in Pero's path. "Yes," Luca said with a sickening grin. His gun aimed at her chest. "Get in the van." He motioned with the gun. "We don't want to keep your friends waiting."

The DITCH

For decades, the DITCH served as an all-encompassing, ultimate-security prison for the enemies of the Blessed Path. Since the inmates were detained indefinitely without the faintest whiff of a trial, as well as the prevalent practice of 'heightened-questioning' within the facility, the operations of the DITCH have overwhelmingly been considered a major breach of human rights by anyone with a soul.

While the smoldering ashes of the Blessed Path's supporters insist that the DITCH is a complete fabrication in the chronicles of history, there is no doubt that the facility did in fact exist. Located deep in Arizona, what remains of the DITCH is now just a burned out, mile-wide trench over a seven-mile stretch of the Sonoran Desert. The scar left in the earth is perhaps the best representation of the facility's impact on human civilization. Unfortunately, there is still much left unknown, like, for starters, what did DITCH mean? Was it an acronym?[67] If so, what did it even stand for?

"We used to joke about that all the time," Neef said in Darien Ogletree's documentary, *Resistance Is*. "We would have fun trying to come up with our own possible meanings." Neef looked away from the camera and smiled wistfully. "Like: Divine Intervention Truth Clearing House. I think that was Nas. Or: Dirty Illegal Technical College Hell. That was definitely Davy's. Then Remi had: Down In The Church Halls. And Brie: Dehydrated Interjection Torture Committee Haven." Neef chuckled. "None of them really made any sense, but that didn't matter."

"What was yours?" Ogletree asked, off-screen.

---

[67] The Blessed Path sure loved the tidiness of acronyms.

Neef's smile disappeared. "Determined…Interpretive…Territorial Communal Hogpen? I'm not sure. I had a lot of guesses, but none of them came close to what that place really was."

Chapter Fifty-Two: Chyron, the Devourer of Hope

Sirens bled through the concrete walls as the Futile clambered down the staircase. Despite the booming laughter and whoops from her bandmates that nearly drowned it out, Nas couldn't help but focusing on the high-pitched wailing. They were coming for them. That was to say: They, the ever-present THEY, the *they* that loomed in the shadows, the gravity pulling out her fingernails in every anxiety fueled fever dream. They, whose presence was often more felt than seen, were finally coming for (capital T, proper noun-ed) Them, everyone and everything she loved. Forgive her if she couldn't quite work up the enthusiasm of her bandmates. Celebrations would be saved for when they were all safe and sound in a remote location far away.

No, fuck that. Nas shook it off. Even the smallest victories deserved to be recognized. With that, Nas let out a whoop to rival even that of Neef. This spurred her bandmates on further. Even Remi who was shuffling down the best he could with the help of Brie, yelled out with joy. Their laughter reverberated through the vacuous stairwell. The sound was among the most pleasant things Nas had ever heard. There was no need to wonder this time. She knew there would be something of them left behind.

When they started the descent, they were the five masked members of the Futile, wanted dead or alive. Before they reached the bottom, after shedding outerwear the whole way down, they resembled five regular, well-mannered Young Apostle Academy students visiting the Capitol for no reason other than seeing Voting Day in action.

Thankfully, the blocks that Pero had set up to each stairwell door held up. The OCT had made it into the lobby. Shouts of frustration could be heard as the Futile approached the first-floor landing. It was quite the buzzkill. The Futile's good mood and celebration promptly ceased. No need to give them further reason to burst through just yet, not until the Futile could access the service level and undercut it all just as they planned. Nas couldn't help but stifle a laugh though as Brie flipped the door off as they passed it by.

A full three blocks down from their performance site, the Futile emerged into the open city air. Chaos lurked everywhere Nas looked. Just to her left, four peace officers held down an unarmed man for his discarded sign that lay in the snow. Moisture ran its bleeding letters together, obscuring the meaning. Five cell phones attached to as many people filmed the ordeal rather than helping. Various insignia and patches of the Dissent decorated their coats. Before Nas could act, a group of teens in brightly colored ski-masks ran into frame, tackling the officers off of the man, allowing him time to scramble away. A fifth officer then drew his gun on the youth, firing off one shot before barking out a threat that he would shoot again. Nas watched slack jawed as the youth cried out, holding his side. His mask was promptly yanked off to reveal a boy of no more than twelve. Nas watched for blood, trying to find solace when there wasn't any.

"Nas, we have to get to the checkpoint," Neef said softly over her shoulder.

Brie, Remi, and Davy were already halfway down the block. Nas looked to Neef before turning back to the scene, helplessly watching as the youth were shackled together. The boy holding his side grew paler by the moment.

"What've we started?" Nas asked.

Neef frowned. "Looks like a revolution, like it or not." He offered his hand. "Come on. We still have a bit to go and Remi's hurting." Together, Nas and Neef jogged to meet up with them.

"Trains are shut down for the day," Brie said.

Nas nodded. "Checkpoint B it is then." Plumes of smoke snaked toward the sky. The further they walked into the city, the further they got away from the bedlam of the impending riots, the more Nas felt responsible. That boy was even younger than Aria, the look of his eyes as...

The sun was a hazy orange cough drop. Despite not being good for anyone, the air smelled medicinal. It tasted like it too, chemical and bitter. Nas wet her lips. Just minutes ago, she had been so joyful with her bandmates in the stairwell. Though she could remember the feeling, it was impossible to fully recall.

"Check it out." Davy pointed at one of the many large billboard screens posted around the Capitol. "They must've gotten TBN going again."

Nas stopped in her tracks. The chyron running at the bottom of the screen read: "BREAKING: HEAD OF THE OFFICE OF CULTURAL TERRORISM, J.R. RANKIN VICTIM OF DISHONEST CONSPIRACY TO UNDERMINE REELECTION CAMPAIGN."

"Well, shit," Brie and Remi said simultaneously.

Nas clenched her jaw. It was more or less what she expected, so why was it still so disappointing?

"Yep." Neef sighed. "It seems they still remember who the real bad guys are." Neef put his hands on his sides as the screen cut to live footage of the Futile performing on the roof of the former Migrant Registration Center. Exaggerated blurs covered Nas' hands as she flipped off the TBN drones.

Remi balanced his weight on his one good leg, cocking his head up at the screen. "That was pretty bad ass though."

Nas managed a slight smile. "Did you expect anything less?"

With a shake of his head, Remi returned her smile. "Nope."

The overwhelming urge to cry came upon Nas suddenly, tightening her throat.

"Uh, folks, act natural," Neef said under his breath.

Dust swirled as a black SUV skidded to a stop in the street beside them. The doors flew open. OCT vests covered their chests. "We're going to have to see your papers and identification," a young agent with windswept blonde hair said.

"We're from the Roanoke Young Apostles Academy," Brie said, reaching into her backpack. "We have the proper forms right he—"

"Save it," interrupted a voice from the backseat. The sun glistened off his bald dome as he stepped out. "Just do a retinal scan and be done with it," Rankin snarled.

"It's illegal to scan a minor without their consent according to Article 4, Section 8.2 of the House of—" Neef started before the young agent stepped up and began the scan.

"Matches one of the youths performing on the rooftop, sir," he said a second later.

Rankin grinned at Nas. "Excellent."

Chapter Fifty-Three: Driving Etiquette for Nightmare Scenarios

Four years prior, in a two-door Kia Optima, on an icy country road, Pero learned to drive at the age of fourteen. With a warm smile, her dad took her through different nightmare scenarios. Some were probable (*here's what you do if you happen to run off the road*). A few were unlikely (*here's what you do if a bridge gives out and your car begins to sink. You're gonna want to roll down your window or kick it...*). And the rest were impossible, said just for his own amusement (*now if you're driving and you find yourself being chased by a T-Rex, you're gonna want to drive in a serpentine path.* "I thought I would want to stop entirely because then he'll be blind to me." *Ah, rookie mistake. Also, don't automatically assume the T-Rex is male. You're better than that, Junipero*). Still, nothing he could've said would have prepared her for this.

Don't start, c'mon, don't start, Pero willed as she turned the key. Without a hiccup, the school van roared to life. *Traitor.* Pero shifted into reverse. Her stomach knotted as she saw Luca's stretched-out-silly-putty face in the rearview. A stylish haircut topped it off. *Of course, it does,* Pero thought. Below-average young men have tried for centuries to obscure their mediocrity with style and confidence. It made sense for this guy to fall into that category. Still, Pero could work with that. Even though she went to an art school, boys like him had surrounded her for most of her life. Actually, especially since she went to an art school. Pretentiousness practically oozed from the walls when the school was still open. The thing about guys like Luca that pissed Pero off the most though was how they thought they just had her, themselves, and everything else completely figured out. They were so predictable in that every one of them always believed that they were the smartest person in every room. *That's okay, I can use that to my advantage.*

Step one of Pero's plan was to catch Luca off guard.

Between her and the douche-to-end-all-douches sat Aria. As the van pulled away from the parking garage, Pero kept trying to sneak glances at Aria in the rearview, hoping to convey with her eyes that everything was going to be okay, that she had it under control, that she wouldn't let that asshole hurt Aria, or Duckworth, again. However, each time she looked back, Luca caught her eyes instead. Even though the gun was out of view, she knew it was still there, probably pointed at the back of Aria's seat. Pero wondered if it protruded through the vinyl, cold and obtrusive, like some phantom limb in a haunted house movie.

"Who are you?" Pero opened the floor up for questions, even though she already knew the answer. Everything about Aria's actions, the recognition on her face, the sag in her shoulders, told Pero that this was the pathetic blogger guy that had kidnapped her. The second part of Pero's plan was to regain the power in the van.

"Don't worry about that. You just drive to where the rest of them are. I saw the stunt you all pulled. Pretty impressive," he said, cocking his head with more condescension than praise. "Pretty impressive."

"Oh, I know you!" Pero slapped the steering wheel. "You're that Acolyte guy. How's that been working out for you?"

Luca's jaw tightened. "Just drive."

"I read some of your work once," Pero called back as she eased toward the train station. Hopefully she would figure out what to do somewhere between spaces. "It was this article defending business owners' rights to kick gay people out of their store if they wanted."[68] Pero caught his eyes again in the rearview. "It was good."

Luca scoffed and shifted toward the window. *Good*, Pero thought, watching him squirm. Finally, Aria looked up, narrowing her eyes at Pero. Tears lurked on the perimeter of her eyes. With a quick wink, Pero tried to convey: *Don't worry. We got this.*

Pero cleared her throat, retightening her grip on the steering wheel. "You're a pretty talented writer, you know?"

"Oh, yeah?" Luca said, without turning from the window. Asshole speak for: I'm far too cool to agree with you, but please go on.

"Yeah, by the end of the piece, I was actually agreeing with you."

"You were, were you?"

Ugh. The whole process of turning a declarative sentence into an interrogative one was the verbal equivalent of chewing tinfoil with a mouthful of fillings. Pero shook it off. "Uh-huh, I kinda just wished everyone would be as up front with their prejudices. Everyone's racist, sexist, biased whatever. It's refreshing when someone's actually brave enough to own up to it. If you don't like someone, let them know so they can dislike you right back." Pero resisted the strong desire to rub the sticky-looking dinosaur that dangled from the rearview mirror on her tongue. The lingering taste of her lying words lingered there instead. Despite this, Pero gritted her teeth and pushed the issue further. "That's the problem we used to have in this country and still have with some young people like us…" Pero dug a fingernail into her palm at the statement that bound her to Luca. "They're too idealistic."

---

[68] If this somewhat vague article description from Pero seems cliché and reductive, well, good, because that's the kind of low content work that Luca regularly churned out. It isn't worth further elaboration.

Luca's thin lips parted to show his shark white teeth. Pero's eyes shot back to the road. Most of the Capitol's streets were blocked with people. *If the roads are shut off that means the trains have already stopped running, which means Checkpoint B it is then.* Pero turned the van around. Brightly colored balaclavas stood out of the crowd like fans wearing the jerseys of their favorite players at a sporting event. *Was that all this was, politic as sport?* No, it was more than that. Lives were at stake. This wasn't a game. Rows of officers lined the sidewalks, keeping the mass of people corralled together, bumping into each other like spinning tops. With so much ego and emotion trapped there, it was only a matter of time until the scene spun out of control. The batons and riot gear, the military grade vehicles blocking the streets, told Pero that not only were the officers ready for it—they waited in gleeful anticipation. If the world were a just place, the children would be out of the crowd before anything popped off. Unfortunately, Pero knew better than to believe that.

In the rearview mirror, Luca had finished his assessment of her. "You don't believe that."

Ah, Pero had him. It was her turn to do the questioning. "Why wouldn't I? If the truth is the truth then why doubt it?"

"Because you're…you're with them."

Pero raised her eyebrows at him in the rearview. "Well, it sure seems like one of us is assuming too much."

They didn't know it, but Luca and Aria gave Pero the same look of doubt in the rearview. *Good.* Pero decided to leave it at that. If even Aria was doubting her then Pero had done a convincing enough job.

It was on him to ask questions after that. Another four city blocks stood between Pero and the next checkpoint. The heavy stream of traffic attempting to leave the city was choked off by a logjam of OCT SUVs foolishly checking each vehicle for the rogue members of the Futile. The only vehicles heading into the city were military grade hummers and riot tanks. They were as preventive to the impending riot as a sneeze on a vitamin C pill meant to ward off a cold.

Damn it. Pero slowed to let several hummers pass. There wasn't much time to act. If she didn't get to the next checkpoint soon, Nas and the rest of them would conclude the worst and attempt to evacuate the city on their own. It was now or never.

Time for step three of Pero's plan: do something incredibly dumb.

"I know it's been a while since you've been involved with the BP," Pero called back. "But are you familiar with the Okhrana Contingent?"[69]

Luca's left hand gripped the back of Aria's seat. His right hand remained unseen. A reminder to Pero that she would never fully have the power in the conversation so long as a gun was aimed at her girlfriend's little sister. His eyes ticked forward to hers in the rearview. "Uhhhhhh, yes. Are you familiar with it?" Luca batted back.

Pero navigated around another roadblock. They would be at the pick-up spot soon. She couldn't take this dude right to them. Not with his gun. Not with his head full of ideas as bad as his haircut. Not with his mere presence likely stirring up PTSD for Aria. Not with all that was going on in the city. Also, what if he saw them without their masks, would they then have to kill him? Like some old mafia movie?

---

[69] At the time, few actually knew about the top-secret spy network of the Blessed Path meant to infiltrate the ranks of their enemies. It was mostly heard about in whispers and over-conflated bouts of gossip. Those who really knew didn't talk about it and those who talked about it didn't really know.

As satisfying as that would be, that couldn't happen.

"I wonder…" Pero started, allowing the ellipses to trail on just long enough for Luca to draw his own conclusions, wondering again if it was better to stop talking while she was ahead. "What would your father think if you were to spoil a years' long undercover operation?"

Luca's green bomber jacket that was already at least one size too small got tighter as he hunched forward onto the back of Aria's seat. His breath had to be on the back of her neck. Aria winced.

"You think you're going to trick me?" Luca coughed out a laugh. "You think this shit could work?"

Doing her best to ignore Aria's obvious discomfort, Pero shrugged again and glared back at Luca in the rearview. "Here's the real difference between you and me—and it goes further than skin tone or upbringing or economic class. It's this: one of us is playing like they don't give a fuck and the other one really doesn't, so I suggest you drop your little daddy issues bullshit, because you're out of your league here, and whatever game you're playing to redeem yourself is only going to get yourself ki—"

Luca cackled. "Did you practice that monologue at your little art school? Yeah, that's right, you're not the only one who knows something. I know all about you Jun-i-per-o."

Okay. Maybe it wasn't worth underscoring the point any further. She had already said either too much or too little. There was only one option left. Step four: do something incredibly dumb AND dangerous. Pero pulled the van onto an empty back road. She ramped the speed of the van up from twenty-five to thirty-five then forty-five miles an hour. She checked the rearview again. *Yep, Aria's got her seatbelt on. Okay, good. We're going to do this.*

Recognizing that he had a literal captive audience, Luca continued with his rant. "If you really were in the Okhrana, why would you even say anything about it? Huh? Do you think I would even care? Is that supposed to impress me? Do you know how many people I've helped get on the BP's side? How much my efforts have helped their recruiting drive, influenced their policies, dictated their relations to the public? Do you have *any* idea?" Luca gestured with one hand. Her goal had been achieved, he was angry and acting irrational, but it still wasn't good enough.

Pero watched him, waiting for the right moment. The red needle on the speedometer stretched towards nirvana. She remembered at fourteen, practicing driving with her dad, because he wanted to make sure she knew how before he...She could still picture him coughing into a handkerchief as they concluded their lesson in a snowy parking lot. *Now's the fun part,* he said. His blue eyes rimmed in red.

"Treating me like I'm some impressionable idiot. Do you not know who the fuck I am?" Luca's voice rose to a shout, unaware of the engine's whirr. "DO YOU KNOW WHAT I'M GOING TO DO TO YOU ALL?!" Luca raised both hands over his head, including his gun. *Now!*

Pero slammed the steering wheel to the left into a patch of ice. The van spun in a half circle flinging Luca from his seat. With a sharp bang, his cantaloupe head cracked off the side window. Luca fell over in the fetal position and let out a low groan, cradling his head with both his hands. *Gun? Where was the gun?* Pero shifted into park and jolted around. Aria steadied the barrel on Luca's bleeding face. "Now, I suggest you get the hell out of our van, asshat!" She opened the double doors, pushing him out with her foot.

Luca fell from the van into the sludge of the parking lot. The doors shut and they drove off, leaving him behind amongst the dilapidated buildings and melting snow.

"What can I do with this?" Aria climbed into the front seat holding the gun as though it was covered in feces.

"Here." Pero offered her hand. "I can take it."

"What was all that Okhrana stuff?" Aria asked without handing over the gun.

Pero gave a short laugh. "That convincing, huh?"

Another second of hesitation before Aria passed off the gun. "Do we need to ditch the van? What if he calls us in?" She unzipped her hoodie. Duckworth crawled out and laid in her lap.

"That's a solid point." Pero tucked the gun underneath the driver's seat. "If he was going to call us in, he probably would've already done it. Still, we can't risk it. We need to make this quick."

Aria nodded then looked out the passenger window. Pero watched her for a beat from the corner of her eye, hoping that Aria was okay.

Hoping that she had bought it.

Chapter Fifty-Four: Blood In Yr Mouth

The zipties cut into her wrist. The deeper they dug in, the harder she had to work to keep her panic at bay. Nothing pushed her closer to the edge of freaking out than being restrained. Inspiration to stay strong was found in the examples that her bandmates set by refusing to answer any of the questions Rankin sent their way. If it wasn't for them, Nas wondered if she would've cracked and told the agents the rest of their plan, what their names were, what their favorite foods were, how often they had bowel movements, where their families lived. Like the best of us, Nas was much stronger than she gave herself credit for. Like the best of us, she credited others for whatever strength she found. Deeper down, she realized that everything they provided to her, she had to reflect back for them.

If one broke, they all would.

Boots crunched in the gravel towards them. "Get'em up," Rankin barked to the four agents that stood before them. He was done with his phone call. It would only be a matter of time until the peace wagons would be there to haul them away.

"I can get myself up, thanks," Brie said to the agents as she got to her feet. Then she turned to Rankin. "I doubt you can say the same, huh, bud?"

As calm as the Pope on Christmas, Rankin walked over and smacked Brie hard with the back of his hand. Brie hunched over. A line of red dribbled from her mouth to the ground. With her head bowed, Brie spit out a glob of blood. "I got you." She looked up at the Commander with blood in her teeth and smiled. "I got to you," she sang. "Someone does have emotions."

Nas knew what Brie was doing, but still she willed her to stop. Each blow that Brie received affected them all. Like a waterlogged, sagging floor, there was only so much they could take before the bottom dropped out.

"Get up!" He said again, before turning to Brie. "Try that shit again and I'll shoot one of your little friends in the kneecaps. Think I'm playing?" He arched one bushy eyebrow into the blank sky of his never-ending forehead. "Please try me."

Instantly, the strength drained from Brie's posture.

Davy stood before the agents got near him and Nas did the same. Remi struggled, unable to gain his balance with his hands bound behind him. Neef attempted to help him until an agent promptly slammed him in the stomach with the butt of his rifle. A whoosh of air escaped Neef's mouth. He faltered for a moment, falling to one knee, before helping Remi to his feet by leaning underneath him and rising together. Neef stared a laser beam at the agent who knocked him over. The young man, once brash enough to hit Neef in the first place and bold enough to brag to his fellow OCTers that he would "beat the fuck out of those Futile pussies" if they ever crossed his path, was now more interested in the smoke-filled Capitol skyline.

Rankin looked down the street in each direction. Sweat poured off his oven-coil-red face. Watching him, the damn default settings of trying to humanize Rankin kept coming upon Nas. How much bitterness? How much sadness and brokenness must one feel to go through life like this? What drove him? Heartache? *No, stop that.* Nas halted the train of thought there. *Some are deserving of the labels placed on them. Some people are just soulless husks driven by nothing other than their fear of mortality and irrelevance. Motivated solely by their own selfish desire to acquire as much as possible before they die. Indifferent to the suffering of others for no reason other than they just simply can't be bothered to give a shit.*

Sirens rushed by. An ambulance plunged into the bleeding heart of the city. Rankin exhaled as it disappeared from view. Then he snapped towards the band with the four fresh-faced OCT agents at his back. "This is how it's going down. When TBN gets here. You all will look at those cameras and you'll admit that your little video was a lie, all of it was a lie. You do that, and maybe certain arrangements will be made. Maybe you'll be placed in a facility together with annual visits for a ten or twenty year sentence. That doesn't sound so bad, eh? Better than most get." He lunged closer, putting his face in each of theirs one at a time. "But if you fucking cross me—" He pointed in Nas' face, his breath hot and foul, "You won't live to see your next birthday."

Nas wanted so badly to put him in his place. To cut him down effortlessly like she knew she could. But what good would it do? No doubt he would actually shoot one of them if she pushed him. Plus, if nothing had yet to change his mind, it was unlikely anything could. That's the thing about soulless husks; they operate off of animal instinct, abject fear, and irrational ego. She would have better luck arguing with one of the Blessed Path's Blurt Bots. No, Nas' focus was better spent on just how in the hell they were going to get out of this.

Rankin paced up and down their line like a caged lion. "You all think you've got everything figured out. That the Blessed Path's this big bad evil making your lives shit," Rankin continued. "Some time in the DITCH will do you good. You're the ones making life more difficult than it should be, getting people all riled up to where they end up hurt. If you would just fall in line, then life would be easier for you and everyone you love. That's what you don't understand. That's what my opponent—" Rankin pointed to the billboard screen where a highlight reel ran about Rankin's biggest successes as head of the OCT[70]— "Didn't understand. Everything I did, I did for the good of my people and my God and if anyone can't see that then they're the ones standing in the way, not me. So, stop whining about the way things should be and start appreciating the way things are, because trust me…" He paused in front of Remi, before kicking him hard in his hurt thigh sending him to the ground. "Shit can get much worse and it will." Rankin spit on the cement, punctuating his rant.

The comlink on Rankin's lapel began beeping rapidly. He squeezed it silent before calling over his shoulder, "Donovan, give me your rifle." With a snort, Rankin thumbed his nose, staring at Remi as he waited for the gun.

In Nas' peripheral, Remi struggled back to his feet. Nas shot a look down the street. How much longer would it be? The peace wagon, TBN, any of it would be a safer alternative to waiting there with Rankin, whose sanity was obviously being held together with alcohol and painkillers at this point. Wherever Pero and Aria were, Nas hoped they were far away. *Hope?* Nas regarded the word. Yes, she still had it, same as always.

The click-clack of a rifle being cocked drew Nas' attention front and center. "So, tell me again, what're you going to say to the cameras?" Rankin growled.

Tell him again? They hadn't even agreed with it in the first place. Nas could feel her bandmates looking to her. They would follow her lead. In a

---

[70] Some unmentioned "successes" included: the shutdown of a harmless 'sports-talk' podcast show that once made a passing reference to the Loyal Defender's truly embarrassing first pitch at an Aberdeen Iron Birds' spring league game twenty years prior; the seizure of over thirty thousand Loyal Defender action figures manufactured by an Ohio factory that greatly embellished the LD's muscles but got his mustache wrong; and the immediate (and continued) imprisonment of forty thousand citizens who thumbsed-up an anti-Blessed Path post on the social media site Acquaintances before it was taken down.

split second, Nas auditioned the possible outcomes. Her options were pretty much:

1.) Not say anything. Pro: deny giving Rankin the satisfaction he so desperately craved. More than anything, it would please Rankin immensely if he could "break" the Futile. It would prove correct all his preconceived misconceptions. Con: he may shoot one of her friends.

2.) Spit directly in his stupid face in place of answer. Pro: it would feel really really, really awesome to do that. Con: he would definitely shoot one of her friends.

3.) Agree to tell TBN it was a lie. Pro: they would possibly survive long enough to figure something else out. Con: if Rankin was this concerned then he must be catching heat somehow. If they were to say it was a lie, it would undo everything. Rankin could maintain his good standing with the Loyal Defender. The status quo would continue. Thus, making all this—Nas glanced to the pandemonium that had consumed the city—meaningless. That wasn't an option. The Futile weren't the only ones who had sacrificed something that day and Nas wouldn't allow those losses to be made in vain. Besides, it was just as likely that Rankin would kill one of them anyway.[71]

4.) Stall, stall with everything in her, hope to goad him into one of those awful villain soliloquies that allowed him to forget about time and space long enough for them to come up with another plan. Like that ever worked.

---

[71] In conversation with Neef, this author, finding themself quite clever (per the usual) asked why Nas didn't consider another option such as agreeing to lie and then not do it when the cameras actually showed up. To which Neef looked at this author as though they were the stupidest person alive (accurate) and said: "There were already cameras everywhere, on the agents, on the lampposts, on their guns, everywhere. If Nas would've said that then it would be all they needed. They could, and did, rip any stray comment out of context to justify whatever they wanted to do. Nas knew that. Also…lying would never be her first option, regardless of the situation. That's the difference between her and the rest of us."

"Why do you even care about this?" Nas asked. It wasn't a good plan, but number four was the only way.

"What?" He spat the word out as though such a question was beneath a straightforward answer.

"It's just there's so much more to life. You don't seem happy. Capturing us, turning us in, ensuring our imminent deaths, seeing to the unpleasant deaths of everyone we know and love, et cetera, et cetera, it just seems so exhausting and for what? This?" Nas glanced side to side, hardly taking in the full scope of destruction. "None of this means anything. There's more out there worth living for." Nas shifted her feet underneath her. The constraints on her wrists continued to cut off circulation to her fingers. "What's the point?"

"Thank you for asking," Rankin put on a caricature of girlish affectation. "No one ever asks how I'm doing." The rifle jostled as he tightened his grip on it. Rankin's voice dropped back to his normal tone, "I imagine I'm doing this for the same reason you do what you do, a purpose, a reason to live, an enemy to hate, sex, power. We're not all that different, blah, blah, blah, but tell me—" Rankin aimed his rifle at Remi. "Why don't you just say what I need to hear? Or else I'll shoot this traitorous-fucker right here and write him off as collateral damage to bring y'all in."

"Don't!" Nas shouted. "I'll say we lied. I'll look right in the cameras and say it. Please, you've already caught us, just…"

"What'll you say?" Rankin kept the barrel steady on Remi.

The comlink on the blonde-haired agent squawked to life. He leaned away to reply, the way someone may try to conceal a sneeze.

"Nas…" Remi stared down at the rifle held to his sternum.

"I'll lie. I'll say we lied," Nas said again as static commands bled from the other four agent's comlinks.

"No!" A bead of sweat fell from Rankin's jowls. "Say the exact words."

"Nas…don't," Remi said.

A clap of thunder, Rankin lunged forward and bashed Remi across his forehead with the butt of the rifle. Remi crumpled to his knees. Rankin swiftly kicked him in the face. Remi sputtered and coughed, unable to turnover. A grin spread across Rankin's face as he raised his rifle to do it again. The agent referred to as Donovan clasped Rankin's arm and whispered something urgently to him. Rankin jerked away, raising his fist to hit Remi again.

"We lied! Okay!" Brie shouted, her voice breaking. "Stop!"

"Sir!" The blonde agent stepped forward. "You need to—"

"I want to hear it from her." Rankin pointed at Nas with his rifle held at arm's length before turning it back on Remi.

Nas stuttered over the words, she couldn't say them fast enough. "I—we—lied. All of it."

"Sir! You need to c—" the blonde agent tried again, grabbing Rankin's arm.

Rankin shrugged off the blonde agent with ease. "Actually, you know what? This kid isn't even that important." Rankin repositioned his aim on Remi.

"Sir!" The blonde agent drew his rifle on Rankin. "You're to come with us immediately! Per the LD's orders, sir!"

"Fuck you and fuck him," Rankin said out of the side of his mouth without letting his eyes off Remi. "What'd you say, kid? You ready to go with me?"

"We lied! We lied, okay?! Don't!" Nas and Brie yelled together.

"Drop the rifle now, sir!" The other three agents drew their weapons on Rankin as well. "Sir! Now!"

"You ready?" Rankin asked Remi. His finger applied pressure to the trigger. Neef and Davy dove in front of Remi at the same time.

"No!" Nas screamed. Multiple pops followed. The highest of pitches rang in Nas' ears, the likes of which she would never hear again. Then—a bright flash like a star collapsing in on itself blew Nas off her feet.

Chapter Fifty-Five: Mad World

A flatline droned on. Brie craned her neck to assess her body for any injuries. Hurt was everywhere, but no blood, a small win. Breathing hurt. Brie fell back. The sky above was sepia-toned like they had been blown into a post-apocalyptic world where water was the primary source of power and people drove badass tricked-out death-mobiles for whatever reason. The kind of scene deserving of an orchestral, string-swelling soundtrack, but all Brie got was the incessant ringing in her ears.

Brie stayed on her back, trying to summon the strength to get up. A blue-masked face appeared inches above hers. Its mouth moved, but Brie couldn't make out the words. *It—It's me. Am I dead?* Brie blinked back at the girl's face, unable to put together what was happening. The face above kept trying to tell her the same thing.

The blue-masked girl pulled Brie to her feet. "Sorry 'bout that," she said. "It looked like it was going bad for you folks with those Octagoons so Kay—" She tilted her head to a green-masked girl standing a few feet off. "Tossed an Airpop to break up the scene."

"Thanks," Brie choked out. Her throat burned as though it was full of sand.

"Don't mention it. It's time to unite, right?" The blue-masked girl raised a fist in solidarity before jogging towards the smoke-filled city with the green-masked girl. "Sorry 'bout your friend!" She called as they disappeared in the swirling dust.

What the hell? Brie watched them a beat longer.

"Brie!" Nas called out, strain apparent in her voice.

"Nas!" Brie jogged over with her hands still bound behind her back.

"You good?" Brie asked.

"Think so." Nas struggled to her feet. "What was that?"

"I'm still not su—" Brie jumped in front of Nas and stopped.

Through the dust, the four OCT agents dragged an unconscious Rankin to the SUV before stuffing him in the backseat. The blonde agent locked eyes with them as he shut the driver's side door and drove away.

Brie and Nas exchanged a look of confusion.

A groan rang out from nearby.

"Neef!" Nas called. Brie and Nas ran over. "Are you alright?" Nas asked, kneeling to assess his wounds.

Neef leaned up. Blood oozed from his nose. Dirt covered his face. "I'm...fine...Davy?" Neef called out.

"Yeah?" Davy answered from a few feet away.

Brie went to him. "Davy, you okay? Your arm looks a little fucked up."

Davy rolled to his side. "Were we in time?"

Oh, god. 'Sorry 'bout your friend'—*Remi!* Brie spun around. There...twenty yards back. She sprinted to him. A trail of blood leaked across the pavement, gaining more ground each second. Brie fell to his side.

Remi attempted a smile. "I'm okay."

"No," Brie said, wanting more than anything to take his hand. "You're not, Rem."

"No." Remi winced with a chuckle. A large wound in his side pooled with every struggled breath. "I'm not."

Brie leaned over him to make eye contact. "I'm with you." She kissed his forehead. "I'm here."

The gravel crunched next to Brie. Nas, Neef, and Davy knelt down with her. "We're all here," Brie said, choking up as Nas placed her head on Brie's shoulder. Reality began setting in. "We love you. We're here," Brie said.

"It was worth it," Remi said. The light in his blue eyes paled as the pool beneath him darkened. "All of it was worth it." Remi coughed. "Every second."

"We couldn't have done it without you," Nas said, trying, but failing, to hold it together. Neef leaned into her.

"You could have," Remi said to Nas. "But I'm glad I got to be there."

"Remi..." Brie started but didn't know what else to say.

"I'm not scared," Remi turned to Brie. A tear ran down his cheek. "It's okay. I'm not scared." He fought for breath. "It was worth—" Remi coughed. "I—I love you, guys. Thank you...for all of it."

"We love you, Rem," Davy leaned forward. "I'm sorry. I tried. Wasn't fast enough."

"I know." Remi looked to Davy. "I'd rather...I know you tried."

"I'm proud of you," Davy said despite his sobs.

"We can't do this without you," Neef said through his tears.

"You can. You have to," Remi choked out.

"Remi," Brie leaned in. As the end approached, she found it was just as hard to accept as she remembered. Fighters tend to fight against all things, regardless of what they're up against. There was so much she wanted to say that the words jumbled up, duplicating as they bumped into each other, piling up in her throat, forming a dam that was near impossible to break through. "I didn't tell you the end of my story." Brie sniffed. "That morning after mom passed…"

"Did you see one?" Remi asked.

Brie nodded as tears flowed down her face. "There were so many. They were beautiful."

"I hope I see them too," Remi said, locking eyes with Brie. "You think I will?"

"Rem…"

"I love you."

"I love you." Brie laid her head on his chest. "We're here with you. You're not alone."

"I'm not scared."

"We're here."

"I know. I—I'm not…scared. I'm not…"

And Now...the Hosts of TBN's "Bless This Morning" Have A (Very Small) Change of Heart (A Transcript)

Greg: Good morning, welcome to the (deep sigh) fifth hour of Bless This Morning.

Kelly Anne: Bless your morning, Greg!

Greg: (forced smile) Yes, Kelly Anne, it's still technically morning.

Kelly Anne: (puts on deeper, mocking affectation) Yes, it's still technically morning (looks into the camera and laughs while slapping her knee).

Greg: (grimaces briefly) Yes. Well, as we reported at the top of the fourth hour, we have some breaking news. Former head of the Office of Cultural Terrorism, J.R. Rankin has been apprehended following allegations that he assassinated his political opponent and committed multiple acts of treason against our fine country.

Kelly Anne: (puts on a sad frowny face) Well, that's just not acceptable, is it, Greg?

Greg: No (sighs). No, it isn't, Kelly Anne. Here at TBN, we've always been vocal about our lack of support for Rankin, so his new turn comes as no surprise. In fact, our producers have gone ahead and put together a little highlight ree—

Kelly Anne: Blooper reel is more like it! (swats Greg on the knee while he stares dead eyed in the camera).

Greg: A highlight reel of Rankin's greatest failures as head of the OCT. Let's watch.

***Video footage runs of Rankin vowing to capture the band, of the OCT's failed raid on the church, of the Futile fleeing the OCT in their van as three SUVs burst into flames, of the Futile performing on top of the Former

Migrant Registration Center as Red Mask flips off the TBN video drones, then footage of Rankin being led red-faced and handcuffed into a Blessed Path Detainment Center. ***

Kelly Anne: Whew, if that's what he got right then I'd like to see where he went wrong.

Greg: We…that whole thing…was…never mind.

Kelly Anne: The real shame is that the band of rude teens is still on the loose—

Greg: Yes, that's—

Kelly Anne: Now that's what I call a blooper!

Greg: (winces and shakes his head) Yes, as my beautiful co-host has reminded us this morning, if you or anyone you know has any information on the renegade band of misfits known as the Futile then please contact your local…er…uh…as soon as possible.

Kelly Anne: I just don't know why they wear masks, blech, so gross.

Greg: (eyes finally light up) Ah, It's time for a word from our wonderful sponsors! As always, we here at TBN remind you to have a blessed morning. All things in his honor.

Chapter Fifty-Six: Laments of a Thoughtful Bot 5.0

To: *********@****.com
From: itsmeterry@amail.com
Subject: A Quick Note of Glad Tidings / A Brief Word of Regret

Dear Nasim,

First, allow me to ask forgiveness. I have come to understand that you prefer to be called the abbreviated nickname of Nas rather than Nasim. Yet, I am also careful to not be so presumptuous to call you by a nickname that is perhaps reserved for friends and loved ones, so, for now (or at least until I hear otherwise), I shall address you as Nasim or, if you prefer, Ms. Bashir.

Second, do not worry. I obtained this email address through secure methods and no one will be able to track our correspondences (I have finally leveled up beyond the Blessed Path's capabilities!).

Now this would normally be the part of the message where I inform you (as concisely as possible) that I am a reformed nationalist bot. However, it seems as though word of my existence has spread greatly among your membership :)

I was particularly pleased (as much as one can be without having a reward-based chemical trade off system in one's brain) that the video surveillance footage I obtained (and passed on to you all) was used in your inspirational event held on Election Day!

The subsequent takedown of Rankin and the (however temporary) shutdown of the Office of Cultural Terrorism is quite a feat. If perhaps you found a few coincidences breaking in your favor that day (the flying away of drones, the magnification of your video's outreach [worldwide no less!], the brief blackout of TBN, the delay in back up law enforcement so you all could make your escape) and wondered what could have caused such chance situations, then allow me to say (ever so humbly) that it was me (!).

Oh, my, I hope (there was a time when I found that word so strange and sad) that statement of fact does not appear boastful. That was not the intention—rather it was meant to display how much I believe in your cause. Regardless, there are things far more important than my fragile ego.

Unfortunately, this is where we will transition into the difficult part of this message. I watched (via street camera) as Rankin aimed his weapon on your friend, Remington (again, I will not assume to use his nickname here). I hoped (in vain) that the agents would arrest Rankin before he pulled the trigger. Alas, they were slow to act (big surprise there) and your friend lost his life, despite the well-meaning attempt of you, your friends, and some fellow activists.

The limits of my actual understanding of the human experience are (sadly) vast. Yet, I too have lost someone I considered my (only) friend, the sorrowful effects of which linger still. I hope (forever I will) that the passing of your friend has not caused you more heartache than needed, nor lead to doubt in what your band has accomplished.

Instead, perhaps, you can remember Remington as a person (flaws and all) and in that way he will stay with you. That is (after all) what any surviving, solitary being in this world can do.

It will be understood if you do not reply to this email. Regardless, you should know how much good you and your friends are doing. In a matter of weeks, you young people (I am only sixteen years old myself!) have made tremendous strides towards undoing the trouble my (ugh) creators and many of my (former) peers caused.

I will continue rooting you all on from the sidelines and will be watching out for you all the best I can (for example, the Blessed Path was not too pleased this morning when they found all their surveillance footage and data obtained on your band completely fried like the anxious bird they consume quite often).

Please (for the sake of everyone) keep trying.

—Terry

Chapter Fifty-Seven: Digital Witness

To: itsmeterry@amail.com

From: **********@****.com

Subject: RE: A Quick Note of Glad Tidings / A Brief Word of Regret

Hi Terry,

Thank you for the kind words. We're glad to have you on our side and appreciate everything you've done to help so far. We couldn't have done it without you. It has been hard, but your message has helped some, thank you. I do have a request if it's not too much to ask...

By chance would you be able to help us in locating a certain prisoner?

And, please, call me Nas.

All my friends do.

—N.

Chapter Fifty-Eight: The Rhythm of the Road Behind Them

The wheels against the concrete created a new composition, filling in for the empty spaces in the conversation, the words they couldn't yet bring themselves to say, the words they resisted saying just for the sake of saying something, anything. Bumps came at a rate of about one per every ten seconds as they left the Capitol in the rearview. Bronto, the sole souvenir from Woody, dangled from the still unnamed van's rearview mirror, swaying back and forth, a sad, unreliable metronome. Brie watched it, trying to find some consistency to its rhythm, if she could just lock in on its beat, then... A metallic clanging jangled along with the rest of it like the staccato strums of a steady rhythm guitar. It reminded her of Remi. Brie knew it would be a long time before she stopped finding reminders of him. As hard as it was, she hoped that day wouldn't come.

Davy sat next to her, his right arm bouncing in its makeshift cast, his left resting along the seatback. Every so often, his hand would land gently on her shoulder, letting her know that she wasn't alone. She rustled Duckworth's fur again. He panted up at her from her lap. Small gestures meant everything.

Neef sat in the backseat, still sniffing while he looked out the window. The words Neef spoke at Remi's burial site three days prior came back to her.

"Remi knew instinctively what many people spend their lives in ignorance of, and that was that left alone, people can be weak, petty, small, and ineffective. But together...together we can be something more. What confidence Remi lacked in himself, he projected onto us and in that way, he lifted us up so we could do the same for him. As long as we're together, he'll always be with us..."

Brie caught eyes with Neef in the backseat. He nodded back even though his earbuds were in. Nas and Aria sat in the front bench seat talking quietly amongst themselves, catching up on all they had missed in each other's lives. Their presence reminded Brie that there was some good that had come from all of it. Well, that, and…

"Yo, folks, listen up," Pero called back as she turned up the radio volume.

"Until further notice, the Office of Cultural Terrorism will be put on hold while the Loyal Defender personally conducts a full investigation into the allegations of misconduct by former head J.R. Rankin. The Blessed Path reports that the temporary freeze will save billions in revenue. Meanwhile, a worldwide search is still being held for the band known as the Futile for their connection to Rankin's crimes. If you or anyone you know—"

Pero swatted the volume knob off. "Dang! It's official. You all shut down the whole OCT!"

Nas leaned forward. "Correction: We shut down the whole OCT. It was a group effort." Nas placed her hand on Aria's. "It took all of us."

Pero reflected a smile back in the rearview.

Davy's new burner phone chimed. "It's the Dissent again," he said to Brie. "They keep wanting us to play their events. Said they've got more support than ever."

Brie shook her head. "Yeah, I can tell you who wasn't a part of the group effort, the fucking Dissent. They left us on our own to do everything. They never even said a word about Rem either. All they did was try to take whatever credit they could after it was over." Brie called up front. "No offense, Pero."

"None taken," Pero shouted back. "Now that the school isn't of use to them anymore, they're pretty much done with me anyway. So, I'm independent." Pero glanced briefly at Aria in the rearview. "Aside from being y'all's driver."

"Sooooooo…" Nas started, letting the word stretch on between them.

With a sniff, Brie jumped in on the higher harmony. "Soooooo…"

Then Davy on the mid. "Sooooo…"

And Neef on the low. "Soooooo…"

Even with the ultra-high note that Remi couldn't ever hit noticeably absent, the remaining four members of the Futile carried on the harmony until they burst into laughter for the first time in days. "So—" Nas wiped her eye with her wrist as she smiled. "What's the plan next? We can't just drive on aimlessly. Do we take one of those Dissent shows or…?"

"I say we go our own way," Brie said.

Davy patted Brie on the shoulder. "Same. We've always been better on our own anyway."

"Neef?" Nas asked.

Neef popped out his earbuds. "The only people I need are here in this van. We got this."

"Aria?" Nas asked.

"What?" Aria's face lit up. "I get a vote?"

"Of course, you're with us now. At least until we meet up with mom."

"I'm in," Aria said with a nod.

"P—"

"Don't even ask. I'm in too," Pero called back. "But that still doesn't answer the question of where to next."

"Well, there's no shortage of options." Nas pivoted to Davy and gave him a nod. "I've got a good idea of where to start actually."

"Vin?" He asked with hope apparent in his voice.

Nas nodded.

Davy slapped her a high five with his good hand.

Nas beamed. "It's time to right some wrongs, which reminds me—" Nas leaned forward to rummage through her knapsack. "Here, Pero. I got just the thing. Play this."

Pero plugged the Aux cord into the battered MP4 player. The Mindfucks reverberated through the metal hull of the unnamed van. The six members of the Futile rocked out, each taking on an instrument different than their own, or in the case of Pero (keys) and Aria (cowbell?) any instrument. Brie felt a smile come over her. In the window reflection, she swore she could see Remi's jerky movements. It was true; he would always be with her, with all of them. Nothing would ever change that. Nothing could ever take that away.

And I said, 'Here am I, send me.'

A Song of Thanks Sung by a Hack[72]

I would first like to say thank you to the Futile's editor, Emily Fisher, for her keen eye and careful consideration with each line and every word in this thing. Thank you, Emily, for making this book much easier to read.

Sarah Baldwin created the amazing cover design and book layout. It was always a good day to get one of her new cover sketches or illustrations in my inbox. Thank you, Sarah, for helping this book stand out.

Tracy Marchini of BookEnds Literary Agency was my agent when I first wrote this book. Without Tracy's enthusiasm and editorial vision in early drafts, I'm not so sure this story would have gotten to this point, or, if it had, it would certainly be a lesser version. Thank you, Tracy, for believing in this book before few others even knew it existed.[73]

My dear friend, Major Rich, talked me through nearly every plot hole and crisis of confidence, as he does pretty much daily for me anyways. Major also came up with a bunch of funny ideas like AR15 & Pregnant and he wrote the lyrics to "Good Cowboy" on a whim when I wondered aloud if I would get sued for just straight up using the lyrics to "Cotton-Eyed Joe." There are easily a hundred other things in here that wouldn't be possible without his help. Thank you, Major.

Thank you to Romann` Frost, Sierra Porritt, Emily Rich,[74] and Westley Wieland, for being early readers and supportive friends. You all definitely made contributions and suggestions that found their way into this final text for sure, thank you.

---

[72] Credit to Touché Amore and their song, "Is Survived By" for this heading.
[73] Tracy also wrote the synopsis/pitch on the back cover of this book.
[74] Emily thought of all the DITCH acronym meanings and it was her idea for Brie & the Exits to be the name of Brie's possible solo project, among other things.

Thank you to Kalinda Schreiber for always being there to vent about rejection or the never-ending wait of the publishing world, not to mention your advice and kindness. The world will surely be graced with a book of yours soon. I can't wait.

Thank you to the estate of Joe Burgess for the friendship and for once signing me up for random cat facts texts.

Thank you to Joshua Clifton and the Honey Gold Records crew for believing in my work and helping me put it out.

Thank you to my bandmates over the years who definitely inspired parts of this book: Chris Goode, Wes (again), Durf, Josh (again), Taylor Chance, Brady Clifton, Coleman Fitch, Jon Raby, Nick Griffith,[75] Tyler Chance, Payton Clark, and Jacob Cockrum. I'm thankful for our daydreams and adventures, for every practice that I was either the first or last to arrive, for every show regardless of attendance, and for every petty argument about who should get the best seat in the van or whether a song needs an actual chorus or not, may this book forever be a point in my favor. Thank you all.

Thank you, Brice Evans, for bringing some of the Futile songs to life. They sound better than I even imagined. Brice also came up with the ska band name mentioned briefly in chapter 7. Thanks, Brice.

Thanks to David Curtis, Matt Jackson, and Neil Endicott for letting me go along to sell merch on a couple RKR runs, those early trips may not have meant much to you all, but they were a huge influence on me, thank you.

A huge debt of gratitude is owed to the southern Illinois music scene

---

[75] Technically, Nick and I have never been in a band together, but Nick has been there for enough trips, practices, and shows that it certainly feels like we were so I'm counting it here.

as a whole. Long live Hitts and The Creature. Long live basement shows. Long live Dirty Damn Hall.

Thank you to the real life, bad ass feminist punk band, Pussy Riot for being an obvious conceptual influence for the Futile. I considered putting the characters in all sorts of masks (animals, scary movie villains, off-brand-Disney characters, dead presidents, etc) but the truth is that the influence of Pussy Riot was there from day one, so I wanted to honor that rather than hide from it. The book *Words Will Break Cement: The Passion of Pussy Riot* by Masha Gessen helped provide an understanding of the stakes and allowed some insight into the brave people standing up for important causes all around the world.

The short story "Manifesto: A Press Release From PRKA" by George Saunders directly inspired Nas' speech in chapter twenty-one.[76] Also, in 2017, Stacy and I went to a George Saunders reading in St. Louis. He was so kind when we got to talk with him about writing that it inspired me to write the Terry chapters of this story the very next day. Those are still some of my favorite parts of the book. You'll never see this, but thank you.

Thank you to Jake Yordy, Matt Lythberg, Matt Caraway, and Bryan Roscoe Wright for your love and friendship.

Thank you to Diane and Steve Bailey. You two have practically been our best friends through the last several years, guiding us through so much. I'm so incredibly thankful for that and everything else. I love you both, thank you.

Thank you to my sister, Vanessa, for actively encouraging me many

---

[76] Watching interviews with Nadezhda Tolonnikova of the aforementioned Pussy Riot also directly inspired this scene.

years ago when I first mentioned that I wanted to write a book someday. I'm still sorry I broke your caboodle. Much love to the entire Durfee family, Kris, Alicia, Weslyn, Theo, and Fawkes.

Thank you, Mom and Dad. You both always saw to it that I never had to wonder if you loved me or if I made you proud. I could write another eighty-thousand words here, but none of them would come close to conveying how thankful I am so here's just a few that I hope will do: I love you. Thank you.

Thank you to Ezra, Eli, and Ewan. I used to think that putting "musician" or "author" next to my name would be the best thing I could ever accomplish, but the truth is that being your dad is the greatest honor of my life. Thank you for being who you are and for just existing.

To Stacy, my goodness, you're amazing. I love you. Thank you for loving me, believing in me, and for all the extra work you covered so I could write this thing and put it out. Thank you for the proofreads and for building me back up whenever I felt like giving up. Thank you for forever being my first reader and best friend. I could cry just thinking about your love. Thank you.

Finally, thank you to anyone that is reading this. Thank you for picking this book up and giving it a chance. I hope you liked it.[77] If you did, please leave a review online or just tell someone else "hey, this book The Futile wasn't so bad." This is a small operation, and I can use all the help I can get. But also, if you don't feel like doing that, that's okay too. Still, thank you.

---

[77] If you don't like it, I promise you don't have to tell me about it. I have a lot of feelings and you'll hurt every one of them.

About the Author

Dane Johns lives in southern Illinois with his wife, Stacy, and their three children. At one time, he played in several bands that you likely haven't heard of unless you were in very specific places at very specific times. Even then, you probably didn't like them. The Futile is his first novel.

CPSIA information can be obtained
at www.ICGtesting.com
Printed in the USA
BVHW031139070322
630818BV00005B/105

9 781087 927732